I0575242

Joseph Ellis

Caesar in Egypt, Costanza and other Poems

Third Edition

Joseph Ellis

Caesar in Egypt, Costanza and other Poems
Third Edition

ISBN/EAN: 9783337231514

Printed in Europe, USA, Canada, Australia, Japan

Cover: Foto ©Andreas Hilbeck / pixelio.de

More available books at **www.hansebooks.com**

CAESAR IN EGYPT, COSTANZA

AND OTHER POEMS.

CAESAR IN EGYPT

COSTANZA

AND OTHER POEMS

by

Joseph Ellis

Third Edition
Corrected and Enlarged

LONDON

REEVES & TURNER 196 STRAND

1885

INTRODUCTORY NOTE TO THIRD EDITION.

———— *ii* ————

THE Text of this reprint is the outcome of a line-by-line
revisal, whether with regard to metrical euphony, clearness
of meaning, good-sense as the stand-point of fancy, or
punctuation—on which the effect of rhythmical construction
so frequently depends. The labour of this pursuit is known
to the worker if unperceived by the reader who, however,
may safely ascribe to elaboration the satisfaction derived
from perspicuity. *Ars est celare artem.* True to say — a
fine thought can be wasted by ambiguity. even excite derision
when it could have deserved admiration,—grotesque what
should have been elegant! The studious note with chagrin
a high intention or delicate conceit marred by incomplete-
ness. Many there are! who, in everyday life, enjoy lofty
ideas which they feel incapable of wording : the Poet makes
the effort, with greater or less success, for his skill may be
superior to his genius, or imagination exceed the power of
expression : Poetry is in the written, and in the unwritten.

There is a charm in Art for its own sake ; though the
careless reader be blind to faults, he is a loser by them ;

to be uncritical—dull to blemishes, easily pleased—is the 'fool's paradise ;' in the degree of perceptivity we experience more pleasure and more pain.

No result of Art is beyond the reach of improvement. I have striven to render my work worthy of acceptation, my aim being to satisfy the more observant—as the greater includes the less. It has been said an author should himself be his severest critic, but—familiarity is as a veil.

The 'Preface to Second Edition' (following) contains some needful explanations.

J. E.

Monks,
  Balcombe,
    August 1885.

PREFACE

[To the Second Edition,—1882.]

—o—

WHEN first preparing 'Caesar in Egypt' for Press, the Author was advised by literary friends that a Preface was unnecessary, or disadvantageous. The adoption of their opinion did not prove satisfactory, for Reviewers barely recognised the subject; the most generous of them[1] pointed doubtingly to 'originality,' though a glance at 'The Argument' might have removed his doubt,—the Alexandrine War not having been previously dealt with poetically, whilst the Second Part is an invention on slenderest suggestion of history.

A professional Critic had the candour to confess he knew next to nothing of the Alexandrine War or of the association of the great Dictator with Cleopatra ; and recently,[2] an Article entitled ' Former Invasions of Egypt,' for instruction of the public sums up thus: 'Even Caesar was powerless so long as he remained in Alexandria, and had to be relieved by a motley host of Syrians, Bedouins, and Jews

---

[1] *The Times*, February 9, 1877.
[2] *Pall Mall Gazette*, September 1, 1882.

marching on Memphis'—the pertinency (or impertinency) of which will be judged on comparison with the description of same in 'Argument,' and Text.

'Caesar in Egypt,' whilst alone in its theme, follows no model; whereon a learned friend of great literary experience remarked 'I know nothing which, in treatment, resembles it.'[1]

In the endeavour to portray Caesar, the view received from history and apparently accepted by Shakspeare has been pursued;[2] but in describing Cleopatra the Author follows his own ideal as to feature, complexion, and character,—Ptolemaic, Greek in type and training, with no taint of Coptic blood.[3]

---

[1] In combining with the poetic element, the historical, the dramatic, archæology, fiction—and Chorus.

[2] Brutus says—

> 'And, to speak truth of Caesar,
> I have not known when his affections sway'd
> More than his reason.'

And Antony—

> 'Thou art the ruins of the noblest man
> That ever lived in the tide of times.'

> 'He was my friend, faithful and just to me.'

> 'When that the poor have cried, Caesar hath wept.

And Caesar himself—

> 'Know, Caesar doth not wrong; nor without cause
> Will he be satisfied.'

> 'But I am constant as the northern star,
> Of whose true, fix'd, and resting quality,
> There is no fellow in the firmament.'

> 'I do know but one
> That unassailable holds on his rank,
> Unshak'd of motion; and, that I am he.

[3] See medallion at p. 31.

It would seem Shakspeare was undecided ; for in *Antony and Cleopatra* we read 'a tawny front,' and afterwards, 'here my bluest veins to kiss.' Moreover, Artists supposed to be well informed have depicted the famous Egyptian Queen in various shades of swarthy ; Gérôme represented her some years ago as a Negress with woolly hair, etc. Nor should it be overlooked our Cleopatra is, presumably, of the age of *twenty*, whereas at the period of Marcus Antonius the Queen would be *thirty-two*.

> ' Broad-fronted Caesar,
> When thou wast here above the ground, I was
> A morsel for a monarch.'

There is further reason for a Preface. ' Columbus at Seville ' was published in 1869 ; secondly, in 1876 ; and now, for the third time, in this book. In 1880, appeared ' Columbus,' by the Laureate. Admitting some differences, there are more similarities : both are in Monologue, the variation being that one is a soliloquy the other an objurgation. Hence the Author of ' Columbus at Seville ' is on his defence ; he can scarcely be unconscious how, without explanation, he might be accused of paraphrase or, at least, of reverberation : anyone who takes the trouble to examine will grant this. Another distinction should be pointed to — namely, in characterization—of which, if the unanimous testimony of biographers is to be believed, there can scarcely be two opinions.[1]

The coincidence of current events with the publication of a record of ' The Alexandrine War ' is noticeable.

---

[1] A copy of the second edition of ' Columbus at Seville ' was sent to the Laureate at date of publication. [1876.]

Readers will not fail to perceive the resemblances ; such as burning of the City, interference with water supply by Egyptians, operations of native army. For Romans, read Britons ; for Achillas, Arabi ; for Caesar, Wolseley ; for Cleopatra—Tewfik ! With restoration of the Khedive by the English General the parallel is complete.

MONKS,
     BALCOMBE,
          Sept. 1882.

CONTENTS.

———o———

CONTENTS.

CONTENTS.

LIST OF PLATES.

These illustrations are produced in copper by the photo-intaglio and photo-relief processes of the Typographic Etching Company, London.

———o———

1. FRONTISPIECE: Portrait of the Author, Photo-Engraved from a negative from life by Lombardi, London, 1882.

2. SPHINX OF MENÉPTHAH: traced from a photograph of the original in the Egyptian Department of the MUSÉE LOUVRE.

3. HEADS OF CAESAR AND CLEOPATRA: (1) From Photograph of the Antique in British Museum. (2) Fac-simile of imprint of a Medallion in 'Series Cæsarum,' Venitiis, 1708.

4. PROFILE OF CAIUS JULIUS CAESAR: Fac-simile from the series of authenticated Portraits in Tonson's Edition of Plutarch's Lives, 9 vols., 12mo, London, 1749.

5. PORTRAIT OF CHRISTOPHER COLUMBUS: reproduced from 'Ritratti de cento capitani illustri, intagliati da Aliprando Capriolo. Roma, 1596.'

CAESAR IN EGYPT.

F

TO

Professor GEORGE LONG

IS INSCRIBED

'*CAESAR IN EGYPT*'

WITH GRATEFUL ACKNOWLEDGMENT

TO HIM

FOR ASSISTANCE DERIVED

FROM

'THE DECLINE OF THE ROMAN REPUBLIC'

AND FOR

MUCH VALUABLE COUNSEL

THE ARGUMENT.

21

THE ARGUMENT.

———o———

CN. POMPEIUS, surnamed Magnus, after the disaster of Pharsalia escaped to Egypt. He met Cornelia[1] at Lesbos, whence he sailed to Pelusium, having reason to reckon on influence and support there. During his second consulship he had befriended King Ptolemaeus 'Auletes' at Rome. Auletes left the administration of his Will to the Roman Senate, depositing a copy with the Consul. Moreover, Pompeius had ordered Gabinius with a Roman force to restore Auletes when driven out of Egypt in B.C. 58. Two of the legions were left at Alexandria. On the other hand the Egyptians had assisted Pompeius in his last contest by sending ships and otherwise. But the Alexandrines having intelligence of his defeat and flight, from jealousy of

[1] His second wife, widow of Publius Crassus; his first wife was Julia, only daughter of Caesar.

Roman interference caused his murder at landing. Cornelia witnessed his death and escaped with her son, Sextus Pompeius.

The Egyptians were in anarchy. Pothinus (Governor), Achillas (General), and Theodotus of Chios (Tutor), supported the young King in opposition to the Will, which directed that Cleopatra (the eldest child) should reign conjointly with, and wedded to, her brother. The Princess resisted, being then with her adherents beyond Pelusium. Hence a civil war.

Coincident with Caesar's victory at Pharsalia miraculous events were pretended. In the Temple of Minerva at Elis the image of Victory turned towards the portal; at Antioch noises of fighting and trumpets; the same at Ptolemais; at Pergamus, in the adytum of the temple, sounds of drums; in the Temple of Victory at Tralles, wherein a statue was consecrated to Caesar, a palm sprouted from between the stones of the floor.

Caesar with the design of preventing Pompeius from regathering his forces and informed he had been seen in Cyprus—probably on the way to Egypt,—proceeded direct to Alexandria with 3200 soldiers. But his rival was no more. He had, however, other and important interests in Egypt; as Consul and Dictator of Rome it was his duty to administer the Will of Ptolemaeus Auletes, and he declared for the joint sovereignty.

The Romans occupied a part of the city entitled Brucheium which extended towards the sea,—Caesar residing in the Palace with the two Princes, Princess Arsinoë, Pothinus and Theodotus. Although Caesar's opinion was avowedly opposed to the policy of the Ministers they simulated respect and consideration for his wishes. But he had also demanded payment of the large debt due by Auletes to Rome and to himself, which added to dislike of Roman intervention caused him to be unpopular with the Alexandrines. This feeling being displayed, Caesar sent into Asia for the legions there.

The Consul persisted, requiring the youthful Ptolemaeus to plead before him to show on what grounds he refused to reign with his Sister; this displeased the Ministers. Caesar soon learned that Achillas was preparing to assume the offensive; Achillas had command of 20,000 foot and 2000 horse, besides the sympathy of the people, and possession of the City and open country.

Meanwhile Cleopatra continued with her little army. Reflecting on the situation, and how possibly to gain her sovereign rights, she resolved to present herself before Caesar, and endeavour, by persuasion and womanly graces, to conciliate him. Her age was then about twenty; she is described as beautiful in person, witty and courageous, gifted with pleasing manners and a melodious voice. In accomplishing her project she was aided by Apollodorus, a devoted officer of her household, and, with him only, coasted from Pelusium into one of the embouchures of the Nile. Landing in disguise, she was carried by Apollodorus to Caesar's apartment in the Palace. The Consul, entering alone, observed the reclining figure, and then first beheld Cleopatra. After mutual explanations, he ordered the Queen to be suitably provided for and protected. Nevertheless, from this time he insisted more and more on the fulfilment of the directions of Auletes' Will—with some appearance of assent ; but Pothinus furtively opposed his purpose.

The Consul then advised Ptolemaeus to send as ambassadors to Achillas two distinguished men, Dioscorides and Serapion, both of whom had been in the confidence of his Father. Without parley they were killed. On this, Caesar secured the King, and decreed the death of Pothinus.

Achillas advanced in open war against the Romans. Caesar, now on defence, had to send for ships and soldiers. He was in great danger, suffered some defeats, yet seized the Island and Tower of Pharos, with the Heptastadium,—the mole which connected the island with the city,—and burnt many of the Egyptian ships. During this struggle the famous Alexandrian Library was accidentally destroyed by fire.

Princess Arsinoë, having fled to the Egyptian army and assumed royal authority, put Achillas to death and elected as General, Ganymedes, the eunuch under whose care she had been educated. After an interval of cabal and intrigue the Alexandrines, finding the Romans difficult to conquer, offered friendship to Caesar on condition of his releasing the King, whom they said they preferred to Arsinoë and would obey. Wishing to satisfy them, and thinking the concession would scarcely increase their power, he liberated Ptolemaeus, who parted from him with pretended regret and with the warmest expressions of affection, but immediately after headed the army and recommenced operations against the Romans, putting them to some disadvantage. Cleopatra, under the guardianship of Caesar, dwelt in the Palace.

The Egyptian fleet was in great strength at Canopus, whilst the host of Achillas invested Brucheium. Caesar had received reinforcements and was thereby enabled to stand his ground. He appointed Tiberias Nero admiral, with the famous Rhodian, Euphranor, under him. His fleet resisted a furious attack with partial success.

At this crisis, Caesar was encouraged by a welcome message from Mithridates of Pergamus, who, after severe fighting, had reached Pelusium with his army. No time was lost by Caesar in making arrangements to go to his aid. Mithridates had taken Pelusium and proceeded towards Alexandria. Caesar, with extraordinary ingenuity and boldness, fought his way out and joined his ally in the Delta.

Then the final encounter. The Egyptians intercepted

Mithridates and had commenced the battle when the Romans approached by land and sea : victory wavered—till Caesar made a desperate onslaught on the camp, effecting an utter rout ; the King, in attempting to escape to a ship, was drowned. Arsinoë was made prisoner.

After this defeat the Alexandrines submitted ; Caesar established Cleopatra on the throne conjointly with her younger brother, yet a child, — thus fulfilling his duty as executor of the Will of Auletes.

Peace restored, the Consul remained some months to regulate affairs of State, to see the antiquities of Egypt, and for required rest after extremities which had well-nigh brought him to ruin. The lost books of Appian contained the particulars of CAESAR'S progress up the Nile with Cleopatra, including the wonderful relics of Memphis and Thebes, Heliopolis, the Pyramids, the Memnon, the Sphinx, the cities of Lake Moeris, Syéne, and Elephantiné. In Cleopatra he found a companion whose wit and spirit were congenial with his disposition.

But Caesar could not too long neglect Rome. Returning to Alexandria he promptly and resolutely consolidated the authority of the Queen. Taking the sixth legion with him to Syria,—there to oppose Pharnaces,—he left the rest of his army at Alexandria to support Cleopatra.

Successful campaigns in Syria, Africa, and Spain were followed by a Triumph at Rome for the Alexandrine War, conspicuous objects therein being Princess Arsinoë, and a camelopard, (giraffe) then unknown in Europe ;—this the closing scene of a very interesting though little regarded episode in the career of CAIUS JULIUS CAESAR.

CAIVS JVLIVS CAESAR. FROM PHOTOGRAPH OF ANTIQVE IN BRITISH MVSEVM. ✦ CLEOPATRA. FROM IMPRINT OF A MEDALLION IN "SERIES CAESARVM" VENICE 1708.

Caesar in Egypt.

So while away the ages,—come, and gone !
Monuments voices have, the later arts
Yield livelier records of the silent Past ;
Pile up the relics, print the lettered page
In multiples unreckoned till entranced
We see the withered centuries embalmed,
And as in fossil or in crystal shown,
The disembodied Mind :—in vain, in vain !
Mind is Itself alone, emotion springs
As fountain newly from the riven rock ;
Yea, like the petal wakening to the Sun,
The Soul that cometh hath inheritance
Coeval ranking with the birth of Time :
Yet do we fondly ween the passion proved—
Was such as kindles now, and thus assured,
Live in vicarious ecstasy somewhiles
The life of Men foregone, conceive their acts
And feel their mental wounds.

                   Pompeius Magnus !
Who as a Palace in a Fortress rose
In strength or splendour equal, at one stroke
Bared of its boastful beauties,—crash he fell.

Pharsalia lost! how but to die or fly?
'What, even to the ramparts do they come?
Ah, my Cornelia! calm at Lesbos waiting
Me to felicitate—Master of the World:
Away with armour! take the scarlet robe
To change for russet of the peasant sort,
As least derived from greatest—let me go.'

And thus he went, through woods and coverts
　　winding,
First to Larissa, fair Thessalia's pride,—
Cradle of Thetis' son Achilles, erst,
Nor far from where Olympus points to heaven;
Then on through Tempe, to the poets dear,
And to the coast nigh which, by dream forewarned,
Peticius from his bark Pompeius hailed,
And with Favonius and the Lentuli
To Lesbos took him. Of Cornelia's grief
Why tell what every human heart doth trow?
But if he would the conqueror's hand evade—
To Parthia, to Libya, or to Egypt?
Pompeius Magnus! could he overlook
Egypt's indebtedness?—to Cyprus next,
Thence to Pelusium and the youthful King:
Some ruthless Dæmon thereunto him led!

Attended poorly into port he sails,
His ships but few, his men two thousand told—
The Arbiter once feared—a supplicant!
Whereat the fiend Ingratitude took form:
Urged by Pothinus, eunuch, misanthrope,
And hater, hating most the man most loved—
Accurst Septimius, striking from behind,
Abetted by Achillas' surer aim,

Him reft of life whom legions could not kill :
Thus died the warrior in Cornelia's sight,
A swooning shriek his piteous funeral knell !
The mariners hastily their anchor weigh,—
Guarding too Sextus, of Pompeius scion,
And bear them, desolate, to friendlier shore.

Gallant Pompeius ! strong of arm and loin,
Of curly crown and merry countenance,
Giant in muscle or of body or brain,
Charmer of women and men, Earth's favourite,
Save one—of loftier zenith !—must it be
By the strict canon of pre-eminence
To pale and fall before the brighter star,—
Desert the world to make for Caesar space ?

O fated day of fratricidal strife !
The ghostly spheres are moved to visible signs ;
At Elis, in Minerva's sacred Fane,
(Elis, the sanctuary of the nations round,)
The Phidian image to the portal turns;
At Antioch, Ptolemais, Pergamus,
The temples ring with superhuman sounds
Of drums and trumpets and the din of war :
At Tralles, shrine of Caesar's effigy,
A palm-tree springs full-leafed from stony floor.

Now Caius Julius, first and greatest Caesar,
Becomes the Paramount of humankind :
Nor yet ! for from Pharsalia's hateful fray,—
Where with insensate rage the gods of Earth,
Roman with Roman, friend or brother, strove,
Despising death to prove that *One* must reign,—
Had fled Pompeius ! whither— whither gone ?

To Egypt onward ! leave the scattered hosts,
Which like evaporate clouds again condense,—
Haste to arrest the famous fugitive,
In ruin strong, with magic in his name,—
To gain a woeful prize,—his trunkless head ;
Too late for capture, impotent to save !

At this result, to Rome the Consul sent,
And his o'erbrimming heart relieving wrote—
'The crowning comfort of my victory rests
To pardon Romans by mishap my foes.'

'Tis told he wept,—such tears as must be true, -
His Julia's husband and his dearest friend !
Dry, dry the tears—men cannot work and weep ;
Henceforth is vital effort exigent.

King Ptolemæus his last Testament
Committed, haply to secure its aim,
To Roma's Senate—as a sacred trust :
This was Auletes, him ' the Piper' styled ;
Sometime deposed, a guest with friends at Rome, -
Pompeius, Marcius Cato, and Gabinius,—
He, by advice and War's arbitrament,
Gained restoration to the Monarchy ;
And, also, owed he cash to sundry Romans,
Julius Caesar one,—by office bound
To be for Rome his representative.

The Consul, knowing not Pompeius' death,
In Romans by Gabinius left, secure,
To Alexandria came with slender force,
Yet through the City, in the pomp of power
And regal progress, with his Lictors marched,

Fasces before him,—and the people frowned :
' Pompeius no more, why still confess
Roma's authority?'   Stern, Caesar strode,
By bold and trusty messengers heralded,
The Royal Alexandrine House unto ;
There Ptolemæus and the Prince cadet,
Arsinoë, junior Princess of the Throne,
And grim Pothinus, Eunuch-Minister,
Him met with smiles and simulate honesty,—
And there, with dignity impassible,
Abided he in well-pretended strength :

   Soon after said, ' By King Auletes' Will
These, eldest Girl and Boy, conjoint must reign :'
Pothinus with design not all unwise
Forestalled the Salique law, full well aware
That Cleopatra could his craft outreach ;
The Consul urged, ' It is a Testament,
By Rome held sacred, must accomplished be ;
At which Pothinus, in dissemblance deft,
Bent low the knee—' Behold ! a Judgment just :'
So far assented, Caesar pressed his suit
For reimbursement in integrity
Of nigh five thousand Talents to him due :
The Eunuch, politic, gave moneys, then
Among his friends made pleasure of his scorn
In multiplied discourtesies ; ' Deprived !
Had only pottery—silver vessels sold
To yield the requisition ;' clamoured citizens
Against the impost levied for the debt ;
Pothinus prospered in a fool's delight,
Whilst Caesar sent for legions—far away !

   Unmoved by such preventions, Caesar thought,

On surface smooth to Minister or King;
And, in this restful lull, made bland request,
' I would the wonders of this City see—
Projected by the Great of Macedon,
Built at whose hest by skilled Dinocrates,
Myself observe the Works whereof I read.'
The Soma saw he which ' the body ' held,—
' The body ' termed, with just significance,—
None other than the Conqueror of the World,
Regarding whom he once had grieved to tears
That any man his glory should transcend ;
He saw Serapis' Temple, and the Tower
Of their ingenious schemer Sostratus,
On Pharos raised, (with Beacon-fire,) led to
By Heptastadium ; and the Docks and channels
The Palace nearing, (with belligerent view ;)
The Catacombs yclept Necropolis ;
Poseidon's Temple, to all seamen dear ;
The vast Emporium, (to Canopus lost ;)
Gymnasium, Stadium, Amphitheatre,
Pan's Temple on the hill-top towering,
The Hippodrome, the subterranean Cisterns ;
But more than all did Caesar's cultured mind
Rejoice the famed Museum to behold,
Well-spring of learning—scroll on scroll up-piled
Of science and philosophy much loved
And Academe of those who him had taught, —
Though by his act to perish, undesigned.

———

Meantime Queen Cleopatra—self-proclaimed,
Watched with her scant adherents from afar,
Beyond Pelusium, in some strength encamped,
By arrogant Achillas held at bay,—
Unequal chances facing undismayed :

Magnanimous daughter of a line of Kings—
No moment yielding to a craven mind,
A Monarch would she rise, at any hazard :
Of all the Cleopatras foremost found !
Or Alexander's sister,—made a bride
On Philip's fatal day ; or, sadlier, wife
Of royal Œneus' son, doomed Meleager,
Who wasting slow, by magic spell accurst,
For hopeless love of Atalanta died :
As master-minds are prone,—own-counsellor
In things of import grave, she reasoned thus—
'Comes Caesar missioned by the gods for me ;
He hath decreed, and justly by the Law,
My brother me should marry—paltry boy !
A brother too my mate ! it shall not be,
Uncurbed I govern, wed me where I love ;
My Champion manifest ! how gain I him ? '

In thought entranced, her form upreared, transfixed,
Her hands on high, the fingers interlocked,
With lips compressed, looked she intent at nought ;
Then disapparelling, unwittingly
Turned to the speculum a furtive glance,
Her image there espying, fancy-fired
Sank couchant, to voluptuous slumber given :
SLEEP rests not on the spirit at unrest ;—
' What can I offer Caesar ? he is mighty,
Hath fame and wealth and in the name of Rome
Controls the world ; persistence—or despair ? '

Succeeds a waking dream,—Ambition's dream—
Expanding, warming, till the eyelids droop.
Fresh as the floweret to the dawn of day
Woke Cleopatra to her fantasie,

By introspection settled purpose grown
In fashion to her thoughts impersonate ;
Of goddess' visage lit with eyes of fire
And brain to keep them burning, of a mould
Blent in majestic and benignant grace,
Meet incarnation of her dreadless soul,
Like a fair column set apart she stood
Revolving her design :

                        ' No man of mark,
Conformed with me to match, will disregard
A woman young and fair, moreo'er a Queen,
Nay, even Cleopatra—him the least,
Of men the greatest ; Caesar wanteth not,
Myself is all to render—other none !
If to be lorded let my first lord be
The demigod who towers above them all ;
Queen Cleopatra Cleopatra gives—
The single bribe,—so must he melting place
Me on my Throne.'

           Clang-clang ! clang-clang ! the cymbals ;
Dames attend : composed, with courtly gesture
Smiling to welcome them, would fain conceal
Her passionate temper wrought by schemes untold,
Dissimulates with pleasant irony, and says
'Too anxious are they, too regardful all : '
The tiring done, luxuriant tresses plaited,
The jewels and the perfumes ministered,
She bids them, lightly, ' send Apollodorus ;'
He, joyfully, proud of the trustful missive,
Bound to her Cause in fealty, quick attends.

    Seated, so habited, assuming State,—

' Praise for thy promptitude, Apollodorus ;
Thou pitiest my straits, my army weak,
Achillas traps me, and Pothinus worse,
Hates me as eunuch should,—the jackanapes !
Authority complete my birthright clear !
But Caius Julius, noble as he is,
Rules, in observance of my Father's whim,
To yoke me with a boy, to have me reign
In couples ; this, Pothinus and Achillas
Alike debar,—and I am with them there ;
'Tis hard, contending with a Testament,
It loathes me quite ! thenceforth must I rebel ;
Despite of them and Caesar, only I !
The Consul hath not seen me—he shall see ;
Abate surprise, with *thee* I to him part ;
O faithful, valorous helper, canst thou doubt
My last success in what I machinate ?
Caesar is mortal man though as a god
In force and eminence, and I will be
The grandest woman of our God-made Earth,
Of this world's Victor, victor, with one arm
Rout fell Pothinus and his dastard crew ;
Now be attent to learn, the while I tell
Particulars of my arch stratagem ;
Hast thou not friends in the Palace ? ask of them
The Consul's goings out and comings in ;
This done, we coast in menial guise, by night
Unto the gate of my ancestral home,
The princely City of the Ptolemies,
Where, with precaution, safely pass we in ;
A friend worth having must be strong and brave,
Art not thou vigorous in heart and limb ?
Thou canst and wilt whereto I bid, me carry,—
Even to Caesar's chamber ; start not so !

How, thou shalt know anon; but take me there, ·
The rest is mine to do.'

                  As vassal leal,
In purpose firm whate'er the venture prove,
Apollodorus bowed obeisant, saying,
'Be it so,' quickly goes, and reappears—
To tell, 'O Queen! thy project is prepared :'
At earliest chance they sped, in tiny skiff,
Muffled and masked, watchful the verges keeping
Of the Internum, losing not its shore,
Passing seven mouths of Nile, to port of Pharos,
Whereat, unseen, they landed—to proceed
Along the Mole, the dusky ways among
Of busy Alexandria, where, as planned,
The stalwart guardian placed his protégée
In covert safe, for rest and sustenance ;
He to the Palace, she to think of next,
Becomingly enrobe, with care to braid
Her raven locks below the cincture falling
And amplify adornment ; well she knew
To make perfection perfect, and the art
To win.

            Right soon returned he—at command ;
'What more, my Queen?   I but exist for thee,'
A fascinating smile his recompense ;
'Quail not, brave heart! I'll guide thee what to do ;
Am I attiréd as a Ptolemy?'
Beholding, all abashed,—her dazzling beauty
Scarce seeing in the radiance diffused,
E'en as the Sun too bright, a darkness brings,—
Bending, he uttered low, 'Who sees, adores!'
Then the Aspirant, frenzied in fierce hope,—

'Now swathe me, good adorer, as here lain,
In some coarse canvas, seeming merchandise,
After the custom delicate things to cloke
In rude outcovering ; straightway with thine arms,
Thy muscular limbs, transport me till I bide
The rightful tenant of his Domicile,
Nor less than occupant of Caesar's Room :'
Effrayed, the staunch, obedient servitor
Inwrapped her tenderly, with timid touch
Up to his shoulder raised her, and away !

In garb of slave, his precious burthen bearing,
With crouching form his devious course he threads
As one on errand bent who goes his way ;
The Palace knew he, and the helots there
Unheeding passed him : Caesar then in council,
Apollodorus knew the Sanctum void,—
Therein, the curtains closed, with cautious speed
On silken couch his living load disposed ;
Expertly then with scrupulous carefulness,
As o'er a lovely flower, constrained to leave
Its perfume and its petals unimpaired,
The rough envelopment he disengaged
To loose the dainty members, folding her
Closely in pallium of royal woof ;
So thus the body in brocaded coil
Lay like a mummy vestured for the Bier,
The features left unshrouded : 'All is done !'
'Veil me, yea, look upon me, haste, depart,
Thee I forget not,—to my people say
Their Queen is soon to reign,—they have my blessing !'
With lowly crest retiring, backwardly,
Apollodorus softly draped the door
And fled the Palace.

                              Sacred Silence reigns :
Listening for footfall Cleopatra drowsed,
And drowsing hears eftsoons a manly tread,
Soldierly, measured—yes ! it must be He :
The Consul enters, in disrobing pensive,—
Rapt, slowly walked, and walked, and presently
With sharp glance marked an object—in surprise :
Thy nerves fail not, great Caesar ?—'What is this ? '
Observing curiously the pallium,
He, statue-like, the dormant figure scanned ;
(His towering forehead, his far-searching eye,
His firm-set lip made, voiceless, to command.)
The while he ruminates impassively,—
With indecisive hand the veil withdrew
And met, full blaze, two black refulgent eyes
In passion or intelligence supreme !
The placid countenance, immobile, spake,—
Not to the outward ear,—the world is hushed !
Gazing he wavered, turning, gazed again,
In deep tone uttering—'Thou ? Cleopatra ; '
A moment's pause, — the sunny cheeks grew
         sunnier,
Flashed forth fresh sparkles the significant eyes,
The ruby, pouting lips to music parted,
Pronouncing only, 'Caesar : ' wonder-struck !
As doth a mountain in the Earthquake-shock
The frame of Julius quivered, signing not
His wildly-throbbing heart its pulses found,—
The man who dauntless had confronted death
Dissolved to weakness by a woman's smile !
With mute respect and kingly dignity
Raised he the Queen,—unwound her, taciturn,
Put her at rest, and, with a formal bow,
Sat, at decorous distance.

'Royal Lady,
Caesar is here; superfluous to declare
Thee Princess Cleopatra,—who beside?
Less than myself could such event divine;
May he then humbly ask—how camest thou?
What can he do, of good, for her so fair?'
In dulcet tones,—'Great Caesar, King of Men,
Consider my distress! Executor
Of Ptolemæus Sire, thou bidst me live
In wedded link,—a brother-boy withal!
Say'st thou it is his Will?—it is not mine!
Wed not I with the stripling were it shown
Pothinus and Achillas not opposed,
Or Caesar had decreed it shall so be;
Am not I First of Egypt? thus to wive
No Queenship other than the Slave of slaves:
In thy told purpose, Consul, thou art just,
But know'st not Cleopatra,—her behold!
Do I look one ordained to reign by halves?
Mate I with equals,—may with Caesar mate,
Elect my Knight, my ægis, and my Jove!'

With hesitance, reflective,—'Well thou speakest;
By Nature gifted to be dominant,
Wilt, of selection, gain ascendency,
In beauty regal, as by birth a Queen;
Lady, for else, thou know'st my Mistress chief
Is Rome; take comfort—let it wait to-day;
To-morrow shall decide what course is best.'

Hereat, the intrepid Princess prudently
Her manner easing to a genial humour,
Complaisant, jubilant-smiling, 'Yea, most true,
Thy mistress Rome of me precedence boasts—

Which I accord ungrieved ; thy mistress Rome
Exacts obedience, Egypt prays thy help ;
Be love and duty equal in regard ;
The pleader at thy feet hath Woman's plea
Of feeble to the strong—who overawes
The hundred Nations, and may add to these
Egypt in Cleopatra,—when she reigns.'

'Sweet Sorceress ! sweetly conquer,—better so :
Shall he preferring loss desire to gain ?
Yet would I conquer only to obtain
Sole sway with love's subjection in thy heart :
Established shalt thou be, though men may say
Thou dost prevail o'er him who doth prevail ;
For, less the halo of the Crown of Egypt,
Thy Seer foretells unto the end thou wilt
Excel as Cleopatra.'

　　　　　　　　Rose he then,
Elate, as gallant courteous kissed her palm,
(Holding the taper fingers wistfully,)
Whereat she laughed exuberant, carelessly
Clapped hands for joy—mistaken for a call,
Bringing attendants, him the Quæstor one,
To whom advancing Caesar drily said,
'Tend well this Lady,—for she is the Queen,
Conduct her to the Matrons, let them mind
To lodge her suitably—my order this !'
The Quæstor signed assent, and Cleopatra
Moving with stately reverence to all,
Dumbly him following, went.

　　　　　　　　Along the floor,
Chromatic, tesselate with marbles rare,

Pacing, on-pacing with uncounted steps
As one who finds new pabulum for thought,—
Caesar somewhile irresolute, suddenly
Summoned his officers.

              The morning next,
Discoursing with Pothinus and his Ward,
Unchanged he urged the reconcilement due
In prosecution of the Father's fiat,—
True to his duty as Executor :
Pothinus temporized, in form agreed ;
Moreover, at a banquet this same day
A guest in proud array our Heroine shone
In grace supreme, if not in title so :
The King, nor true, nor wholly confident,
Accomplished Alexandrine in deceit,
Leaned to Pothinus and Theŏdotus—
[Or Minister or Tutor of one mind,]
Feigning consent to Cleopatra's claims :
The Consul said, ' But Ptolemæus must
Substantiate his right by Self to reign ;
Auletes' Will is Law, myself am Rome : '
Whereon, Pothinus angered made cabal,
And with the General Achillas leagued,
His mandate to the army reckless sent—
By land and sea Brucheium to invest.

   Caesar, still earnest for a friendly close,
His armaments unequal to resist,—
Ambassadors despatched, the King's known friends,
(Serapion, Dioscorides, important men,)
To parley with Achillas, who uncaring
Said—' Let them die ! '

Hence must he, Rome's Dictator,
Signalize Rome.   The Alexandrines flushed,
In numbers horse and foot, munitions—strong,
(Some Roman soldiers also, of Gabinius,)
May not be openly fronted ; ' Fortify
The Palace ; guard ye the fort and harbour :
Inspire our combatants to utmost valour,
Or win by strategy where force might fail.'
[Now were Pothinus and the boy-King held
In durance.]   Bold Achillas bolder grows,
Surrounds the Palace,—in audacious pride :
' Will he not vanquish whom Pompeius vanquished,
Pompeius' murderer greater Caesar slay ? '
In vain his onslaught ;—to the Harbour next :
The Fleet ablaze ! wherefrom the fateful firebrands
By Æolus wafted—on the Palace fall,
Igniting soon the Treasure-house of Wisdom,
Library priceless—by the studious prized ;
Destruction dire ! Who dares such loss compute,
Who conjure back the thoughts then immolate?
Will genius regenerate a conceit—
A once evolvéd germ be born again ?
Then were annihilate immortal parts,
Even as the burning of the souls of men :
Forth with redoubtable ardour sallied Caesar,
Seized Pharos' Tower and gave it garrison,
Razed all impediments Bruchcium nigh,
And, for the nonce, Achillas kept aloof.

    Amid those perturbations of dismay,
Whilst in the doubtful fray confusion ruled,
Princess Arsinoë to Achillas fled
And, with inherent Ptolemaic spirit,
Declared regality, and wore the Crown ;

For shrewd Achillas felt his own defect
Of full authority to popular view,
By Caesar's wise detention of the King;
And hereupon, Pothinus criminate
In traitorous missives to Arsinoë,
The Consul doomed him to a felon's fate.

Howe'er alluring Cleopatra's charm,
[Why should a hero beauty underprize?]
The Consul diligent, scanning incidents—
Offensive or defensive, War foreknew;
To Rhodes, Cilicia, Syria,—for Ships;
To Crete for Archers; e'en to Nabathæa
(King Malchus, of the line of Ismael,)
For Cavalry: meanwhile, the outworks guarded,
Intrenchment, bastion, gabion, all devices
For safety indispensable, are done:
Wellnigh to hopelessness the danger grew;
Shut out from land, and harassed from the sea,
The cisterns rendered brackish,—so he might
Heed the misgiving murmurs,—doubt *himself;* '
But he was Roman, and with Romans joined;
'Sink wells,' he said, 'retreat before these caitiffs?
Forget not Rome! bring in Pompeius' Legion.'

Arsinoë (compassing Achillas' death,)
Made Ganymed General,—sagaciously,
For with much art he wrought, in tactics quick
To baffle and to hold; untrammelled all,
With multitudinous host,—the stranger pent,
Obstruction either side, entrapped and caged;
The City like a cliff too straight to climb,
The Harbour blocked, and watched unceasingly:
Romans exasperate, break away to Sea;

There Ganymed, 'gainst whom the Chief of Rome
In petty warfare his renown imperils,—
Determinate, the same for small or large,—
The odds accepting, fixed the game to win :
The strife is hot, the Consul's ship surrounded,
For life he swam, his scarlet chlamys losing,
His tablets bearing,—with a charméd life !
He masters, and the Alexandrines quail,
(Craven at sight of Roman fortitude,)
Appealing to him, 'Give us back our King ;
We love nor Ganymed, nor Arsinoë,
Send Ptolemæus,—we are reconciled :'
The Consul, counting on his legions near,
Consents, preferring as an Adversary
Even though beardless boy in name a King,
Instead to combat with a headless host
Whom to discomfit were inglorious,
Whom to be beaten by left honour none ;
So went young Ptolemæus, streaming tears,
Egyptian tears unreal and unimpassioned
As those their crocodiles' ; he 'could not go,
To be with Caesar cared for more than all
The rights of kingship ;' thus away ! and soon
Unmasked his nature, like a tiger-whelp
Freed from the toils, and in short term of days
Made clear his motive—threw aside pretence :
The tears so lately feigned as his lament
Were, prematurely shed, real tears of woe !

———

Caius, in pauses sweet of leisure strained,
With Cleopatra weighty counsel held :
In such dilemma well it was to have
So fair a Chancellor, withal so wise ;

Taught in all Coptic wiles, adept in craft,
Quick to unweave the meshes of their schemes
And circumvent their projects, knew she not
Methods and men of Egypt? who outwits
Egyptian like Egyptian? land or sea,
Leader or follower, every trick of war
To her apt cognizance not idly shown ;
Expert in tongues, enabled to discourse
With stragglers any, all intrigues to learn.

The Brother gone, the Sister freely breathes,
And thus at ease, the riot set at rest,
For fit reception of the Consul cares :
With fervent eyes, as Sybil when inspired.
Imbued with light as one to love resigned,
Her raiment flowing free, of silver tissue,
Anklets and armlets serpent-like of gold,
Her white well-moulded bosom half revealed,
Fair neck begemmed,—yea, jewels laid on jewels,—
Her ebon hair abundant, braided part
And partly loosened,—she, in merry mood
Awaits his advent ; list ! his footstep sounds,—
A sound familiar grown !

                            Both hands held forth,
'Welcome ! most welcome to me art thou, Caius,
Timely adopting to release the Boy—
Their King awhile—for me preparative !
Nor will thy praise be poorer at the tale
Who their fool's errand prompted,—dost thou
          frown ?
Was it not good ? nay, blame me guardfully.
For thou hast done the thing I pre ordained—

Designed to practise Cleopatra's thought !
Dictator thou, she thy Prime Councillor
Hath disentangled thee—as time will show :
The silly child on sole dominion set
Will head against thee the Egyptian host,
Thy rival he and Roma's enemy !
Then how will fare the futile Testament ?'
Her arms outstretching, laughed she,—Caesar laughed
In chorus sympathetic, echoing,
And, lost in loving admiration,—said,
' Hebe of Egypt ! rooted in my heart,
As thou affirmest Caius is in thine—
He had thy view but told thee not, for love ;
Wished to be chided by thee, bear thy gibes,
Biding the rapture of thine after-praise,
Forsooth, for news thou didst anticipate !
Ah ! Charmer mine,'—then rising to her eyes,
Transported madly his reflection saw
In those ink-mirrors—

      ' Dearest, *I am* there !
It is myself,—to be Caesarion named,
The Son of Caesar—King of Kings unborn ;
Of Cleopatra born a Son shall be !'
Then in the glow of love's beatitude
Caressed her, murmuring fondly, ' We have loved ;
Is it not strange the long divided years
Do not ill-match us ? such thy Caius was,
His fate accomplishing in manhood's prime,
Strong in the greed of empire—so art thou !
Fret not nor fear, for whatsoe'er the balks
Thou'rt born to prosper—thought he thus, thy Like !
Howbeit, dear, the striving is not done,
Nor past the peril,—but the die is cast,
" For Cleopatra, Caesar !" hence the cry.'

Gladdened, ecstatic, the Incomparable
At instant impulse close enfolded him :
' Mine earthly Jove ! look at me, kiss me thrice :
May'st thou not love me to thy heart's content ?
Be with me quite for now and evermore !
Thou hast adventured for me ; I am vain
Beyond my kindred pride of Ptolemy
To be enlinked with him—the grandest Man :
Must—must we part ? thy Mistress Rome preferred,
Thy Queen—lorn Mistress—Mistress lost her Lord !'

The Consul, gently loosing, seriously—
' Be great ! of Rome's Republic Ruler he,
(For so again have they their choice declared,)
Or thou of yon bright region—which to see
A duty is, this brawl ignoble past ;
Then shall we visit Egypt's confines far,
Love on and on each time we meet or part,
More loving part—perchance to meet no more :'
With drooping forehead Cleopatra, silent,
The chamber quitted, as oppressed with grief,
He her attending—to the gates of Sleep.

Though hours fly gaily Time the future broods,
As tranquil air forebodes impending storm ;
Howe'er, at peaceful seasons we relax
And quaff and laugh oblivious of our cares :
Nor were those easeful hours all profitless
With Egypt's paragon ; at eve reposed,
In pensive mood—
                        ' Awhile this pause of peace
We may forewarn of things about to be ;
Some notice have I from my native friends—
Eftsoons the leaven of our brother King

Which you or I, or both,—nay tell not either!
Have thrown among their ill-assorted host,
Will breed a ferment not to be allayed;
Protect thy ships, secure thy water-ways,
Or they will starve us—with the rats shut in!'

Response prelusive an approving sign,—
'Prophetic Mentor! it is organized;
Their schemes know I, esteeming what thou say'st;
Our Fleet is at this hour in all prepared,
The brave Euphranor Captain, unsurpassed,
Tiberius Nero General in command;
Though they exceed us much on land or sea,
By higher spirit shall we overpower,
And thou, enthroned, wilt glorify my name.'

'Forgive! forgive me, woman, fondly straining
Even beyond thee,—for the stake is mine;
If I preserve the courage of my race,
Would I not furtherance yield at any cost
And prove me Cleopatra? who though young
Is resolute to die for greater life,
Or doubly die Caesarion to bestow!'

Beyond himself exalted, he arose,—
'Be thou contented! no forebodings heed,
For our Caesarion shall protected be,
Unborn or born secure, and comforted
In thy maternal soul's serenity;
To my impervious Shield thy faith commit.'

———

At dawning hour the sounds of contest ring;
First with the Navy, for along the night
With boding message had the scouts returned;

Aggressively proceedeth Ganymed,
Seizing the Transports ; Romans stand at bay ;
Their Ships well-manned attack with onset fierce,
The Convoys rescue,—less Euphranor, lost
In death.

        Now Fortune smiles on Rome !
Prince Mithridates, styled of Pergämus,
Whom Caesar somewhile sent in search of succours, —
A constant friend deserving of report,—
Had with his gathered force Pelusium gained,
(The barrier main 'twixt Syria and Egypt,
Lately by foresight of Achillas armed,)
Its Fortress captured—his defence secured ;
Ingress to Egypt from the Sea through Pharos,
From land Pelusium, after late success
Held by the Romans ; onward Mithridates—
In every march subduing.

                To the field
The Consul quitting, doubtful solace seeks :
‘ Queen, sad adieu ! I leave thee in good hope ;
The risk is equal be the clash whate'er ;
The law of Fate it is to satisfy
The world's demand ; fair one, for *thee* I go,—
And for myself, for true it is to say
My will is with it ; sorrow some to think
And motive most to urge, *thy* maintenance
Is in the hazard,—ill the gods forefend !
Or if to fail, for thee 'twere best endured,
Rely on Mithridates,—he hath virtue,
Will for my sake uphold thee ; failing him,
The Carsulenus—those I shall instruct :
The while Rome needs me,—though the rapturous
    beam

From thee proceeding is as draught of Lethe,—
With no more fooling must I check this feud,
To save if next to lose,—ah, first to save!'

'Caius, thy love is proven,—and be sure
Thy debtor in it, whatsoe'er betide,
Will not dishonour thee; herefrom I watch,—
Here is my eyrie, whence with eagle-eye
Anent the motions of their King I search
To aid thy strategy; invincible!
Add to thy titles, if in glory least,
"Of Cleopatra Saviour;" kiss me, dear,
And say thou *wilt* return!'

Comes pitiless war!
The Boy-King, with his General, in full strength
Confronting Mithridates at the Delta,
(So named because like "Delta" circumscribed,
A fertile plain, profaned as battle-field!)
Advances skirmishing, retires the worse;
Meantime the balance trembles,—the Egyptian
Rich in supplies and force numerical:
The Consul, vigilant, with prescient aim,
(Egyptian Fleet to Lower Nile removed,)
Combining all resources, sped by sea,
Resistance crushing, landed, so to join
His coadjutor—superadding Caesar;—
Copt against Roman measured, arm to arm,
The contest desperate—the issue final;
Shall Rome at such be humbled? Ganymed
To test extreme their skill and valour goaded,
By pertinacity the stroke delayed;
Then Julius—'To their Camp! at end diversions,—
Assail intrenchments! round them—flank and rear!

My Carsulenus, take thy troop above,
Their bulwark seize, inform us when 'tis done,
Whilst I assaults redouble till they fly ; '
Dispersion utter—hither, thither, where ?
Scared runagates ! for safety to the ships !
The King, a fugitive among the herd,
In the tumultuous escapade is drowned.
Now pæans sing ! the vain entanglement
Portending Caesar failure and reproach,
Begets him gladness and access of fame.

————

Zephyrus with swiftest wing and balmiest breath
To Cleopatra brought the word sublime—
'Success ! Thou'rt Sovereign sole :' a Mother too,
For at this season was Caesarion born,—
Proud Mother of a male to Caesar's line,
Knew she the ecstasy of hopes fulfilled,
Love and ambition in the climax wed !
Contemplating her infant's winning smile,
She pondered dreamily, then thought aloud,—
'Myself I gave thee, how to give thee more ?
None else than thanks to proffer—poor indeed !
But there thou art, Caesarion,—*our* Son !
Were not my babe a ransom for a Crown ?
Why lingers he, my Caius ? '

————

Soon he came,—
In form triumphant as a Conqueror,
Of Egypt Master, Rome's Autocrator :
Withheld the Alexandrines service none—
Pleased at relief from irksome ways of war ;
Abase the spear, forsake the battlements,
In suppliant livery go forth : proclaim
The Consul ! Priests, submission testify,

Bring out your idols,—leading, carry them ;
Then he who hath the power will stay his
    hand.

    Caesar, just, merciful, before them bent ;
Bestowing amnesty, their love he won :
The Ptolemæian City traversing—
Impeded only by the cheering throng,
He gains the Roman quarter,—to receive
Congratulations from compatriots dear :
With recognition to his soldier friends,
Rome's Consul gladly the Expectant seeks.

    Pass to the Palace—and its anxious Chief ;
Her last, as in progressive happiness,
Climacteric consonant ! Not oft in life
To men such moments hap, or seldom, sooth,
Are in fruition worthily esteemed ;
For at the crowning hour we underrate
Successfulness by earnest cares achieved,
Occasion scantly use, or let it slip,
Our peace embittered by regret—in vain !

    Eager, resplendent, listening she rests :
'Salute thee, Victor ! as but *one* presumes,
As Cleopatra may—from ruddy lips
Repayment full, in love and gratitude :
Doubt not thy happiness is mine, my King—
And in perfection is for me enough,
E'en as my pride is in thine eminence ;
To Fate subdued, awaiting its decree,
(How could I fear of him who faileth not ?)
Disquietude for other, half thyself,
The dangers rating of the contest dread,—

I re-exist as one new-born, to bless !
Seat thee, O Consul, whilst I hear thee speak.'

   Impressively, apart he seated her,
Sedate retired, with reassuring smile
Her hand compliant raising to his lips ; —
' Queen Cleopatra—*so by me declared,*—
The chance of war is, to the wisest, blind,—
We have the gods to thank for good result ;
Granting all skill and bravery and strength
May be misfortune past retrieve of man ;
A soul born wrestle was it, and my heart
Hath sometimes quailed *for thee ; I* had to lose
A life already by mankind apprized,
The best part spent, the rest of second worth—
Thirsting for vantage whensoe'er it be
How more for thee—*and thine !* '

              Hereat, uprisen
She o'er him leaning,—' Guardian Angel mine !
Were not I mean and poor in thankfulness
Possessed none other answer than my love,
Which soon to thee the tide of time will end ?
Thou goest to thy glory, leaving me
A gilded puppet—of my Soul bereft !
I knew it sadly in the lonesome days
Chequered by hope and fear, misgivings drear
For our two selves and, further, next to tell ; '
Then gliding from his side approached a cot
And lifting coverlet breathed out—' Our Son !
Thy guerdon see, dear Caius ; we shall cease—
Perchance not far between, for I am rash
And of a nature not for long enduring
Here, who somewhen shall memorize us both,

Caesar *and* Cleopatra ! he who won
The world at will,—and she his Commandant !
More great than thou, were't possible, behold ;
Ah, did *thy* mother, Caius, equal his ?
See—thy Caesarion—him I grateful grant,
Exceeding kingdom !'

                    Nigh the cradle bowed,
In meditation absent,—' Worthy *her !*
A goodly child it is, a princely boy—
Proof of thy matchless wealth in witchery,
A gift beyond thyself ; Caesarion, hail !
Supernal Augur who thy future limns ;'
The babe he kissed, urbane the Queen embraced
And with complacence, his discourse resumed,—
' Be we exultant ! after war's turmoil,
Dolour and danger and the sight of death,
A while of comfort and repose were well—
The compensation of our anxious hours
With her, associate of the world select !'
At this he met the warm, enchanting rays
From grand, black, luminous eyes—enraptured paused
At ready blandishment—and after, said,
' Why yes dear, most with thee ! what mortal man
Since Saturn's reign was otherwhile so blest
As I in thy benign companionship
And love ? for, e'er so long we roam to love ;
Together go we, ay together go,
Thinking no close of our consented Heaven—
See thy Egyptus at the banks of Nile,
The same I read of in Herodotus' page,—
Antient to him as antient now to us,
Antient ere Roma or Athenæ rose,
Ere strong Achilles strove or Homer sang,—

Seen once by him thy glorious Ancestor,
Of Aristotle pupil, Philip's Son,
Unequalled Alexander, demigod,
Whom would I rival in desert of fame ;
Dear one, his race I love, and thee I love,
Am I not, loving thee, with him akin ?
Yea, will we wander to those hallowed scenes,
Hallowed by Time who hallows if he spares ;
In union wander—body and spirit one !
Erewhen,'—whereat, composure reassumed,
' Much must we regulate, to secure thy Throne.'

' Dear King ! my only Lord until thou goest—
Shut out the thought—my Lord as now, for aye !
Thou hast in virtue earned glad interval
With her from Hades rescued by thine arm ;
Forget we circumstance—inhibiting
The wretched premonition of the next,
Forbidding pain and caring not for care,
O'erlooking not how Earth as Heaven can be
Whilst we ignore the after and the past ;
What were Elysium than a livelong day ?
The present value and the present seize,
For respite so serene may not recur ;
What counts thy glory, thy Dictatorship,
Compared with life by Cleopatra's side ? '

' O subtle tongue ! timing a tuneful voice—
Affecting more than man may dare to own ;
Ah, fair enchantress ! my ambition fades
When thee I touch and look into thine eyes ;
My Lotus thou, I on thy graces feed
Unmindful of the worship of the world !
Consanguine with the Great of Macedon

Thou hast a hero-heart, and I would reign,
Sweetheart ! within *thy* heart,—than over Nations ;
Be it so—as thou wilt ; to Nilus speed we—
Observance, joyance, pastime—Sybarite !
Yet not unblent with purpose ; we shall seek
What Caesar ought to know ; he thanks the gods
Who season to him yield to view with thee.'

 'Caius, thy words are strains from Helicon !
Thy prisoner onetime fetters thee as hers ;
(Her captive constant, if she had her will !)
Next shalt thou prove what is thy neophyte
When she doth play the Queen ; the Triumph o'er,
By thy wise influence the State confirmed,
A Royal Progress have we on our Nile.'

———

 As now, so then, success is deemed the right,
The cause is spent, and men forget the cause,
War is an evil, discord is distress ;
Come peace ! as rain the arid earth to fresh,
Or as soft zephyrs to the ailing frame :
The Alexandrines, pacified in all,
For Cleopatra clamoured ; she, appearing
In beauty well bedight, won popular love—
Their Goddess tutelar !   Nor Caesar less
Obtains their homage ; he with sage attent
Good counsel gives to satisfy their will,
And there is rest.

———

                    A banquet by the Queen :
The Consul at her side as honoured guest
Pretension none assumes in rank or power,
The singers and the minstrels have one burthen,—

Praise to their youthful Mistress, benison
To Rome's Dictator.
        Next day, a People's Pageant :
Went first the Priests of Thoth and of Osiris,
Each with his sacred idol, treading true
To sound of lyre and timbrel well-attuned :
In gorgeous Chariot (whereunto were yoked
Six Elephants milk-white, in silver trappings,)
Sate Cleopatra and, with solemn mien,
The noble Roman, as the Nation's friend ;
For escort, soldiery of horse and foot
The prime of Egypt's army; after these,
A Car by Leopards drawn, supporting high
The youngest Ptolemæus, but a child ;
(Princess Arsinoë a prisoner kept ;)
The Nobles, Officers of State, Mace-bearers
With the Regalia of the Ptolemies ;
Ædiles and Præfects, and the Palace helots
Carrying the banners of the Dynasty;
Came the prætorian cohort, veteran men,
Stalwart and grave, methodic in their motion,—
As 'twere to tell, or first or last, of Rome ;
Along the teeming streets are groups all eyes,
The smiling eyes of welcome ! house-tops filled
With zealous women in their holiday gear,
Gay garlands throwing as their votive gifts
In Cleopatra's lap—or half for Cæsar ;
Sidelong the happy people dance and sing
Whilst skipping maidens strew the way with flowers ;
Unto Serapis' Temple, there to pay
Accustomed adoration to the gods ;
Then Temple of Hephæstion, built to him
The friend of Alexander,[1] lost too soon—

[1] Hephæstion.

At Alexander's will a demigod ;
On, o'er the Heptastadium, to Pharos,
Passing the Harbour, where the doubled Navies
Tell with concurrent shout the Sailors' glee :
In festive trim the Ships alike rejoice,—
Their sails and pennants, conscious of their Queen,
Swelling or flaunting in the sycophant air.

Back to the Palace, [a delirious throng,]
Whereat descending, forthwith Caesar called
A Synod of the Archons, summoning
With gracious frankness to him—all who would.

'Ye men of Egypt, recognize your Queen ;
Give homage to the gods, beneficent ;
My part it is, in pleasure and in pride
To render you a Monarch such as none,
No kingdom can compare ; your country, favoured
Above all other in this world's delights,
Displays a Sceptre bright as is its Sun ;
Prize her much, men of Egypt, prize her well !'
With deafening cries hilarious rang the walls—
The utterance of devotion !   Cleopatra,
In beauty beaming, with commanding presence,
Instant held Court ; the recusant vassals flocked
With courteous readiness to kiss her hand,
Thereby to seal their troth.

———————

From Storm—to Calm :
Reclined, in stillness of the darkling hours,
Grateful surcease of care, spake Cleopatra—
'All bankrupt am I, Caius, gift or praise ;
Let us inaugurate felicity—
And every hour improve ! the day's the day ;

Oblivion of to-morrow ! I will show
Much to thy wonder—and by me unseen—
Of Egypt in the Past ; appreciate
Dear Comrade my design ; on Nilus' breast
Like swans afloat and better less their toil !
Lodged in a Palace, which my Galley is,
Will we have halcyon days and halcyon nights,—
Nay, look not so demure ; not void of drift,
Pursuit of knowledge, or for wisdom more,
To thee, at least, will fleet the sunny hours,—
For thee, for me alas ! but I have said,—
We will not think to-morrow.'

As she ceased,
From musing, Caesar takes her yielding hand,—

' Most loved, and lovely ! in this troublous life
We mix to-day, to-morrow, and the gone,
Unseeing where they tend ; 'tis very good
To make the best of boons the gods bestow,
With our scant vision searching not too far ;
We know the present, the relentless done
Is with the Powers above ; whate'er our acts,
For aye we make a past, and it is well
Our lightest pleasure hath some consequence :
Thebae and Memphis ! let us then survey
Their broken grandeur, justly to compare
Ourself with other ; for I tell thee, dear,
There is no gain in pluming ignorance
Leading to measure higher than we are ;
This but the quest of Truth, (whole Truth is not,)
To follow fearless where perception guides,
Minding not though it dwarfs us and impugns
Our fondest faith in seeming verities :

Yea, on the banks of thine old Nilus' stream
Whose fountains none can tell, welled up the springs
Of learning, science and ingenious art,—
The gnomon and the monthly march of Time,—
Philosophy of earth, air, sea or sky,
Or the dark destiny of the unbound Soul.'

    '"Tis very wise, O Caius; wiser I,
More wise discerning less; for me enough
The objects near, which I can grasp, enjoy,
Take pleasure from by eye, ear, every sense,
Whilst thou so keenly noting, too far seekest,
Neglecting means of momentary joy;
Confide in her thy faithful patroness,
And thou shalt kiss the Earth where'er she treads.'

    'Fair sophist! let *thy* wisdom have full sway;
In thy fresh flush of perfect womanhood,
Of vernal bloom, thou see'st with hopeful eyes—
A healthful vision not yet inwards turned,
The dreary introspect of withered loves—
Lucific orbs! whose Circean influence
Lulls as Nepenthean anodyne my brain,
Expelling all but blissful memories!'

    'Thou lov'st me Caius! go we to our rest;
To-morrow prove I *my* Philosophy.'

                ————

    This was the night when Caesar met the shade
Of fallen Pompeius,—by his thoughts upraised;
His bed on lain, in moments somnolent
He muttered, dreaming, cabalistic words:
'Where hidest thou, Pompeius, dearest friend?

The danger past, to thee again I turn ;
If we did hate, our hate had spring in love—
We scorn to quarrel with the thing we scorn :
Why didst thou spurn me? thee did not *I* spurn,—
Regarding thee but second to myself;
Why wouldst thou wish thee greater than thy Peer ? '
Then, clear to vision (in his mental eye,)
Saw he the figure of the famous Chief,
His crispéd head, and aspect debonair,
His model form, of stature eminent ;—
' Dear Brother, *salve !* henceforth reconciled;
If to communicate—'twere not to chide ;
Thou dost forgive me errors unexplained,
Undoubting I did love thee—ever loved ;
When in blest Leuce's Isle our Manes meet,
Forgotten all than friendship and accord :'
The Apparition smiled,—and Caesar woke.

END OF FIRST PART.

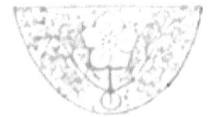

Caesar in Egypt.

PART THE SECOND.

THE phases of our life as chapters end ;
Ourselves we find pertaining to a world
Whereof, at first, we think it alters never ;
Then cometh change,—as in Kaleidoscope,
And our next chapter is a sphere fresh found ;
Again it shifteth, and again we live
Calmly—as native to some strange new things,
Until, of Earth the changes being rung,
Betides the latest chapter of our time,
Putative Proem to—a life beyond.

    Genial the hour when travel shall begin,
Be over labour, care the while debarred ;
A time of gladness is it, unconfined,—
Pending the day when caring is renewed :
Our chronicle regards the signal morn
Of gaiety and splendid circumstance,
When Caesar linked with Cleopatra sped
To view the unspent glories of the Nile—
The central figure of the world in man,
With Egypt's Sovereign—by him invest.

Movement where'er in Alexandria seen :
Told is it not their Queen on Nile embarks,
Her guest the Victor?   Streets to River tending
With banners blazoned, lined with curious crowds
To see the Hero pass ; within, without,
Laborious bustle with diversion vies—
A festive holiday to pleasure lent :
The Consul's Officers and Men of State
Of Egypt, join in cordial brotherhood—
In mutual approval : ensign raised,
Wends the procession, ringing tongues around,
Unto Eunostus' bay, Cibotus' Port,
Where wait the ships, in proud preparedness,
To bear the noble Travellers Nilus through ;
A glorious Flotilla, uncompared,
Rigged in gay colours, decorate with flowers ;
Not as for sea, the brunt of winds and waves,
But inland-bound, for corporal ease contrived,
Complete if Epicurus were its lord !
A Water-palace Cleopatra's Barge,
A Palace moving with indwellers moving ;
Above the deck a canopy o'erspread
With silver thread inwoven flashing sheen ;
Pavilion cool, luxurious, for Herself
And Consul ; chambers underneath hung round
With draperies sumptuous of hues well blent,
For feast, for sleep, for bath commodious ;
The prow Hawk-beaked, as type of Horus, god,
Guardian of crownèd mortals ; at the helm
Displayed an Elephant's head in beaten gold—
The Ptolemaic symbol.

Pioneer—
A pilot barque, with music-men and maidens,

Melodious harbingers of happiness !
Singing they go, to notes of lute and shawm,
Rare perfumes casting to the Zephyrs round,
Scattering Earth's blossoms on the face of Nile ;
The Royal Galley next, and in its wake
The Servitors—a numerous company—
With multifarious aliment supplied,
Succeeded by a minor ship of war
Manned by the body-guards—a jovial crew.

Now Hapimou, beneficent water-god,
Prospers aërially the floating team,
Enough to swell the sails, and but enough ;
Sun-god Osiris gives his sanction full
By radiance unshaded ; winding on
Through Marcotis' lake, and noting there
The water-flowers and vari-coloured birds,—
The sacred Ibis, Heron, King-fisher,
Or, to the instant humour, vineyards near,
The source profuse of Mareotic Wine,—
Biding the festal hour, until the night
Which comes to men, at most, as given for sleep.
Though some have eyes for night as eyes for day,
To do what best is done whilst others drowse,
To see the splendours of the skiey host,
And much dame Nature worketh in the dark ;
Moreo'er there is for Night to humankind—
It maketh a to-morrow !

　　　　　　　Morrow came
To those Nile-revellers ; they hailed the day
At Sais, (noted of the great Amasis,
And, earlier still, for Bocchoris the Wise,
Lawgiver, founder of prosperity,)

By loss of commerce hastened to decay,—
Presenting curious remanents of the past;
The Fane of Neith, onetime of Earth the greatest,—
The Fane of Neith 'the Mother of the gods,'
An area vast with columns scattered o'er
Of Palm-tree fashion; tombs of god Osiris,
And Hophra; giant monoliths, set up
Where native stones exceed not grains of sand;
Near these the sacred Lake whose glassy face
The lamp-lit mysteries of Isis mirrored;
Nor far Busiris with its temple-towers,
Which, at the feast of Isis, all excelled.

See now Bubastis of the Hierarch-Kings,
Shishak renowned, the noblest of their race,
Who to King Solomon a daughter gave,—
Bubastis high up-raised by felon hands,
Devote to Pasht (by Greek, Diana named,)
Whose Fane begirt with Groves conspicuous rose—
As telling, truly, it had been supreme.

Fall'n Heliopolis! City of the Sun,
A shattered sepulchre—a wreck of Shrines:
Here Caesar, zealous, 'This we must not pass!
The hallowed spot where Plato and Eudoxus
Conceived new thoughts, where Moses, Legislator
Derived his wisdom, to instruct mankind,—
Moses, prime leader of a tribe heroic,
Who told of Heaven and Earth in god-like words:
This City, first-named On, whence Joseph took
For Wife the high-priest's daughter, Asenath,—
Whence later, Baruch, Jeremiah sang:
The seat of learning where sage Manetho wrote,
Abode of Solon and Pythagoras;

Where somewhile dwelt sublime Euripides.'
So saw he vestiges of those grand Temples
Built to the Sun-god Re, and Monuments
Admiring seen by Moses and by Plato,—
To European shores transported since.

O'erpast exertion or of limb or eye,
For Caesar, as the Barge on smoothly glides,
Well-earnéd rest in calm companionship
Mid sights and sounds of pastime and plaisance;
And soon, afar outlined, by distance dim
As ghosts of objects next to be beheld,
The simple forms of those stupendous Deeds
Told of, described, unseen but half-believed,
Pi-Rama—Pyramid,—the Mountain-tomb:
Great soul of Time! his pure delight we share
At thought of such a soul's desire fulfilled,
Beholding them when consecrated more
By revolution of two thousand Suns!

Onward to Memphis! old, to be so old
As to be old when older Thebae fell:
Further, yet further, and to Moëris lake;
The mystic city Crocodilopolis,—
To Sebek sacred, Sebek, Crocodile-god:
Memphis—a wide expanse of measured miles,
Ornate with solemn Shrines, colossal Forms;
Temples of Pthah, and of the Bull-god Apis,
Where Apis in the holy stable lived;
On hill Sinopium temple of Osiris—
Of Isis, nearer, by Amasis raised;
The Pyramid of Suphis, Cheops named,
Guarded by Sphinxes of proportion huge,
With lineaments of quietude divine

Demonstrative of a resolvéd will—
Unchangeable,—or was, or is for ever!
Symbol of Human mind with Lion force.
In stone made manifest—inspiring worship,—
And countless tombs gigantic o'er the plain,
Each rivalling each in largeness, by the Lake
On whose green Isle a stately Palace rears;
The wond'rous Labyrinth, step by step revealed,
Of archéd cavernous chambers all-adorned.
A maze of devious passages and halls
For rites hieratic delved,—extending far,
To Moëris Island reaching,—therewithin
Sad tributes of esteem outlived their mark, —
Gone to the state of empty nothingness
Concluding human toil!

           At eve to say—
' Here, Cleopatra, find I travel's charm,
Less blest, for more is not, than thy consent;
Thou hast a land of wonders which excel
Foreknowledge heard or seen; those earliest
    men
Of thine Egyptus giants must have been,
Had stature of Colossus—equal brain;
They acted as we dream, built up their thought.
Bold in the God-ward search aspired to Heaven:
Their stepping-stones, if rough, up-mounted high
Toward the Empyrean, and their yearning
Betrayed a virtuous instinct of the mind;
I am sublimer man by sight of such,
Advantaged in a priceless, deathless meed
Of quality to aggrandize my soul;
Enough to-day; enjoy we our repose,
And whiles the After-glow sheds quiet spell,

Amusement, music and the time-struck dance !
To-morrow more of old Egyptus' marvels.'

  Spake Cleopatra, in low tone, affectioned,—
' Dear Caius, thy contentment is as mine,
Comparing not contentment with my love,
Wherewith I fain would pay thee, though alone ;
Come forth, come forth !'—and came the sounds of
     mirth,
Frolic and melody ; the stars shone out
Primordial lustre from a sky serene ;
Moon-goddess Ashtaroth with clearest ray
Smiled on the revelling ripples, when the Barge,—
Unrivalled burthen borne on Nilus' breast,—
Its pennant lowered for the stilly night.

  To view the glories of the opening day,
E'en as the Orient Globe made gold the hills,
Caesar alert, whilst on the Galley speeds,
Regards the river-banks with thoughtful heed,
Till, a fair prospect seen, he signalled—Stay,
' Tnis is Abydos, of the Tablet-famed ;'—
And to declare intent the Queen rejoined.

  ' Here must we pause, for 'tis the home of Menes,
Egyptus' primal King—first naméd This,—
Of him pronounced "the Eternal,"—sacred ground
Whereon I needs must stand ; the conscious earth
Hath whisperings of centuries bygone
Anear the birth of Man ; it seemeth shame,
Meanwhile the tree of knowledge yieldeth fruits,
The soul no greater groweth,—mightier who
Than Menes ? yea—one Caesar, and one Menes !

For every soul is as the gushing rill
Outchannelling its course toward the Main,
Again to find the source wherefrom its birth
For dissolution in infinitude :
Each man fulfils his own inceptive part ;
He apes another ?—still to be himself :
True virtue, dear, is not acquired by rote,
Caught from the rostrum or the portico,
Or from stale maxims vaunted on the walls, —
" See, it is written, therefore it I hold ! "
There is no virtue in a hackneyed phrase
Conventional, or imitative forms
Derived at second hand and glorified
In practices of superstitious rites ;
It is not virtue to keep safe oneself—
Boasting as " good " what self alone affects,
No pain endured for other than oneself,
Good let alone lest it should harm oneself,—
As virtue claiming merely *not* to do
Some things which perpetrate were hurt to none,
Which unperformed saved not a pang or tear ;
Or, with sly semblance meekly to refrain
From works whereto our temper doth not tend,
From deeds wherein to act exceeds our wit,
From things, desired withal, beyond our power—
Perchance whereto our mettle doth not mount !
Why, dear, the virtue is,— if virtue be
In actions at their best but negative *right*,—
Moved by spontaneous impulse of the mind
To do what men call " good," forgetting self
For others' weal—regardless of reward ;
Not by design to gain at other's loss
In diminution or of fame or purse,—
To stay from punishing, lest justice needs

Nor causing mental pain to slake revenge ;
To wish no harm to other,—to forgive,
To be sincere —whene'er we safely can,—
And crowning all, the closing of my tale,
Ne'er to neglect the calls of gratitude
To fellow-mortal or the beneficent gods :
Virtue—in justice, courage, nobleness—
Includes the godlike attributes of man.'

    The Sun is up,—no day without its mark :
The morn's repast—in Cleopatra's smile ;
Fruits and confections rare and delicate meats
Of Earth's most perfect produce ; wanting not
The wines of Mareotis and Thebaid,
Of Tenia and of Coptos : then to view
Majestic ruins and eternal tombs—
Mementos of the Past ; the Temple-palace
Raised by Oimenepthah, and what remained
Of Menes.

———

    Envy rightly is dispraised ;
Howe'er, we emulate blithe pilgrimage
With Queen and Consul through those shining shores,
Man's crumbled greatness noting as we pass :
The famous Fane of Antæopolis
Shrouded in Palm-tree grove ; the gorgeous
Tentȳra—Temple vast, throughout enriched
With art in form or colour, where was found,
In later age, the curious planisphere
Celestial of Zodiac symbol-pictured :
Coptos, first stronghold of the Troglodytes,
Strange Cavern-tribe untamed,—and on to Thebae,—
Grand Thebae ! grandest relic of Old Time.

'Queen, my astonishment with pleasure blends,
Unsatiate am I—eager still to see ;
Here shall I witness monuments described
By him shrewd traveller of ages gone,
Father of History, Herodotus,—
With Homer and Demosthenes well classed.'

'Yea, Consul, truly, and awhile we pause,
Our fervid, faithful subjects gathering round
To hold high festival in regal State,—
Revels and courtesies ordained to serve
Thine honour and disport ; for Thebae glad
At the event of thine august approach,
Warm welcome gives thee to her classic soil.'

'Be praise thrice told !—for thine ingenious care
To make our working holiday complete ;
Prior, to see the wonders, for 'tis well
To satisfy the conscience ere we play,
When work is done the after-rest is keen.
Lightsome the heart, content the duteous mind.'

So, with a troop of comrades, chosen friends,
Led by an aged Hierophant well-versed
In scrolled, recondite records of Egyptus,
And Hierogrammat of linguistic skill,
The Consul hied in sober merriment
To view the skeletons of ages fled,—
The giant bones denoting giant minds ;
Those unexampled Temples sempitern—
Luxor and Karnak, joined to be in one
By avenue of Sphinxes multiplied
In numbers infinite : first to Luxor, built
By Ammonophin ; through the propylon huge

Prefaced by two tall obelisks and two
Gigantic figures human-form ; beyond,
The temple-tomb of Ozymandias,
And unrecorded cenotaphs self-told ;
When, as through lines of Sphinx and Obelisk,
To Karnak Caesar came, amazed he said,—
'Too wonderful this vision to be real,—
The work of necromancy, or a dream ;
This grand confusion, these colossal forms,
Wide wilderness of ruin ; how could die
Men who had life so much ? not wholly die,
Fate fails to cast them to forgetfulness ;
Here granite-kept they live ; bare silent walls,
Mute graven monoliths with meaning rife,
Weird prostrate statues, and still columns stark,
Speak from remotest time to us who see :
Are not these hieroglyphs, somewhen improved,
The origin of language writ by me ?
To those ingenious men is honour due
Who taught me how to write ; what loss for me !
Confessed my labours, all my perilous pains,
Less their divine invention of the pen
Whereby to tell,—and tell as suits the will,
Though truth my beacon be,—of acts and thoughts ;
Withal, I know not but my humble work
In form destructible, will fade away,
Whilst these strange anaglyphs survive to show
The energies foregone ; what claim have we
To dwell as they the sumless ages through
Upon the Earth ?'

          This homily ended,
The Hierophant proceeding warily,
With courteous motion would direct attent

To estimation of a marvellous scene,
The relique of King Ramēses—sometime named
Sesostris—Palace, Citadel, and Fane ;
With Temple added by the great Nitocris,
Psammetichus' Consort—ruling o'er her King,—
Comely as brave ; her mounting pillars twain,
Moreo'er, in outward form symbolical,
The Hall of Ancestors,—dimensions vast,
Exceeding all or Greek or Roman dared ;
The lofty portals, columns intermixed—
Ghastly erect or wildly overthrown,—
Unbounded desolation ! everywhere,
On, on—too far for sight.

                      Away, away !
The tongue is dumb-struck by the mind o'erwhelmed :
Next search the Libyan shore,—for new surprise ;
See the Memnonium—Ramēses' temple-tomb,
In Court-yard reared the famed, enormous stone-god.
(Grandeur in size by just proportion ruled.)
Its hand alone threefold the corporal bulk
Of him who raised it for his effigy,[1]
(Fit emblem of their greatest warrior,
The largest hewn in stone ;)—see galleries
To all the arts of culture dedicate,
The sacred Library, on front inscribed
' Dispensary of the Mind ;' then further go
To view the twin Colossi of the plain,
One, the renownèd Memnon, told about
By antient men with superstitious awe,
(Of Memnon by the great Achilles slain,)
At sunrise giving forth its vocal sounds,

[1] In the British Museum.

Somewhiles tears shedding, with oracular words ·
Creations destined centuries to front,
On, onward gazing in unending calm :
Passing by groves of Palm, and monuments
Part by Acanthus and Acacia hid,
And oft with thorny Zizyphus o'ergrown,
They find the mansions of the mighty dead
Mid ravines rocky and the mountains bald—
"Tombs of the Kings ; " whereat the Hierophant→
The vaulted chambers threading reverently—
In erudite phrase his stirring story told
Of walls in colours picturing, still clear,
The acts and triumphs else forgotten, lost—
Worker and memoir in same place embalmed !
Immense sarcophagi of ebon stone
Graven with symbol characters, within,
Without, around, to tell the tale and praise
Of their once animate tenants, there entombed :
But chief was one (to Britain borne away,)[1]
Of Alabaster, whole, magnificent,
Shrine of the first Menepthah, mighty king,
Found by Cambyses erst and desecrate,
Devote to Neith their goddess most adored,
[Neith, of the upper firmament Supreme,]
Wherein the 'Book of Mysteries ' is writ,
The war of Soul with Typhon, cause of Sin ;
This, and some other read the Hierophant
Of history by no tradition marred,
Far—far and secret as the source of Nile ;
Roaming these dark, sepulchral palaces,
These aphonous habitations of the dead,
Great Caesar viewed, in manly sympathy,

---

[1] To be seen in Soane's Museum.

Affection's token in eternized loves—
Mummies of memories, memory to outlive !
There saw he pictured, as an object new,
The tall Giraffe with slender neck upreared,
Whispering his Quæstor, 'Seek we one of these
To deck our Triumph when to Rome we come.'

Search for the day be o'er,—to Nilus back
For rest and thought, engendering fresh resolve ;
Soon seen the Galley hoist with flying flags,
Its jocund music speaking cheerily—
Concord with Caesar, honour to him all !

Hey-day ! for revelry and heart's delight—
The feast, the song, the timbrel and the dance,
Whereat the accomplished Queen adroit presides,
In Tyrian robe appareled regally,
Her hair confined with annular Asp of gold,—
Agatho-dæmon, type of Majesty :
On silver platter and in golden chalice
Went round the generous juice and dainty cates -
(Potation prompting merry quips and antics,)
Wines of Egyptus or of Thasian grape,
Ambrosial Anthylla : thus the Barque,
A busy microcosm, with joyance teems !

But hark ! the ring of laughter from the strand,
As the declining sun with shimmering ray
Subdues the motions of the sprightful scene :
'See Consul, here my virgins, thee to charm,
Doth not the breath of Spring refresh thy soul ? '
Advancing now the maidens modestly,—
In gauzy garments, counterfeit disguise,

F

Bespangled, glittering, and betricked with blooms,
Their brows with wreath of lotus-blossom bound,
Neat ankles circumvest with silver bells,—
To Cleopatra and the Consul courtesy :
Blithely they dance, well-timed by castanets
And cymbals and the synchronal clap of hands,
Or by the agile tread of foot unworn—
In supple web of interwoven limbs,
And wavy movement of voluptuous guile,—
When one, the cynosure in symmetry,
Taia named, from forth the group alone,
With arch acknowledgment to Caesar, sang.

INVOCATION.

Gods of Egyptus' stream,
Gods whom of Earth we dream,
Gods of high Heaven supreme,—
  To Caesar glory !

Osiris ! who doth shine,
Isis ! his Queen benign,
Horus ! her son divine,—
  To Caesar glory !

Lights of the glowing sky,
Earth which doth food supply,
Zephyrs that round us fly,—
  To Caesar glory !

Men who of Rome command,
Men of Egyptus' land
Or from remotest strand—
  To Caesar glory !

Camel and *Elephant,*
Ye Beasts *the desert haunt,*
Couch your strong limbs and vaunt
   To Caesar glory !

Behemoth, Crocodile,
Fish of our sacred Nile,
Ichneumon and Reptile,—
   To Caesar glory !

Ibis and Birds that sing,
Eagle with soaring wing,
By tune or plumage bring
   To Caesar glory !

Butterfly, Scarabæus,
(It doth from evil free us,)
All things with eyes to see us,—
   To Caesar glory !

Lotus our Nile's delight
And flowers *in colours dight,*
Odours *of balmy night,—*
   To Caesar glory !

Land of the mighty past,
Of Tombs and Monoliths *vast,*
Give glory, first or last,—
   Caesar and Cleopatra !

Her song out-sung, the pretty minstrel bowed
To Caesar lowly, and with native grace
Around his head the myrtle chaplet tied ;

He bending to receive the proffered kiss,
Nor disinclined, a jewel gave her, saying
'This to remember Caesar :'   Taia blushed.

   The feast is over, and the gleeful throng
Have left the night to silence ; only Two
Mingle harmonious converse, unrestrained.

   ' Beloved mine idol ! I beheld once more
Thine Egypt's wonders, Roma so excelling,
I doubt me great ; we scantly judge the past
By those mere relics,--surely they were gods !
Men of superior nature,—larger soul ;
In their still Tombs they live ! with sturdy will
Contended they with Fate—nor quite in vain ;
They would not cease, would half-immortal be,
Survive in stone, or in their frame preserved,
Thought petrified,—themselves their monuments ;
In hybrid type or artful symbol-sign
Would fain perpetuate material forms
To designate the forces of their minds ;
Fresh from the sacred fount they deeply drank,
Took inspiration at the Source of Prime
Erewhen my Fathers of a faded age
Imbibed of Hippocrene ; exemplars they,
It doth misgive me—doubting, part ashamed—
How I in action do but simulate
A perfect archetype ; shall I bequeath
To men who follow—if the world endure—
Some semblance of those Titans gone before ?'

   ' Fie ! Julius, to thyself art thou unjust,
Though just to others, as the world doth know ;

Thine acts are models, as thy thoughts are new ;
Whereas Sesostris of uncertain date,
Mere dust, is lost in doubt and mystery,
Thy name illumines the historic scroll
For myriads of mortals unbegot ;
Even so Cleopatra—fearing none !
Cheer thee, my Caius ! there is much beyond
To urge thy soul for more heroic deeds,
Which will the splendour of thy fame increase
And, like a comet blazing in the sky,
Constrain the world to gaze at thy career ;
Prithee let past be past, secure the time—
We have the best who live ! enhance thy life,
Good chances seize lest never they recur,
Waste not the fleeting moments meant for bliss.'

———

   Pale gleam of dawn beheld the Argosy
Astir with workers to perform intent ;
Well known this day their gay Flotilla speeds,—
On either shore excitement early seen,
And o'er the face of Nilus ; now pursues
The Fleet its project ; with the freshening morn
Came the Thebæans, thronging countlessly
To render generous service unbesought,
And bless the Royal concourse.

               Shone the sun,
Egyptus' deities propitious proved,
In sacred pinnace sailed the Hierophants
With the Hieraphori their Standards bearing ;
Music and song on river or on bank,
Flowers strewn athwart the waters, and the word
' Long live the Queen and Consul !'

Off! away—

The zest of travel is to seek the next ;
Pass by Hermonthis and Latopolis,
And onward sail until to stay enchants ;
Apollinopolis Magna,—there to see
Edfou's grand Temple by the Ptolemies raised,
Wide-spread as full in graven histories
Of hierogram and symbol-shape occult,—
To be unriddled in efflux of Time ;
Here, a huge mass, the stone much ornate cage
Wherein Hawk-headed Horus grimly sate,
And the swart Crocodile—elsewhere adored,
Abhorréd as of god Osiris foe,
Of Typhon emblem, genius dire of Evil,—
Was oft devoured in horror's deep despite !

Reposing, when the day's sight-work is done,—
Deserved repast enjoyed, the careless hour,
Evening of day or life, for idle ease,—
The Queen, in lightsome spirit, lightsome spake :

' List thou my Caius, when a dream I tell,
A dream for thee and me—not all a dream,
Which to fulfil, my fancy pleaseth much ;
Progressing further, on the Nubian land,
There may be found, not far as we can speed,
Objects stupendous of the antient days—
I mean the Subterrenes of Ipsambul ;
Know'st thou these, erst, were sought and self-inscribed
By one thy compeer in celebrity,
Precursor fit, in wisdom or in power,
(As noted aptly by our faithful scribe,
The Greek of Greeks most skilled in Egypt-lore,)
Psammetichus ? himself a King o'er Kings,

Like thee subduing all than him the less ;
Wilt thou not see what he, foregone, did see ?
Those Cavern Temples of Cyclopic thought,
In painted story and in carvéd lines
Adjudged than of Egyptus more refined,
Scooped in the banks of Nile where bank is rock,
Fronted with effigy each whose shoulders' breadth
Equals the measure of ten stalwart men,
In honour of Osiris Hierax formed ;
The Cave a multiple of sculptured Halls,
Roof upheld by figured columns, graceful
Though colossal, showing on eloquent walls
The Hero's legend ; with artistic hand,
By pencilled colours or the chisel's tongue
Extolling the achievements of their King :
Such shouldst thou view, dear Caius.'

'Cleopatra--
What else than praise for thy seductive scheme !
Poem of promised pleasure—hard to lose ;
Yet while melodiously thy voice persuadeth,
And whilst I charméd listen, I *must* think
Of governments and Rome—too long forsook !
If to be happy were, in all, the lot
Apportioned unto men, most blest am I
With thee, O fairest fair ! nay, there is more,
We do profess a tribute to the gods
Which part as gods we pay ; it is for us
To render back for all the boons they grant
Some service to the world whereo'er they rule,
Some benefit to other ; poor is he
Of heart and brain and soul whose force is spent
Regarding only a diminutive thing—
" Myself," pretending to a separate self ;

For each is part of one unending scheme
To graft the next on what hath been fulfilled ;
We of this age are debitors beholden
To our fore-runners, from whose ashes sprung
(Apart Dame Nature who doth constant bless !)
The mighty men thine Ancestors among
Who taught us lessons, and by noble works
Have left their footmarks in the clefted rock
Whereby we mount to higher thought and knowledge ;
Gem of Egyptus !   Caesar owes the debt,
And must acquit it—or he will not hold :
Dear love, I am o'erblest to be with thee—
With her the darling of the Graces trine,
The peerless One, her only parallel !
Behold yon archéd sky with brilliants set,
Mysterious, infinite,—of them I seek
The star most bright, beneficent, beautiful—
To name it Cleopatra ! dost thou hear ? '

' Yea Consul, kindest kind,—profoundly grave :
Let me encourage thee—to warm thy soul !
Is this to me denied—alas, alas !
Another plan have I, so well designed,
Thou canst, I think, scarce fail to execute.
It is, dear coz, to seek whiles sad return,
(As meet divergence for variety,)
Oasis Ammon ; 'midst the desert sands
An Island rises fresh and flourishing,
Of palms and groves, and water-springs and flowers —
A paradise of verdure ; thou shalt see
Temples and gardens, with a Palace joined—
The famed Ammonium with its riches stored ;
Let us on Camel mount—our manner here—
"Ship of the Desert" sometime quaintly called ;

We shall have retinue for company,
And after pastime novelty doth yield
Our Vessel find and float where we would go ;
Dear Caius, this a timely thought I ween,
Born to prolong our friendship? say thou wilt !
Hath Rome not waited?—surely more can wait,
Thus Caesar wends where Alexander went?'

'Cease—cease beguiling Angel !—I to Rome ;
Not so to match thy greatest Ancestor,[1]
Wandering, though with thee, to Oăsis Major,—
Nor to be hailed like him as "Amun-Ra !"
Whilst Caesar Caesar is, he'll Caesar be.'

Onward to Ombi—there to note, as chief,
Its Ptolemaic Fane, in pride columnar
On mound conspicuous at those level shores ;
And then to Ultima Thule of Egyptus,
Where commerce, checked by rocky, foaming falls,
Suspends its wonted course ; Syéne this—
Of bold, romantic aspect, rearing up
Amid the waters, shaggy cliffs around,
With greenest groves of palm and lebbek tree,—
Where Nubian girls are seen unheedfully
Cooling their slender limbs in Nilus' wave ;
Syéne—school of Science most remote,
Of first Observatory, Temple eke,—
Wherein the Hierophants star-gazing dwelt,
Or at the Solstice watched their sacred Well
One day illumined by the vertic Sun,—
Its circled marge by classic foot impressed
Of King, and Priest, and curious traveller,

[1] Alexander the Great.

Herodotus, Eudoxus, Manětho sage,—
The day whereon the gnomon fails to cast
At noon its normal shadow on the plane :
Here too the Quarry from whose womb have sprung
In tinctured granite, carved and polishéd—
Obelisk, and Temple, and colossal form
Spread o'er the face of Egypt's wondrous land :
Near, the twin island Elephantiné,—
A sylvan nook—one time the seat of kingdom,
With temples decked and gardens, interspersed,
' Islet of Flowers '—so named,—and then again,
On, to the rocky isle of Philae placed
Below the rushing rapids, in a lake
Serene, translucent of the river's bend—
A swan upon its bosom ! and environed
By granite bluffs fantastic—where is seen,
Shaded by Palm-groves old, an affluent Temple
To Isis dedicate, in earliest time,—
Annext the later Fane for triune worship
Of God Osiris, Isis, and their Son :
The Cataract reaching, Caius Julius stays,
Up-climbs the crags the tumbling floods amidst,
Then motionless, in deep reflection lost—
' Here Menes, Alexander, and Sesostris stood.'

Back, to rejoin the rich Refectory
And give the eve to rest contemplative.

' Dear One ! thou endest well our holiday
With these so lovely, much adornéd isles ;
Earnest in will, against the stream we strove,
And next, unwilling with the stream return :
Now Alexandria !—by the speediest course,
For Rome much needeth Caesar—Caesar Rome.'

'Thy word, O Consul, if against her wish,
Is law to Cleopatra,—doubt her not;
So swift as sail and sturdy rowers can,
To Alexandria; there, if last, she hopes
A respite brief.'

'Ay love,—a respite *brief!*'

The Alexandrines give reception frank
To our Nile-Rovers; plaudits to their Queen,
And to the Roman who hath shielded her;
Here Messengers are found with urgent errand—
From Asia, from Hispania, from Rome:
Whilst in Egyptus' sunshine Caesar dallies,
Fell Faction festers in the wide-spread legions—
Dark-gathering clouds uprisen, presaging storm.

But first to gladden, as we friends rejoin—
A term of absence ended; politic
That Romans, leaving, should familiarize
With the Egyptian Court, and Men of State;
Moreo'er, are sundry farewells of the world
Claiming some tender, ceremonious care.

The Banquet over, in desired repose
Rome's Consul, lovingly, 'We soon must part:'
'No, Caius, no! all Nature inculcates
Development by grade, and like decay;
If its meridian hath our love attained
Let there be such declension, as the Sun's,
Until insensibly, by lessening light
Our night of sorrow cometh unperceived;
When benefits on us the gods bestow,

How may we break with sacrilegious will
The spell they do create?—in just esteem
Do we not rightly make the most and best
Of Fortune's gifts,—to body or to soul?
Shall our reproach be spiritual suicide?
Are we not well together, honoured Caesar—
Who being so mighty should be lord of joy!
Oh folly! shall the happy separate?
Whole term thou know'st is but a longer day
And suffers, last, inevitable doom;
Wherefore permit our ceasing to be slow,
Let there be no to-morrow till thou goest,
Make we the days most long by wakeful wiles
Though happier be the faster!'

　　　　　　　　　'Plead no more;
Thy voice hath Syren tones,—ah, Syren eyes!
How strong his will who subjugates thy will:
The lot of man it is to die in life,
Let slip his longings, as the hours do fleet—
Defenceless losing aught he most doth prize;
Each day resign we somewhat we have loved—
Or flee from us it will despite our care;
One day we cease to all, a final death,
The consummation of those deaths whilom;
Soon must I die to thee!'

　　　　　　　　　'Nay, nay—not so!
May I love Caius, his bald logic hate?
A woman I—not cold philosopher;
To part from thee is as a Ship doth loose
Its anchor—to the Sea, perchance to wreck!
Hast thou not saved my State, and counselled me,
And given me Queenship? more than Father thou,
And more—dear furthermore! to make thee dearer?'

' Queen of Egypt, thy mellifluous speech
Finds echo in my soul ; when we induce
A Heaven on Earth we know it must have end—
Indefinite howe'er the tenure be ;
Nor would we have the gods perpetuate
What our own sense reproves,—which were to take,
Presumptuous, a throne above their Throne ;
(For e'en the gods may not o'erreach the right :)
Oh Lady-love ! illustrious confessed
In boastful Ancestry's fallacious fame,
It is as woman most thy merit shows ;
Why tell thee this ? unless to verify
I have my share of sorrow—losing thee,
For it doth add a pang to parting pain
To think some other in thy heart shall dwell—
To dream some other in thine arms may rest ;
O goddess-born ! offspring of Earth unmatched,
Thou gain'st not subtly o'er the viewless soul
Predominance by highest place and name,
But by thy wise, refined companionship,
The art to please, with sensuous charms in aid,
(On Nature's pet impartially bestowed :)
True tribute yields he to thy Regal grace !
Severing the silken cord in face of death
And war's vicissitudes, to keep his rank
As man to govern man ; love e'er so strong,
Ambition must o'errule, lest else the world
Were lost eftsoons in chaos of decay ;
So, dearest,—doth his grief with thine compare ?
For though I go, to me thou diest not—
To me *thou* livest ever whilst I live ;
At eve's still hour, when graver thought is o'er,
The vision of thy presence will appear,—
As a melodious song somewhile well sung

Hath lodgment ta'en in Memory's mystic cave,
(Guarded above by blest Mnemosyne,)
Resounding in celestial cadences—
Of unison divine—to mental ear.'

'Speak on—speak on O Caius ! for thy voice
Comes to my senses as the breath of Heaven
Chanting supernal pæans through the grove—
Entrancing while we scarce ken what it tells;
Oh thou excellest by thy wit too much
For her, but woman, nathless thy esteem ;
To-morrow, if to-morrow ! we shall part,
And thou wilt witness Cleopatra's tears :
It is the hour of sleep,—so long at least
Be we for all in all,—and all forget.'

—————

To-morrow—their to-morrow—signs of haste
And sound of action round the Palace walls,
Not of rejoicing, but of fixed resolve,
Of dull vivacity—a sense of change :
' The Romans leave us—are we glad or sad ? '
Say it was then as now, and as for aye,—
They are not merry who do wear the mask :
Caesar, on patriot purpose solely bent,
Pressed on the exodus of Roma's legions ;—
General of Generals he !

—————

                              Queen Cleopatra,
Of placid visage though tumultuous heart,
Affects repose, Caesarion beside,—
Aspect of Sphinx—to know, to nought reveal ;
Her hair unbraided and her bosom bared,

The floor bestrewn with lily and with rose,
The Consul's valediction loth to hear.

He erelong coming, with respectful step
To near the couch advanced, and, on his knee,
In silence took her hand—as when they met :

'As first you saw me Caius, so I lie—
To ask—in tristful trust—of *thee*—my fate ;
See thy Caesarion—and our tale is told—
Of love and amity unvarying,—
More, of thy plenteous kindness, kingly aid :
Oh, must thou go—go now? I dread thy speech :'

'Queen, I have something done, and something
     leave ;
For all, whate'er, am I requited greatly
In lustrous sublimations, unforgot,—
In one unfading lustre—in Thyself :'

'Ah, Caius—thou hast struck the jarring chord,—
Drear deprivation, and a living death :'

'O friend belovéd ! let us act with honour,—
In such just pride approving what we are ;
Some part I've told thee of unsettled wars
And Roma's discord—to be calmed by me ;
Caesarion will be cultured in thy care,—
I crave the child, to fondle—look upon,—
From distance shall I counsel and defend,—
Soon wilt thou find a King to minister
And share with thee dominion.'

                              Stooping then

Her lips to press,—she quickened by this token
Sprang from the couch, dishevelled, passionate,
Embraced—and wordless fell: Caesarion slept ;—
Still! as primeval stillness :

                       Caesar stood
Rigid, with saddened eye ; then moved away
Intoning low—' Good-bye dear Cleopatra !
Twice—thrice good-bye,—the world's work must be
    done :'
In-breathing, sighing, he the curtains closed,—
While she among her roses prostrate lay.

THE END.

CAIUS JULIUS CAESAR.

Costanza

Costanza.

Where Æolus, King of Storms, had earlier reigned,
A shining Island of the Tyrrhene Sea
Of rocky aspect, in whose caverns deep
He stored the winds and bade the tempests stay,—
Island whence aye the faint volcano-glare
Sheds, nightly seen, from sources confluent
[In dread arcana of the earth, profound,]
With Ætna's seething pit—abode of fire !
Where Mulciber with Cyclops hammering toiled,
Circled in ardent and sulphureous flames,
At anvils, for the thunderbolts of Jove ;—
'Tis Lipara ;—there dwelt a daintie maid
Costanza named, of noble ancestry,
Much cared for—nurtured in unclouded joy :
For since the gods were gone, and Lipara's fires
Blazed harmlessly, to lighten, not to scathe,
The Isle grew plenteous for the wants of men :
Then, side by side, the turbaned Saracen
Held with the Christian a divided sway,—
A simple age, of manners fresh and free,
When hearts were hearts, and love was love un-
      doubting,
And when emotion sprung from Nature's Soul.

The Maid showed beauty passing common praise—
As though an angel had her mother met ;
Mild-melting, oval, silken-fringéd eyes,
Whose placid sheen, as of a glassy lake,
Denotes unfathomed depths, and purity,—
Whate'er the mood, true beacons of her mind ;
Slender yet strong, and agile as the roe,
And rounded as a Phidian master-piece,
Luxuriant tresses, mantling o'er a brow
Whereon it seemed the Sun, unsetting, shined,
The pride of Lipara, but none her own,
Costanza reached the age contemplative,
Not all the present, when a future dawns,—
A land of promise and illusions charmed :
Ere then a child, of merriest children one,
She had been joyant and brimful of love,
Her kindred loved and all of human kind,
Caressed her pets—or doll, gazelle, or doves,
Flattered the flowerets with endearing words,
And took delight in butterfly or bee ;
She loved the moon, the stars, sea, earth, or sky,
The humpéd camel, or the graceful horse,
Or pretty babe, or squalid beggar bare,
And of the wrinkled toad but saw its eye ;
She had been happy as the roses are,
The dew-drop drinking, perfume paying back,—
Until there grew a void within her heart,
The loves whilom were not enough to love,
Nor yet enough for her to be beloved ;
Her mother loved her fondly,—not enough !
It must be love—in love responsive, whole.

At Lipara they held high festival
To vaunt the birthday of the Æolian King,

Whereat went forth the Island Chivalry
In holiday trim and warlike pageantry
For games athletic and the frolic joust :
Costanza with her kinsfolk forward placed,
In simple-hearted, girlish joyfulness
Bred by the changeful motions of the hour,
Forgat the hungering void, and looked, and laughed,
As one uncaring, save to be amused ;
Then, in the final fray, the victor proven
Had, for his meed, the circus round to ride
And yield the guerdon to the fairest fair,—
Martucci Gomito,—reining a milk-white barb
Of purest Arab blood and proudest pace ;
Gentle Costanza marked his brave, fierce eye,
Broad forehead, clustering hair, and manly form,
And in a moment knew—the void was filled !
As in enchantment, waits she his approach
Bowing obeisance as he moves along,
The myrtle wreath in hand, prepared to throw ;
And still, spell-bound, she gazed, unknowing why,
Curious to note his preference—when, near,
His steed, by fright, or by his heel compelled,
Reared and curvetted—to the fear of some,
Whilst she unscared, in wonder, saw him bend
Low to the girths,—the chaplet on her lap !
Up to his eyes she looked, Martucci looked—
To see the tinctures of her heart suffuse
Her delicate cheek—the primogenial blush
Brought from its sources by the precious dower, –
The efflorescence of her maidenhood !
And then her craving soul was satisfied.

    Erelong, enamoured, brave Martucci sought
A bride in Lipara, and ardently

Declared his palm the maiden myrtle-crowned
Whom he had given Election,—fairest fair !
They said he was not noble, was not mate
Nor fit companion to their royal race,
Nor wealth enough had he to wed with her :
Costanza pleaded, ' My first love is he,
My only love, my only, only love !
Oh Mother ! let me love him—for I must.'

Martucci hot replied, ' I'll noble prove,
The wealth will live to gain, or, failing, die !'
Infatuate, rashly sped with galliots twain
To rove the seas and spoil the Saracen :
Boldly he ventured, and his fame came back,
' Rich prizes from the infidel had won,
And home would bring an argosy of gold.'

Meantime, by hope upborne, Costanza pined,
But one dream dreaming—waking still to dream,
Neglecting much her erenow playful tasks,—
Her many loves in one concentrated.

But bold Martucci hardly fortune tried,
And, by a day, too long delayed return ;
The Saracen in double strength went forth,
His convoy intercepted and o'ercame,
Him straightway bearing to the Afric shore.

To Lipara the tristful tidings came ;
The maiden heard but this—' Martucci dead !'

Then dead was love to our Costanza sweet ;
She moved in light unwitting of the light,
The stars looked cruel, Cynthia only sad,

The sunshine was but chill, the Earth a blank
Of all affections, creatures, colours all ;
The fabric had its lovely form preserved
The while its ghostly habitants were gone ;
She wept not tears, alas ! there were no tears,
Dry were the outshed fountains,—yet she wept,
And sad with weariness no rest could cure,
Rapt rambled hither, thither, as in dark,
Her beauteous eyes unnoting day or night.

Its wonted way, indifferent, wags the world ;
The portals opened, revellers came and went :
One night, Costanza soul-sick utterly,
Her head concealing in mantilla fold,
The parting guests among—among them forth ;
Away she glided, thinking dolefully
· I have no home, for me the wide, wide world,
To me all places are as nothingness,
Let Nature do with me as Nature will ;'
On, on she flitted through the sinuous streets
Obscure and narrow, steep and stony-rough,
Until she knew the dawn, and as the Sun
Uprose she saw the strand, and out beyond,
The sea—and, presently, a fisher's skiff
Rigged for the labours of the wakening day.

With automatic skill the boat she loosed,
Unshipped the rudder, threw adrift the oars,
And pushed away ; the wind blew off the shore,
The sail was set and quick the bark impelled,—
Its freight a thinking, dormant chrysalid
Cast to the hazard of the waters wild.

Costanza knew it all,—not wisely knew,

But as synthetic with her fantasies;
And somewhat reasoned justly when she moaned
'Am I not desolate, withouten hope,
So whither in the finite can I go?
If Earth to me is nought, the Sea extends
And fain may bear me to Martucci's soul.'
Along the boat recumbent, looking to
The sky, illumined, brightening into day,
She had no thought but one—adored Martucci;
Love's first smile, of admiration born,
In fancy pictured clear; the hectic flush
Of scorn, of anger, of abaséd hope,
In being deemed unworthy; his wide chest
With furious storm convulsed—by love of her!
Heroic features cast in Grecian mould,
Herculean shoulders meeting curly locks,
His stature all-commanding, like a god,—
And let the ecstasy o'erwhelm her grief.

  Apace the skiff is drifting with the wind,—
The moon has mounted, and the stars shine out;
Costanza's gazing, ever-gazing eyes—
Stars unto stars! beheld them, unsurprised,
Thinking they looked, and spake, and lighted her:
As soul aflight in æther unconfined,
A dream upon the ocean floated she!
In all so perfected, so dear to Heaven,
A miracle was granted, her to save,—
Two Seraphs hovering round the fragile ark,
Its puny canvas fanning volantly.

  Uncounted hours fly o'er; the charméd maid—
Unnourished, lapsing faint and comatose,—
Translated instantly—to ravishment,

With her beloved Martucci lived in Heaven.
He to an Angel changed, with sapphire wings,
Upon his breast her head, his eyes to hers ;
' My only love, I've come to thee someway,
Oh, happy me, to find thee anywhere !'
When heard she music heard amid the spheres
And knew its meaning, to her fancy thus,—

> ' *Doubt not, Costanza—*
> *Love does not die,*
> *Thy love is reckoned*
> *In thy faintest sigh :*

> ' *Doubt not, Costanza—*
> *Thy love is dear*
> *To us, blest Angels,*
> *Loving ever here :*

> ' *Doubt not, Costanza—*
> *As mortal blind,*
> *Be thou but constant*
> *Thou thy love shalt find :*

> ' *Doubt not, Costanza—*
> *If grieved thy life,*
> *Continue constant*
> *Thou will yet be Wife.'*

Whiles resonant lingering those supernal strains,
Costanza felt a soft encircling arm
Her from her hapless resting-place upraise ;—
The miracle-boat ashore in little bay
Nigh Syrtis Minor gulf :

'What art thou, dear?
Whence cam'st thou, winsome child?' spake Carapresa,
Enfolding her with kisses, mother-like:
This heaven-sent finder was of Christian race,
Of Trápani native, and by garb she knew
The damsel from Italia's shore had sped;
At break of day she would the fishers meet
On whom, as slave, she waited; 'Pretty dear!
Speak, for thy language is, I think, as mine;'
Costanza, looking into space some while,
Breathed out but this, 'I know not—leave me here;'
Then Carapresa, grown compassionate,
Bore the submissive maid with haste unto
A poor yet sheltering cabin; there, resigned,
Upon the scant bed laid her, sitting by,
Fondled her lovingly, and tearfully
To see such beauty in such wretchedness,
Gave her some simple food, as nurse would do
To infant, patient vigil held until
The curtains drooped to grant the weary rest:
A lengthened sleep—wherethrough the watcher watched
The jetty fallen fringes, for she thought
'Perchance it endeth in the sleep of death:'
Bright Spirits glistered near the couch, and smiled
On Carapresa consolation pure;
[Affright, in wonderment, she knew they smiled.]
As some night-wanderer notes the streak of morn,
So our good guardian saw the silky lids
Uplift to light and life, rejoicing much;—
'My darling pet, I welcome thee anew,
Thou hast been slumbering, I have wished thee wake;
Costanza as in vision, reft of sight,—
'Where am I now, and who art thou so kind?'
'Thou art near Susa, of the Afric land,

Lone Carapresa I ;' whereat the crone
O'er-laved her gently, combed her flowing hair,
Chafed the white, velvet hands, and tiny feet,
Enraptured, clothed her, muttering timorously,
' A princess surely,—whence such loveliness ?
An angel is she, fair and beautiful !
Alack, alack ! how guard her from reproach,
From infidel clutch preserve, or lustful look ? '
Next unto Heaven appealed for help and light
Exclaiming, joyed—' Now know I what to do,
To good Alathiel hie we,—if she will.'

[Alathiel, comely Moslem dame high-born,
Wealthy, life-wearied by a broken love :
Retired to Susa, she had there devised
Asylum merciful for maidens meek
To guide the effluent energies of youth
In ways of virtue and industrious arts,—
A guarded, calm seclusion, where no man
Must dare to enter.]

                    In reflection merged,
Her reverie mumbling as the beldams do,—
' Lest she should flee,—I'll keep her as a bird,
The bird this Peri, and my hut the cage ; '
And thus decided, nurturing the maid
With such sparse succours as the poorest have,
Departs to reckon with her masters rough,
The door securing, window screening close,
Returns in haste at eventide, to find
Costanza sitting tranquil and forlorn,
The splendent eyes to no-where searching far ;
' Good heart ! my dear, wilt thou not with me go ? '
' No home have I, so will I with thee wend,

No home have I, my home is anywhere :'
When, in the stillness of the murky night,
The fishers gone to sea, the land at hush,
Close wrapped her Carapresa, tenderly,
And oft supporting, somewhiles carrying quite,
Helped by a market-wain in part their course,
To Susa[1] brought her,—to Alathiel's haven ;
Susa, a city opulent and gay,
With frowning fortress crowning craggy steep,
Across the shore where Titan Atlas lifts,
Transformed to mountain vast, his mighty back,—
Doomed to uphold the firmamental sphere.

  Now struck the early hour when sleep, with most,
Is weak or over, and when cries and raps
Are heard but fright not ; so Alathiel heard,
Perceiving it was nigh the hour of dawn,—
Whispering her nurselings, 'Fear not, I'll descend :'
Soon, through the lattice-bars, in grey-eyed light,
The Donna, heedful, maid and matron scanned,
Gave patient ear to Carapresa's plea,
The bolts and chains displaced with tremulous hand,
Unclosed the massive door, and bade them in.

  And whilst Alathiel marked the scaréd eyes
Of lost Costanza, watched her witching ways,
Heard her weird words of woe, unblaming aught,
Her fair form noted, and her air of grace,—
The most of the romantic tale self-told,—
She added love to chastened charity
Anent the strange sea-waif, and nestled her,
To soothe, or night or day, with comfortings,

---

[1] Ancient Adrumetum.

The maidens warning, 'Give her loving speech
And furtherance, whate'er she hath to do :'
For being asked, in pity, 'Whence art thou ?'
She answered them, 'I know not, I'm Costanza ;
There was a world I lived in, but 'tis gone ;
The people in it were both good and cruel,
And now 'tis past I know not where I am.'

Yet, mid the company she sate their queen,
In virtue sole of saintly influence,
E'en as its fragrance makes us bless the flower ;
A charm had rested on her from the skies
Surpassing reason, having reason none ;
The favourite of some benignant Star,
She by a glance could warm the frigid heart
And quicken it to impulse ; she would work
Among the diligent Sisters, speaking not
Though silently enkindling sympathy ;
Or, with no hindrance, would she stray apart
And plaintive ditties warble to the Moon ;
Their gossip list'ning, she replied by looks,
The inarticulate language of the soul ;
Their love she won at will, with no restraint,—
Though in some awe of her, as heaven-born.

At this same time he King of Tunis hight,
The good and prudent Mariabdela,
By a Granadan prince was hardly pressed.
His title to the throne by arms impugned :
Martucci Gomito, a captive there,
The war foreknew, and wittily conceived
A thought which, acted, promised liberty ;
He, being held a favoured prisoner,
As one of gracious manners, noble birth,

Entreats his gaoler—' Bring to me thy Chief;'
Then to the master boldly outspake he,
' I would the royal presence instant gain,—
Say thou, a stratagem I shall propose
Wins by adoption certain victory : '
The master bore his message, and eftsoons
Into the palace, smiling, rendered him ;
' Accept my homage for this act of grace !
I crave thine ear, to prosper my design ; '
The King,—' Proceed, we have our ears to hear : '
' Thou countest on thine archers,—so thy foe,
And they anticipate, their arrows flown
Thine they can straight return ; hence order thou,
With utmost privity to latest hour,
More fine than theirs your bowstrings, and devise
All arrow-slits alike, the string to suit ;
Refrain whilst they, elate, their quivers void,
Then like a hailstorm pelting, harry them !
Soon will they find the narrow-mouthéd darts
Refuse their bowstrings, whilst your archers shoot,
Doubly supplied, their arrows equally ;
A panic in their hearts surprise shall breed,
When, royal Sir, there is but to pursue : '
' 'Tis well,' quoth Mariabdela,—' give it heed !
And at the battle by my side remain ;
Doth fortune follow, I will say 'tis thine,
High honour shalt thou have and rich reward : '
Martucci to his plan the archery formed,
The battle went as shrewdly he forecast,
Our brave Tunisians the invader foiled
With slaughter terrible—dispersion wide.

Donna Alathiel owning lands at Tunis
Thither was summoned to protect her rights :

Alathiel loved Costanza,—pondered thus;
'She is a graceful Statue, haply I
Could it reanimate to conscious life,
By sights and sounds of stimulant verities
Recall her memory to things foregone
Of streets and marts and sprightly circumstance
Occurring in the genial haunts of men :'
' Dear foster-child, I now to Tunis part,
There speed thou with me, our fair City see ;'
' Mother, I care not whither whither where,—
With thee—with thee for ever would I rest :'
Together they the Town five-gated sought,
Halting betimes at house or hostelrie
Whereat the dame, well known, warm welcome found ;
The while they wended, those the maid beheld
With reverence blessed her, saying 'She's divine !'

To Tunis coming as the conflict ceased,
[Advices then went slow of distant things,]
Alathiel heard how presently would be
A royal pomp of triumph national :
The streets bedizened were in rainbow tints,
As the fantastic Saracen-fancy fits,
The people buoyant in their late reprieve
From the beleaguering host, and in their pride
Of vantage jubilant with dance and song :
Costanza looked, and looked, no smile withal,
Her ever brilliant eyes stretched onward ever,
Nor one side nor the other ; what she thought
None knew by hearing, for she spake no word ;
She breathed as others breathe, and yet the air
Gave not her pulses purpose ; ne'ertheless,
Adroit, instinct with art mechanical,
Her fingers deft the loom would nimbly ply,

Or with entrancing pathos touch the lyre :
She trod the earth as one of other sphere
Whose thoughts and language are to man unknown ;
Toward the Sun she looked no Sun to see,
As things to mortal sight were not to her.

Io triumphe! trumpets sound ! the King
Beside Martucci, leads the cavalcade,
And for the Liparæan, thus proclaims,—
' This noble youth hath Mariabdela saved,
Let him be therefore honoured of you all : '
In order following, ministers and peers
With glittering trappings blazoned typical,
Then captives and the trophies of the spoil.

Alathiel in patrician rank sat grouped
With ladies of the gay Tunisian Court,
Costanza next her, like a Moslem veiled ;
They saw the Triumph moving from afar
Toward the Monarch's Palace glistening
With gilded domes and minarets painted o'er,—
To them directed, for the King had said
There at the close he would the Victor own ;
Alathiel's tent aneared the Column stayed,
Martucci Gomito, his visor down,
Of Mariabdela companion sole :
The King alighting, our Martucci led
With him aside, the laurel wreath upheld,
The visor lifted, then the helmet raised
To place the prize, in manly tone pronouncing
' Lo ! crown for crown, this crown my hand doth yield.'

Rang to all ears throughout the multitude
A startling cry—of joy ineffable,

The cry a word—'Martucci!'   Quick, unveiled,
Costanza, springing from Alathiel's side,
Leaped to the victor's neck, around him clung,—
'He is Martucci!   I have found my love;'
Folding, he whispered,—'Yea, in me thy love :'
The King advanced demurely, and, releasing,
Surrendered her to dame Alathiel's arms;
'We will to-morrow speak of her to thee.'

The lustrous orbs divine now shone to see,
Him first, nor less herself, as two in one,—
To right or left, above, beneath, around;
Admiring hailed the sunshine with delight,
Saw banners fluttering in the lively breeze,
Smart soldiers, horses, brilliant pageantry,
Varied prismatic colours, gay costumes
The Palace by : she heard the clarion ring,
Heard women's voices, (of all music most :)
And raptured knew, of happiness supreme,
The waking vision of Martucci since,—
Her loved Alathiel clearly ; vocal now,
She had outsaid, in new-born, blissful hours,
All Carapresa wot not of,—and next,
'Dear Mother, more than Mother! I awoke
To see thy face, to see thee with my mind,
To know what thou hast done, by grace of God,
For her, a luckless, lorn, demented thing—
My debt too heavy for this world to pay :'
Alathiel clasped her, kissed away her tears,—
'True—true, sweet child,—it was by grace of God.'

Henceforth the dormant loves to sense revived,
Gushed like a fount-spring suddenly set free ;
She praised the Sun, extolled the beauteous world,—

In glad thanksgiving, thought paid orisons :
Alathiel for her cared unceasingly
And spake to her as mother would to child ;
'God hath not, dear Costanza, given to me
A child of Earth, but thee hath sent, of Heaven,
So to exemplify maternal love ;
It is an act of His beneficence,
For thou, not mortal of my body born
Art as my spiritual offspring ; so thou art !
Have I not fostered thee and fed with milk
Of kindness, nursed thee as the cradled babe
When, by misfortune, thou wert babe again?'
' Yes—*Benefactress !* thus in truth it is,—
Immaculate parent of a mind retrieved !
(Oh first, own Mother ! thee I ever love
Although thou hadst no pity for my tears.)
Am I not doubly blest in loving thee
With love scarce lesser than my deepest love ?
Ah ! I have learned, by grief, in lacking love,
Whate'er the gifts, this world is dark and drear,
A barren wilderness—nor sight nor sound,—
Withouten love no glories in the sky,
Withouten love no music in the air,
Withouten love no blossoms on the mead.'

The King with pride Costanza sweet beheld,
Esteemed her as a jewel to his Crown,
Nay, even as a daughter to his heart ;
Yet, told of all the marvellous history,
More, how Martucci would the maiden wed
And, wedded, to his native land repair,
Him freedom gave, as friend or prisoner,
Endowed with wealth and titles adequate—
Granting his nuptials royal countenance.

Martucci to Alathiel homage tendered ;
One hand to her, and to Costanza one,
Between them, smilingly, ' I love you both, —
Shall not I love the saviour of my Love ?
Donna Alathiel, wilt thou with us dwell ? '
Alathiel answering,—' Saracen am I,
But, can we separate? my single child !
Bestowed by Him whereto my duty flows ;
Yea, I will go, for whatsoe'er the strain,
'Tis nought to loss of my celestial boon.'

A day of mourning was it when they went,
The Monarch sorrowful, the people sad
To lose their champion and miraculous maid ;
For transport safe the Royal Barque is lent,
Alathiel, Carapresa, and the pair
    The port forsake mid tears and blessings rife,
The wind-god favours, and Costanza fair
    To Lipara returns,—Martucci's wife.

A Flight in Space.

A Flight in Space.

A Rhapsody.

METHOUGHT, abroad the vast ethereal void
   I was upborne without the need of wings;
A charmed bewilderment my soul employed
   And I became mine own imaginings;—

On, on I floated, wisting nothing where,
   Filled with a fearless ecstasy, and soon
Mine eyes gazed, wonder-struck, in sweet despair
   Upon the serrate surface of the Moon;
Well, well I knew the ramparts gaunt and grim,
   Though much exceeding our extremest guess,
And forms amorphous clung about the brim
   Of black abysses broad and bottomless;
Ah! what a weird and joyless scene I scanned
   Of bald reflection and of shadows dark,
Great Tycho flung his figure o'er the land,
   And Dorfel showed, miles high, his vertex stark;
No cloudy vapours veiled their lofty crests,
   The stars were shining in the long, long day,
The Sun, which to those summits never rests,
   A blazing ball suspent, without a ray,—

A blazing ball suspent in vault of gloom !
   And, where he shone I saw adown adown,—
Although his beams reached not the depths of doom
   In those chief craters titled for renown—
First Ptolemy, and next Copernicus ;—
   And all was terrible, unearthly all,
Nor sight nor sound imparting bliss to us,
   No song of bird, no splash of waterfall,
Nor wind, nor river, nor of motion aught,—
   For those dread creatures moved not to mine eye,
Even to think of them I am distraught,
   Nor can I tell if they did creep or fly ;
Like are they not to entities of Earth,
   For in their airless world none is there breath,
When they began to be they had no birth,
   And if they cease, it is without a death.

At this being comfortless, I thought of home,
   And saw my loved Earth as a silvery sphere
Ornate with crepuscule of frothy foam,
   And lucent, with a lustre very clear ;
Such was its splendour, I confessed aloud—
   ' Rightly, O Moon ! our decimal thou'rt shown,
And surely, if thou know'st, art very proud
   My native Earth thy primary to own : '
Then to my vision was, in part, revealed
   The hemisphere from Earth for ever hid,
Whereon, I think, were mists which half concealed
   A champaign vast and varied, in whose mid
I dimly saw an ocean spreading wide,
   And shores productive, and constructed things ;
Now fell the two weeks' night, so fallen to hide
   Beings to whom the dark not blindness brings,—

Not as the torpid creatures next our globe
   Existing scantly in a vacuous waste,
But as th' Allwise Creator doth enrobe
   For joy complete—as there more gladsome placed.[1]

Of motion sentient, I unnoting time
   Beheld the orb men dote on from afar
And ever give a place in loving rhyme,—
   Hesper or Vesper, morn or even-star ;
It is a beauteous world, than Earth more fair,
   And, nearer to the Sun, as heaven more seeming,
Like Earth would be excepting cloud or care,
   E'en as we think of it in happiest dreaming ;
The Sun, in grandeur twice our god of day,
   There doubly blesseth, in a surface clad
With glory human language cannot say—
   Such if the poet told he would be mad ;
Nor fogs nor storms nor biting frosts unkind,
   But constant Summer or perennial Spring,
And light in which our eyeballs would be blind,
   And warmth that would to us prostration bring ;
There, among scenes of nature consonant,
   Are organisms dowered with grace supreme,
Whereof my puny praise irrelevant
   Would but conjecture or a mockery seem.

Abashed I looked, then floated on and on
   Until, in holy awe, I came anear
The Fount of Light, Creation's paragon,—
   Resting, enravished, on the outer sphere :

[1] This is derived from the hypothesis of Hansen.

I saw the lustrous comets come and go,
   The planets in their fealty swift careering,
The meteor ring anent the zodiac glow
   A whirling mass, a phosphor zone appearing :

Then, in a moment, was I changed to be
   Within the photosphere, the home of light,
(And, henceforth, seeing, scarcely did I see,
   But trulier knew, as whiteness knoweth white.)
Within the dread abode of Force unspent,
   In primal Life and in the womb of Cause,
Amid the nether worlds' arcana pent,—
   The ruling Medium of Nature's laws ;
Amid the colours prime of various hue
   Which in the things of Earth, reflecting, bide,
And herb, or flower, or maiden-cheek endue,
   Or paint the Rainbow in prismatic pride ;
Amid the odours of the odours' spring
   But faintly touching ken of mortal sense,
The heavenly harmonies' perpetual ring
   By men o'erheard somewhiles, unknowing whence ;
Amid the sheen outshining aye unshaded,
   And, shadowless, where time is never told,
In elemental glories undegraded
   Whose antitypes are diamond and gold :

And so, entranced, by inner sight I knew
   The high Intelligences of the Sun ;
Angels I name them not, nor were it true
   To term them as of flesh, or fancy-spun ;
Words fit them not, for they are not as we,
   Wherefore describe I them with modest fear, –

They are all eye, and hence I say they see,
　　They are all ear, and so I say they hear :
But their quick consciousness is not of sight,
　　Nor are they aught impressible by sound,
Perceiving, ever they perceive aright,
　　Their least perception passing thought profound :
[Are there not tones on Earth which some not list,
　　Redolence subtile only few may know,
Phantasms the eye inspired alone doth wist,
　　Thoughts that from germs not of the Earth do
　　　　flow?]
Or of their language exercised unspoken,
　　If I should say they speak, 'twere wrongly said
Of attribute whereof we have no token—
　　Communion voiceless and unlimited :
Or if I say they love, it were not well
　　So to express a faculty to blend
One in the other's nature, and to dwell
　　In perfect unison with never end ;
Were I to say they have a face or frame,
　　'Twould be but telling a terrestrial dream,
For I have, with amazement kin to shame,
　　Beheld the Intellectual Presence beam ;
Their splendent world of light they permeate
　　Unknowing motion, effort, space, or time,
Transformed from zone to zone, from state to state
　　At instant impulse of a will sublime ;
Less than omniscient all untaught they know,
　　Less than omnipotent need no control,
Less great than God they cannot greater grow,
　　And yet no greater can be than The Soul :

Yea,—in My Soul, I their co-equal live,
　　Albeit incorporate with mortal clay,

In kindred sympathy I homage give,
  Nor know I not but I shall be as They;
With human Minds I think they converse keep,
  Genius through Nature's influence inspire,
And, or in waking thoughts or dreams of sleep
  Imbue them with the empyrean fire;
Forth from their glorious home they subtly shed
  Rays which perforce through crust corporeal shine,
The body quickening as with manna fed,
  The spirit yielding sustenance divine:
O Sun! I know not all my debt to Thee,—
  Great Source of joy! and of this reverie fond,
For in Thine awful flame I seem to see
  Thy God, and God of all the worlds beyond.

Columbus at Seville.

'A CASTILLA Y A LEÓN
NUEVO MUNDO DIO COLON.'

129

CHRISTOPHORO COLOMBO

From Photograph of a Print in British Museum.

Columbus at Seville.

A.D. 1505, ÆT. 70.

Is it the end?—so mundane honour faileth :
Lacketh my chief meed,—the Holy Sepulchre
Will not by me be rescued ; or the Land,
Which much exceedeth, which I yet could find,
Not whilst I live be proven ; or the Harvest,
Golden-sheaved ! not by my hand ingathered ;
The reaper hath the glory, not the sower ;
To track the pathless ocean needed one,—
A host can tread the track, and share the gain :
Diego, Fernando,—equal as my Sons,
Fruit of two Mothers[1] equal in my love,
May ye inherit, and deserve the guerdon !

O Thou, beneficent Father !   Thou, my God !
Hear now my plea, forgive my discontent ;
Is man to man ingrate ? how baser far
Ingratitude to Thee ! forget I not
The joyant day-dreams of my rising life,
My marvellous salvation from the deep,—
Saved, to disclose some secrets held by Thee !

---

[1] He was not married to the second.

O'erlook I not Thou didst in me implant
The clear, fixed knowledge of those unknown shores
Whereby the Earth shall be a grander Earth,
The True Faith, haply, save unnumbered souls.

My God ! Thy goodness to me hath been great :
How had I surer thought of Atalantis
Than Plato the divine, shrewd Marco Polo ?
Or than of Marinus and Alfraganus
Of the rotund formation ? ay, the GLOBE !
How could I doubt a message deigned by Thee ?
Didst Thou not give to me, by Martin Behem,
My help for sailing,—in the Astrolabe ?
Didst Thou not call up then dear Toscanelli,
And Juan Perez—at the Convent gate ?
He who, as 'twere Thine angel sent to aid,
Foreran me to the Royal Ysabel.

A pricking pain it is to scan those years
Of fretful waiting and vexations vain,—
Eighteen they were—of earnest hope suppressed,
Dull, droning years—of fullest pulse of life
Outspent in care, and penury, and scorn :
Well I remember thee, cold Cazadilla,
And thy repulse for John of Portugal ;
Some better men there were in those drear days,—
Gonzalez de Mendoza of Toledo
Whose intercession to the Queen me brought ;
And thou De Quintanilla, thou, kind host
Who with the good St. Angel beckoned me
Whilst, in a brief despair, from Spain I fled.

What clamorous strife of tongues at Salamanca,
When I stood forth the Junta to dumbfound !

To tell the dolts of schools and catechisms
What God had taught me—God alone could teach;
'Ha, ha!' say they, 'so thou dost well believe
When sailing *down* thy globe, thou wilt return,
By God-sent gales compelled, up-hill forsooth!'
Or, 'Thou dost think some men feet upwards walk,
Like as the flies upon the ceiling there!'
Subdued to silence by an egg on end![1]
Yet wert thou one, friar Diego de Deza,
Dowered with a soul receptive of the Truth;
Nor was I daunted, though it hurt my heart
To think—the wisest of the world reject me!
How wiser thou, Columbus? not thine own,
Not thine own wisdom,—for how dared I else
Give promises all undemonstrable
As things beyond the grave?

      Ah! happy next,
Like a triumphant song, the contest o'er,
Rang out to me the message of St. Angel,
Returned to tell the royal heart's resolve;
'For mine own Crown of Castile will I do it,
E'en though I pledge my jewels.' Noble heart!
Bless thee, St. Angel.

      Straight the Queen to see,
For aye her gracious, sympathetic smile
Is printed in my soul; for aye her words
Even as of honey with soft music blent,
My spirit soothing; as a flood came joy,
Forgot I then seven years of vassalage
In one blest moment—ever fresh and fair!

   [1] His own illustration of ingenuity

I

In gratitude supreme the Throne I urged
To let the treasures of the new-found world
Redeem the Holy Sepulchre, and wrest
From him, proud Soldan false! the sacred shores,
No empty boast was this, nor vainly said;
Let man propose, 'tis Thou alone permittest.

Come Juan de Coloma, courtly scribe,
Bring thou the parchments, let the words be writ,
Use well thy pencraft on a novel theme,
Note in indelible characters that I,
Columbus, am henceforth 'High Admiral,'
Viceroy and governor of those lands and seas
Far-reaching, fertile, affluent, serene,
To-day unknown—but surely to be found.

Now speed to Palos, to the bounteous Sea,
To seek the Ships, to call my Mariners;
The Sovereigns say it,—read the royal rescript,
'This is Columbus, fit him for the Ocean,'
Will ye not do it? nay, it must be done;
Men unconvinced will lag at a behest,—
How feign to prove what only God can show?
Dear Martin Pinzon, thou for one hadst faith,
Dear brother of the sea, if afterwards
Was somewhat to forgive, I have forgiven,—
Is not forgiveness truest test of love?
I love thee ever.

            Here my second Spring!
Erenow a dream, wherefrom I woke to act;
No more the days of hope unsatisfied,
No more for me the life of common things;
Passed the meridian of my mortal years,
I breathed as one who newly trod the earth,

Elastic, strong, my spirit fresh as air,
Prophetic soaring over hindrances,
And onwards looking.

            Next, the solemn day,—
Of my Inheritance! Great God, Thou know'st
My faith was firm, the consequence assured,—
To search? ah! no—but certainly to find;
To Thee I knelt, with all my company,
The words from them of prayer, from me were thanks,—
Thanks for the mission I was crowned withal:
Our auspice was to prosper—blest of Thee!

  Yet, in delight immortal, was I man,
And justly weighed the burthen of my task;
My fellows had some heat not wholly pure,
Fed by a fuel burning out too soon,—
A flame which rose and fell with lessening light,
Not, as the diamond, blazing unallayed:
The old, familiar world had won their trust;
Like the retiring shore their manhood faded,
The land was lost, the trade-wind sped to west,
And they were drifting—into an abyss
From whence perchance no wind would ever waft,—
Behind them all they knew, before them nothing!
Hard to inform of things beyond their stretch,—
Who shall unveil the mystery of faith?
Yea, unto me, in secret, all was well,
Whilst prow kept pointing to the destined coast;
The needle varies! whither do they go?
A ——— they say, where Nature's self hath doubt!
What painful sweet contention in my soul,—
Those faint, rebellious spirits, murmuring loud,
Advancing blindly to the fated goal,

Threatening to stay, and do they knew not what,
Exasperate, fearing it were doom to turn—
Till, on the day of desperation came
The singing-birds—as heavenly harbingers!
And herbage floating as from neighbouring strand;
No land descried—no farther will they sail!
I told them I was serving God and Queen,
And forward must they with me to the end.

The Light of Heaven was in me, and I saw
An earthly light, like signal from a shore ;
Ah ! quoth I.—also a new world of men :
His name be praised ! oh, uncompared to-morrow !
Hath other mortal known of such to-morrow ?
O night no night but as a day eterne,—
The fruiting of a life within the grasp,
The long, long happy dream at last fulfilled !
At earliest break of dawn they shouted 'Land :'
Delightful thought ! when, first, I lifted hands,
And kissed the soil of *my* new hemisphere :
What ? foolish worshipers ! am I a god,
To be bowed down to as did those of old
To Paul and Barnabas ?

　　　　　　　　　　　Nay, but yet great !
Monarch of boundless regions unexplored,
To be re-peopled in the faith of Christ,—
Elect of God to spread the truth afar !
There dwelt in me a soul to reign and rule,
Howbeit perhaps my function was *to find.*

The sordid throng among, alas ! once more,
From ecstasy reduced to mortal cares,
Warring, heart-sick, with lust, and pride, and greed

Ah, save their base turmoil, I had some joy
Belike to human heart not oft is given;
Shall I misprize the rapture of my soul
From visions of a virgin world foreknown,
Region to me revealed, and by me found?
The gorgeous birds and flowers, the luscious fruits,
The verdant groves' melodious choristers,—
Eke, but for man, a heaven terrestrial.

This deed accomplished, to the East again
I set my keel : ah, Pinzon, one-time friend!
Martin Alonzo, and dost *thou* forsake?
Wouldst thou indeed outstrip me in the race
And play the herald? no, it must not be;
Away to Spain, away! whate'er betide.

Shall I forget, oh dread extreme of peril,
When mid the horrors of the raged Atlantic
I wavered in my faith, and, doubtingly,
My record trusted to the floating cask,
Lest with me and my toil-worn mariners
The firstlings of my labours should be lost?
Shall I not own my tremulous content
When, next, I saw the Lusitanian King?
Shall I such contrast with black doubt despise—
When my return to Palos was acclaimed?
Or, happy day supreme! Columbus called
With greeting to the Court?

                    To be a King!
For, verily, a royal progress had he;
Still to my sight the signs of welcome glister,
Still in mine ears the shouts of welcome ring,
Brilliant the cavalcade through Barcelona!

Came forth the choicest chivalry of Spain—
A cohort of grandees and caballeros
Colon escorting for the conqueror's palm :
A memorable day for him who led,
Above the throne,—a missioned prophet-king !
Under a canopy of gold were waiting
Sage Ferdinand, and gracious Ysabel ;
To me rose they—as Sovereigns to Sovereign,
When I would offer homage, me upheld,
And bade me sit beside, as one with them—
Reigning o'er realms more vast and rich than theirs :
At last, when I th' eventful tale had told
They both in thankful adoration knelt,
Due fealty yielding to the King of kings :
The *Te Deum* went to heaven, praising Him—
Great Giver of the glories of the World.

Then uttered I the vow—to pay to God
Out of revenues unto me assigned,
Suffice the Holy Sepulchre to save.

Bright Barcelona ! to my vision now
The same mine eyes have seen ; thy sunny ways,
Thy pleasant palaces with open doors
To him the first of men, thy windy walls
Washed by the blue Internum, where I rode
Betwixt the king and prince, as equal man—
O'erlooking not the Providence on high ;
And, happier far, where oft-times I conversed
With the benignant Queen anent the past,
And limning the beyond.

There had I honour !
When they endowed me with a brave escutcheon,

(I pray my heirs will bear it worthily,)
My own insignia quartered in their shield,—
Castile and Aragon :

> A CASTILLA Y A LEON
> NUEVO MUNDO DIO COLON.

Then had I honour ! for the questing mind
Wherever learning grew was vivified—
Possessed with phantoms of new things to be,
I the elect enchanter ! everywhere
' Praise to Columbus, Christopher Columbus—
To whom was given knowledge passing knowledge,
He who hath dared to fathom the unknown,
Hath made conjecture real ! '

                              Again away !
With no scant trappings, but in wealth and power :
The Sovereigns, Columbus and Fonseca,—
Who would have licence let him ask of these ;
Them to deny less easy than to grant !
Who could resist those high-born, proud hidalgos
So fervent to be first in ways untried ?
[I see thee now Alonzo de Ojeda—
Thy prowess testing ere the need began.]

A deedy conclave were we closeted,
The Admiral, De Soria, and Fonseca,
Francisco Pinelo the treasurer,—
Beginning works of sequences untold,
The prelude planning of a birth of Nations ;
My labour great—proportioned to its purpose,
Not less than to explore the hidden Main
Where he, Great Khan, and Prester John held
kingdom.

Our schemes complete, soon in the Bay of Cadiz
My seventeen caravels proudly floating wait,
Equipped in all to colonize the Indies
And marry well the new world to the old :
All men gave reverence to me, for I wended
Of Squadron uncompared 'High Admiral.'

O sunrise fair ! as omen opportune
To hail the entrance of a Sister-sphere :
The Isles Canaries, then awide, afar
Until the first-born of the new delight
Dominica ; and further, mid the Antilles—
Gladdened with odorous gales and sylvan shores :
There found the rich anana, and there too,
As if to match the bitter with the sweet,
Saw we the limbs of men prepared for food ;
Next, passed uncounted, came the Virgin Islands,
And soon our Western home, Hispaniola,—
For rest once more at my La Navidad.

Rest in unrest ! henceforth too well I knew
How this sublunar sphere with trouble teems
Wherever man doth turn it to his uses :
O cherished idols of inventive thought !
Are ye to be the origin of pain ?
Gone my first footprint in the land of promise,
My fortress and my garrison no more !
Yet had I hope and courage, forward pressed,
Took firmer stand, and on the watered plain
Builded to thee, O Royal Ysabel,
The primal city of the new-found shores :
How like a fevered dream the chequered days
Ere my unwilling, irritant return,—

A vexéd dream—of pain, pleasance and sorrow,
A tangled web, an incoherent tale :
The cry for gold, as 'twere their all in all,
Ships back to Spain their thirst to satisfy ;
Dark discontent of men who looked no higher
Than transient enjoyment, yet fulfilled
Their part as instruments to future good ;—
The plot of Bernal Diaz, well revealed ;
And otherwise, I do bethink me now
Of that entrancing passage mountains o'er ;
Great God, I thank Thee for a wondrous scene
Which with my soul I think eternal lives,—
The flower-enamelled plains and branching ferns,
Those giant cedars centuries murmuring,
The towering palms, broad rivers, beauteous birds :
More gold, and more, unsated still my need—
My need for favour in the eyes of men ;
Found had we not the earthly paradise
And bent ourselves to furnish it with woe ?
Behold a problem difficult to solve,
How grand results of benefit to man
Must the ordeal pass of sin and pain :
Next sailed I forth to Cuba, and, more south
First saw the lovely Isle Jamaica named ;
And presently, a labyrinth of islets,
Like an enchantment the wide sea adorning,
Henceforth by men to be ' Queen's garden ' named .
(Told of by Mandeville and Marco Polo,
From the Great Khan perhaps not far removed.)
Yet were these days of dolour, for delights
Outweighed were by trials pitiless ;
My much-loved mariners, uncomforted,
Unblessed with Heaven's supernal visitings.
Took not sedately their privations dire,

Hard toil of day, misgivings of the night, —
Sustained alone by wonder at new things,
By Self corrupted to inconstant aim ;
And I, unstrung, a tranquil sea attained,
Swooned in collapse—a sickness like to death :

They bore me to my city, as one dead ;
Mine eyes re-opened—oh the sweet surprise,
Angel of Providence, Bartholomew !
Whence cam'st thou, brother loved ? divinely sent,
For, in good time thy presence, when my power
Is threatened, e'en when Pedro Margarite
Took ships and fled with falsehood to the Throne ;
Be thou Adelantado, rule with me
To give me double strength—from Thee, my God !

Here I recall intrepid, strong Ojeda,
Who seized, with guile, the brave chief, Caonabo,
And brought him [lashed together] to the Town.

At this some happier days ; the royal pair
By Torres an approving missive sent,
And with thee, dear Bartholomew ! to aid,
I strove to form and regulate a State,
And as a king did rule, not all in vain ;
Yea, to the Indian people gave we battle
They boasting much to drive us from the land—
Our little band against uncounted thousands !
But thou, Ojeda, wert invincible,
Supporting us to hold, and to subdue ;
Then fell the yoke upon them, and henceforth
Paid they their tribute in the longed-for gold ;
Here breedeth some compunction in my heart,—
What rights had we above these simple men

To master them, and next their curse to be?
May we, for good, cause any creature pain?
It is the will of God that o'er the earth
The faith of Christ shall spread; the cry was 'gold,'
My power was gold, and power must be maintained;
To cultured minds how strange a charm has gold!
Hath not its touching some Satanic spell—
To poison blood, and make man less than man?

Now I remember thy pernicious sting
Wretched arch-traitor, Pedro Margarite;
Thy lies had rooted, and their fruit evolved
In thee Aguado, once my favoured friend,—
Juan Aguado, 'High Commissioner,'
Dominion vaunting o'er the Admiral!
Ay, and he had it, and I gave him place,
Well nigh a fatal blow; howe'er 'tis sure
There will be verdict for me in this world;
So thou wilt go as Censor of thy lord
Armed with the budget of my misdemeanours,
To tell them I have not done what I have,
To tell them I have done what I have not?
I will go with thee there, there thee confront
And put to shame thy foolish, false report:
My God was gracious to me in this pass,
And gave to me a boon, by Miguel Diaz,
No less than those exhaustless mines of Hayna,
The same, I think, as onetime Ophir named
Sought by King Solomon for the Holy Temple.

To brand me alien—st
How alien, as the catholic citizen—
How   , who had brought them wealth and
    fame?

The whole earth his one country, man his nation,
Whose pure, sole purpose is to serve mankind :
None else I love thee well my native Genoa,
E'en with the love a man his mother loves ;
Genoa *la superba*, Genoa, my first home !
City of mountain-side, and ships, and palaces,
City of commerce and of sea-going men.

God blessed me onward, and despite the storms,
· (Which must be for the things surpassing man,)
Vouchsafed me passage safe to Cadiz' Town :
My mariners ! would ye your captives slay—
For food to sin, your trust in Heaven forgot ?

Eager, the people to the Harbour throng
A sick and sorry company to see
In tattered guise, with cruel hardships worn ;
Colon among them a Franciscan monk
Corded, begowned, and bearded ; was not he
Reft of his power, his office stultified
By weak Aguado's charter ? therefore now,
Until restored, a man unpropertied ?

Keen smart, soon over ; not for long I wore
The garb of deprivation ; on to Burgos,—
'The Admiral' in lowly gabardine,
His escort proud, with gold, and captive men :
'Columbus, welcome ! why this humble mien ?
Our Admiral, our Viceroy art thou not ?'
My grace to thee, O traitorous Margarite,
And wily Boyle ! so ended your designs.

Wise Ferdinand, sweet-smiling Isabella !
Well did ye estimate the gains foreshown,

Incline the ear to my prophetic tale,
And grandly grant equipments for the search.

Through *thee*, Fonseca! Oh if called to judge
    thee,
Thy doom should not afflict with torture more
Than thou hast caused my soul by thy delays ;
A Bishop hinders what a King commands !
Two years of waning life, unfruitful—lost,
The rich, far-stretching Continent unfound ;
Now on the threshold of my last reward
Thus, thus to be impeded—it was pain.

The struggle ended, and again I went,—
E'en as a greyhound straining at the leash
To break the cord and seize upon the game :
Here am I blameful, if exasperate
With base Fonseca's minion, Breviesca,
He following with insults to the strand,
I struck the dastard renegade to earth ;
Why in that lofty moment did he tempt me
To loose on him my pent-up agonies ?

Forth from San Lucar, on a new-marked course,—
He who the new would gain must quit the old ;
One cask of water left—but God is good !
So on our day of need loomed Trinidad :
Then found I Paria, which I think must be
Near to, or part of some far-spreading shore ;
For there are freshets as of mighty rivers
Whose sources are not islands, and I deem
The influences benign throughout, around
Splendours of earth and sky, exuberant,
Amid the beaming of unclouded suns,

Cooled by soft zephyrs like the breath of Heaven,
Betoken here or hereabout was fixed
The Eden told as man's first dwelling-place;
I say not but that hence the current flows
From out the fountain of the Tree of Life.

The past grows dim,—henceforward meagre hope :
Ah me ! such griefs to but forget were bliss,—
They cannot be forgotten, yet it seems
As life extendeth Time accustoms sorrow,
Emotion dulls, or sweet or sour come liker,
Our world grown dearer, more is part with us,
E'en as ourselves have largely merged therein,
And so events have less disparity ;
The first Ingratitude impresseth deeply,
All ingrates following are grouped in one ;
The early joys have each a separate being,
The later joys blend like the hues at sunset
And vanish as at setting of the Sun.

Not so in all,—my dear Bartholomew,
Not of rejoining thee ! of such I ween,
In youth or age the same, it self-exists,—
Not mixing with the mass of circumstance ;
And healthful vigour came at seeing thee,
Adelantado—ever faithful brother :
How fares then, in this while, Hispaniola?
Too long detained ! a wound too deep for cure ;
Men turbulent, on vicious purpose bent,
Broke up the springs of order, stood at bay
Against authority and mischief bred ;
My soul approveth I was merciful,
And, with much patience, urged them to do well ;

This knew he, Roldan, of vile rebels chief!
But for the just is justice, and I dealt
Strong-handed justice to defend the good;
Wherefore The Admiral, wherefore made a King
If not to govern? this my tyranny;
Bishop Fonseca, thou must know they lied,
Therefore didst greatly lie accusing me
To be unjust—how greatly! when they sent
A Bovadilla to subvert my power.

As once to Job, the messengers of evil
To me came, saying, 'He has seized thy house,
Thine ownings plundered, and proclaimed thee felon:'
Is this Columbus who enlarged the Earth?
Is this Columbus, who expended life
In long night-watchings and in irksome toil
To open wider range for humankind?
You see The Admiral, but he serves the Crown,—
What wills the Crown, whate'er, though wrong, be done.
Put on the manacles, take, take my hands;
And thou too, dear Bartholomew! come—come!
To prison go we—linked as galley-slaves;
I thought, my Saviour Christ was one time bound,
With scorn assailed and flagellate with thongs.

Thus—thus degraded, to Iberia's strand
Brought they their Admiral,—Viceroy undeposed:
Whereat the Spaniard pitiful became,—
Columbus pitied—for Columbus pity!
Merciful God! had I for *pity* lived?
I thank Thee for the power to bear the mock:
Here stayed they not, but warming into zeal
Rose hot with indignation at my wrongs;
Then went a shout of shame, a horrent cry,

A sound of anger which advancing grew,
A people's tumult echoing through the land,—
'*In manacles the Finder of a World!*'

   The Sovereigns heard their cry, and more, had read
My letter to a lady of the Court—
(For shackled hands are powerless to the Throne ;)
So sent they to me, and I doffed my chains
To put on robes for courtly Granada :
From kindly words some scanty solace springs,
And, recking not of verbal penitence,
Sincere regrets can salve indignities,
But when at seeing me the Queen tears shed,
I wept to think those eyes should weep for me ;
O gentle Isabella—noble heart !
I bless my God for serving such an one ;
Hence were the fountains of my soul refreshed,
And I forgave—yea, in my heart forgave,
Whate'er of anguish from her act had sprung.

   Two years they said—my reinstatement full :
Again to common life—it cannot be !
For him to whom 'tis given to open out
It must not be to stagnate in the found ;
For sadly I revolved, my time is brief,—
I must devote with undeclining zeal
Life's latest issues to the work of God ;
Rounding the stormy Cape, had not De Gama
His nation dowered with wealthy Calicut ?
Should *I* not find, as still I hold there is,
A strait extending to the Indian seas
From out the ocean where my lands are known,
And superadd, whate'er the West may prove,
The sumptuous products of the glowing East ?

———————————

The good day came ; forth on the broad Atlantic
With, first, fair progress toward our wonder-land ;
Bartholomew best Brother—Son Fernando—
Praise unto Him who gave, and ye preserved !
An anxious voyage had we, big with promise,
  h comfort to me thy companionship,—
In sooth, keen sufferings were they, lingering sorrows,
Of perils uttermost by land and sea,
Yet now—in memory's cave together gathered,
I do survey them with an even judgment
As doth a watcher looking from the Pharos—
All objects scanning at a moment's glance.

A bitter balk it was when. seeking haven,
   craved admittance at Hispaniola ;
      Ovando ! thou didst well, methinks
To turn away the giver of thy realm ;
Sped we right well without thee, and erelong
The coast of Terra Firma hailed once more ;
Then found we Cape Honduras, and I hoped
Near that peninsula the Strait desired ;
It is not far, or if it be not there
The land is narrow to the Indian seas.[1]

       by raging storms, we found, in time,
The wished-for golden shore Veragua ;
"Twas here Adelantado shrewdly searched
     confirm me in my earlier thought,—
      Chersonesus surely this ;
      didst   with me. Bartholomew,
And hadst   'shed here a settlement

Save some mischance and ills unparalleled :
Back,—back to turn ! yet there the Strait *must* be.
And men one day shall pass thereby to Ind :
God's will be done !　HE lets me mark the way ;
From where Columbus stayed, may others speed !

Lo, then my soul had succour, for I saw
Bright visions of the night, and heard His voice,—
' Why frettest thou, O man, and losest heart ?
Are not thy troubles as of man with man ?
Is there not surety thou shalt be sustained ? '
Wherefore what mattered when the woe befell,-
My ships ashore, my faithful company
Left unprovided on the Indian strand ?
And here it was, denied supplies of food,
God gave me the Eclipse, and hid the Moon
To show the Indian I must be preserved :
Now bless thee, Diego Mendez, constant friend.
Who wert the chosen means empowered by Him,
My heavenly Father, to go thence and save ;
Not thwarted by one failure, thence again,
This time with brave Fiesco to thine aid ;
Go then canoes, go fragile boats to sea,
For *me* the day of miracles survives !
Pass weary months, pass quickly in my thought,-
Months follow months, 'tis sure they will return ;
Ah, Porras ! thou wert one who gave me pain—
By thy desertion in our time of need ;
Thou too wert baffled, and the ships *did* come ;
Unto God's mercy, not to thy good-will
Be it ascribed, Ovando ; so I sailed
Once more to mine own city,—' Isabella ; '
There, with some tenderness, some deference
Was I received and fostered, there to wait—

Enough to grieve o'er my perverted plans,
Beknow of cruel laws I had no power
To mitigate, o'erhear of deeds inhuman
Which tore my heart to crying—'Not to me,
O Good Creator! not to me impute
These sufferings of Thy creatures,—not to me!'
With some pretence of fairness didst thou deal,
Boastful Ovando, but thou wert not fair;
I fear—lest thou hast weighted the account
Which I must cast with God,—may He forgive!

In storms to Spain,—it seemeth that my life
Must end in storm; what mind e'er rests at peace
The goal ungained, the recompense withheld?
How rest whilst, lost my care, the evil rule
Yet banes Hispaniola? profitless
My journey to Segovia! for now
My urgent prayer brings no responsive tones:
The Queen is dead—the Court is dead to me!
Ah Ferdinand, thy chilly surface-smiles
Gave doubting comfort to my yearning soul;
What! thou wouldst grant me titles, properties
In this old world, where I have nothing earned.
My just apportionment denying yet
In those dominions I have won for thee;
Is not the compact sacred? thou shalt lose
It breaking, more than thou withhold'st from me—
In forfeit of thine honour among men;
Thy glory is inglorious, O King!
All is in vain! my letters or my voice:
Thou too, O friend, Amerigo Vespucci,
To right me failest, though thy heart be true.

Lost, peerless Isabella! sunk with thee

My last, fond hope ; O truest, highest friend,
Thou best as woman, Lady first of Earth,
Pure pride it is to think thou me didst love
In like of love wherewith man honours man—
The flame of friendship ; why then art thou gone,
Why, why evanished ere the end is come,
Me aidless leaving ?

———►•◄———

               Dear Bartholomew,
I pray thee to the throne to plead my cause ;
Tell Queen Juana how I wait and fade,
The child of Isabella for me cares,
She will give ear and, with a yielding heart,
Restore my dignities ; assert my claims !
Declare I leave her more than she can grant
In wealth or titles, tell her I can do
Whereby to raise Castile in might and glory
Above all earthly kingdoms.

                      He is gone ;
He will achieve his purpose—not for *me*,
But for my heritage ; increasing tithes,
Revenues still enlarging—endlessly,
At Genoa garnered, shall the fund augment
Which I have set apart to be applied
To last redemption of the sacred tomb.

—————

  The body weakens, but the soul is strong ;
O Soul ! what wilt thou do, so resolute,
Left, left alone—bereft thy minister ?
I am *my Soul, I* have not done my work ;
Are there no further shores for me to seek—
With intuition and the will to act ?
Such—such the ways of God, and sure it is

I have been highly favoured ; he to whom
Was given, by faith, perception of some things
Unearned by human learning, who foresaw
Those unseen regions—as he now foresees
The heaven whereto he goes ; shall I essay
To teach men uninspired the graces of
A better Country, where the King is just—
All covenant fulfilled?   The kings of Earth
Owe justice, and should heed this holiest law
Of Him their mighty Prototype on high ;
Him praise I ever ! Him who hath me blessed ;
Has not the beam celestial lit my path ?
Has not miraculous care encompassed me ?
Have I not heard soft whispers from the skies ?
So may I think of thee, base Bovadilla,
When thou wert lost and my weak barque was
        spared ?
Why rise to touch the highest peak of fame
The pit contempt within down-fallen to be ?
Nay, nay ! 'tis well ; forgive me, Thou Most Good !
My dreams sublime and their accomplishments
Have much exceeded all my toils and trials,
And upward gaze I, with a trustful heart
The outcomes heeding of my mortal life :
Yea, on those shores to and through me made
        known
Will flourish puissant empires, unenslaved,
The dark will be illumined, knowledge spread,
HIS Truth for ever permeate my world ;
For me the scope of Heaven is free to find,
And on the Earth to me shall justice come,
To me will come, and men will say—' COLUMBUS.'

150

Sonnets.

I.

Sleep.

THIEF of the mind—he, at the term of toil,
Serpent-like creeps upon the jaded sense
Till, when no longer we can make defence,
He doth us bind; anon we crack the coil,
Fresh as an amaranth the trickster foil
And, with renascent courage, chase him thence!
Ah, then eftsoons his wiles will recommence,
So of nigh half our days he doth us spoil:
O life no life—O death not death indeed,
Is there not joy unsought and love unfound.
Know we all sights and sounds in Nature's store.
Do not our thoughts new thoughts for ever breed?
Else, as the dormouse or the drowsy hound,
Sleep we, and sleep, and sleep—to wake no more?

Silence.

Hush— hush ! it is the charm of nothingness,
A sweet estate wherein there is no sweet,
A music true though no vibrations beat,
A passive mistress cold and passionless—
Bestowing not yet having power to bless,
Until in holy love we kiss her feet :
O joy wherein the soul no friend may greet,
O Thou no comfort yielding in distress,—
Why do we love thee, Silence ? Art thou then
The mystic, ghostly Mother of mankind
From forth whose womb we sprang without a throe ?
Craving for rest and peace do not all men
In Thy serene resort contentment find ?
Art Thou the very Heaven whereto we go ?

Silentium Noctis.

VOID—void—all void ! the things erewhile—are not,
I but as nothing—with myself alone
In the Still Darkness ; not a ray—no tone
To tell of being, or of space, or spot ;
No ghostly glow refulgent,—one black blot
The face of Nature—as no Sun had shone !
The beauteous Universe by me beknown
Lost to the senses, like a love forgot :
Yet—yet I *am*, and, thinking, see, and hear
The tongueless voices in their noiseless tune,
And bask in brilliancy beyond the Sun :
Ah, wherefore is it Darkness bringeth fear,
Wherefore, O ominous Dæmon ! veil so soon
The Life of Light—so soon, alas ! outspun ?

Æquo Animo.

Have *thou* content !—are there not men unfed
Who wander forth in empty nakedness
No pillow owning for the head to press,
The sky their coverlet, the ground their bed?
Are there not some who crave no mental bread,
Whose passive moments no glad dreamings bless,
Whom no love vexeth in enjoyed distress,
Who have no hopes, no yearnings fond, no dread?
Have thou content !—alas, alas ! in vain—
Whilst still I seek and eager seeking fail,
Whilst aspiration gaineth not the goal,
Whilst Life's deep mysteries a blank remain,
And teachings of the wisest none prevail
To satisfy the hunger of the Soul.

Sight.

When oft with closéd eyes I see thy face,
What is it but thine impress on my mind?
And though for ever henceforth I were blind,
Those lineaments mine inner sight would trace :
Or, though on earth no more thou holdest place,
To me unveiléd beam thy features kind
In ghostly state—which cerements cannot bind !
If from the world terrene, or æther space,
Thou comest at the bidding of my will,
Do not I love thee truely and thou me?
Art thou not calling when for thee I call?
O friend belovéd, severance doth not kill,
Come ! let the vision of my Soul thee see
To tell me absence is not death in all.

Analogy.

Was it a dream—the keen undoubting joy
Which I to-night, as 'twere for aye, did know?
Was it a dream—the vision all aglow
In light the very Light doth not destroy?
Was it a dream did now my soul annoy
With anguish of unutterable woe?
Was it a dream deep in my soul to grow
And every subtlety of thought employ?
Kin of my heart! real things, the loved and lost,
How come ye to me, and again forsake?
(As waifs from out the sea of Time uptost,)
Do ye in dreamland habitation make?
Were ye then dreams me bitter tears have cost?
Is such the life wherefrom at death we wake?

Fame and Immortality.

WHAT being hast thou, much desiréd Fame?
Why do men immolate themselves to thee?
Art thou indeed an immortalitie,
Or only what thou seem'st—an empty name?
Art thou in one a glory and a shame,
So to be lauded unto extasie
And yet be but the last infirmitie—
The cause of folly and the source of blame?
Speak, speak! my heart, is there not something more
Than tawdry reputation fame can give,
Some prize for which ambition is not crime?
Ah! is it nothing when this world is o'er
To reign in mortal bosoms—so to live
From age to age unto the end of time?

Peace.

Peace is to man not peace but torpid soul—
Idlesse corporeal, or a mental sleep;
It is to be as happy as the sheep,
Supine, contented with an earthy dole :
Alas, alas! how shall my heart control
The strong unrest of doubt suffice to keep
Disquietude amid compunctions deep,—
Attaining to so little of the whole?
Of Heaven is peace!—Oh, sunny, ripply sea
Withouten shore,—till then the normal strife
Of false and true—the contest, ceaselessly,
Against the wrongs wherewith the world is rife,
The struggle of the Conscience with the Me :
Peace is the stagnant pool. the rivulet is Life!

Double Life.

In many a mortal life are blent two lives,
One is a life of toil, and trick, and gain,
Of vapid pleasure and of skin-deep pain
Along a miry course—as Mammon drives,
A life which after the Material strives,
Up-building works desertless to remain,
In heaps of gold or monuments as vain,
To be but nothing when the end arrives :
The other life is life of heart and soul,
Of passion and of poetry and song,
Of depths and heights of sorrow and of mirth
No profit bringeth, seeketh not a goal,
And, though it all doth unto earth belong,
Subsists but in oblivion of the Earth !

Experientia Docet.

One said, ''Tis well when life hath early end,
To die ere yet the Soul has ta'en the taint
Of sordid commerce, guileful, base restraint,
For gain to truckle and for place to bend,
Erewhen ingratitude had shamed a friend
Or broken love had made the heart to faint,
Erewhen dark doubt had whispered its complaint
Or hope, declining, could no more contend :'
Oh ! foolish Monitor, oh ! rash desire,—
Doth not the furnace prove the metal true ?
Hath virtue worth that hath no test withstood ?
Were it not better to outlive the fire,
Profit by trials which thy faults subdue,
And die, at latest, when more wise and good ?

XI.

Music.

Voice of the Air, though silent ever near,
Which somewhen inly to the mind doth speak,
And resonant to those who wishful seek
Comest at call from thine æthereal sphere,—
Music, Attendant-Angel of the ear,
Missioned to breed oblivion sweet, and eke
Subdue the frantic, animate the meek,
By fitful change to bring the smile or tear,—
Hast thou not part with the celestial frame
Whereto by hidden ties the soul is kin?
Thine the one language of the heavenly choir,
Thine the one utterance to all hearts the same
Whether outspoken in the thunder-din
Or the harmonious accents of the lyre.

Mystic Harmonics.

SOMEWHILES, when into vacancy I gaze
And seem bereft of life or lost in thought,
My soul is with divinest music fraught—
Soft accents hearing of celestial praise ;
In notes unwritten and in wordless lays
Anthems are singing to me all unsought,—
Each time I listen new vibrations caught,
Till I recline in joy and sweet amaze :
Whence are ye then, ye tones of heaven? for sure
Ye are not visitings of humankind ;
Are ye embalméd memories sublimed?
Or, of the Hereafter, do ye come to lure
My soul from sensuous seekings unrefined
With strains supernal by the Angels chimed?

XIII.

True Love.[1]

(RESPONSE TO A SONNET WRITTEN BY THE AUTHOR OF
'ORION.')

LOVE having once been Love will ne'er expire,
What doth not die the Soul shall not forget,
And though Beloving should not Love beget,
It lives,—an inextinguishable fire;
Friendship forgotten were unreason dire,—
As if to say they part who never met,
Or whoso never owed should own a debt,
Or creatures of the midden will aspire;
Wherefore, O Man or Mistress, tell me not
Thou lov'dst me erst but love me now no more,
None eye hath seen a non-existent spot,
What never was leaves nothing to deplore;
Tell me the Diamond in its Mine will rot
Or virgin Gold will perish in the ore!

23rd Jan. 1880.

---

[1] See Appendix.

Of God.[1]

FATHER of all, by beings of Earth once named,
Albeit they cannot know Thee—what, or where,
To Whom mankind in hope or in despair
Appeal in simple ignorance, unshamed,—
Though truth and reverence be thus defamed
By loving adoration, vow, and prayer
Vaguely devoted to the viewless air
Lest men for worse ingratitude be blamed ;
Father of all, why seek we—not to find ?
Why list we, ever yearning, not to hear—
Save in the wonders of the Earth or Sky ?
Why to Thine Omnipresence are we blind,
Why to Thy children dost Thou not appear ?
Is then eternal Silence—Thy reply ?

---

[1] This and the three following Sonnets are intended as a sequential
series.

XV.

Arcanum Animi.

WHEREFROM, to Whom, or what, we owe our being,
Conscious we are of such we do *not* know
Of whence we come or whereunto we go,—
This, this the fruitless end of our far-seeing ;
Shall we then frankly from delusion fleeing
Confess the humbler creatures wiser show,—
The Steed to whinny, Chanticleer to crow,
In full contentment with their lot agreeing?
Not so, not so !   Doubt is immortal Thought,
Life unexpectant were in life to die,
Fate cannot Prescience from the Future sever,
The restless still-voice speaketh not for nought,
A sound undying is the human Sigh,
A Soul creative is a Soul for ever.

XVI.

Knowledge of God.[1]

Thou great First Cause, in causing Man, with thought
And insight of a Future that *must be*,
Didst Thou endow him to be Fancy-free—
For nearer knowledge of Thee to be sought?
Or is Thy Will he shall remain untaught,
Nathless a Soul with eager yearnings fraught,
Gazing upon a dark and shoreless sea
All valueless unto his vision brought?
Enough O Man! accept the Law of Fate
Content thou art enabled to *desire*,
To know thou dost not know is grandly thine,
Next the creative thy conceptive state—
At highest flight unceasing to aspire,
This, uncompared, thy faculty divine.

---

[1] See Appendix.

XVII.

Fiat voluntas Tua.

THEREFORE, proud Man, shouldst thou pretension lower,
And, for thine honour, bend to the decree ;
Were best presumption, or humilitie ?
Lov'st thou obedience or rebellion more ?
Accept, in thankfulness, the plenteous store
Of Gifts by Nature's God bestowed on thee,
Melt as the rain-drop in the measureless sea,
Rejoicing though thou knowest not its shore ;
Grateful, confiding, fatuous fears forsake
Assured the Cause will not the Work belie,
Be Fancy's boundless realm thy bliss supreme ;
How know we of our sleep but when we wake,
Exhibit we have lived but when we die ?
Who dreams he wakes—doth only wake in dream.

Cathedral of Cordova.

As in a forest seeming infinite,
A portal and an altar everywhere,
The soul is moved to lofty thought, and prayer
Unto the Omnipresent One of might,
So had the pious Moslem purpose right
Who did at Cordova this temple raise;
For when he wandered in the vasty maze
Of columns rich, in every hue bedight,
He knew no spot where he must offer praise,
Nor where he last was prostrate, nor the door
Wherethrough he gained the labyrinthine floor—
Unnoting which among the nineteen ways;
Nor found he there incitement to adore
Than as the thankful heart its homage pays.

BEN SEVILLA AND BADAJOZ,
    4th May, 1860.

XIX.

Lincoln Cathedral.

I've seen the Lyncolne Mynster—on the hill
For seven told centuries by it ycrowned,
And in regarding such delight have found
As our forefathers' pious minds did fill
At the evolving from a fervent will
A work yet onwards, endlessly, renowned :
Æthereal Fancy ! thou art here unbound,
Roving from human deeds of subtile skill,
Pillar and lancet-arch and tracery rare,
Proportion whose perfection bears a spell,
The votive chapels, proofs of holy care,
With roof by worthy Willson carvéd well,
Unto the destination of my prayer—
Where Thou great God beneficent dost dwell.

On the South Downs.

A song to thee, O Nature! whilst the hills
Render my senses fullest sympathie;
Above the world of men, dissolved in thee,
A joy thy joy serene my bosom fills,
And claim I sonship, mindless of 'the ills
That flesh is heir to;' nought is now to me
Than the primeval sward, and sky, and sea,
Boundless—as thy companionship instils:
O Mother Nature! melt my heart in thine,
O Mother Nature! I in thee am lost,
O Mother Nature! own me as thy child;
Why know I this sublimity divine
If not from thee? me take at any cost!
I had not loved so if thou hadst not smiled.

Richmond Hill.[1]

WAKING, I saw a valley far and wide
Outspread beneath, the vision of my dream :
It was of Earth yet not of Earth did seem—
None having mark of toil ; on every side
Fair mead and forest lay, in verdant pride,
And, as a pearl mid emeralds, a stream,
O'er whose broad face the glorious Sun threw gleam,
Athwart meandering did calmly glide ;
No pain was there, no false exciting charm,
But joy serene that might eternal be,—
Whereat, much wond'ring, I inspired did rise
Into a frenzy, and with sweet alarm
Knew I beheld the long-famed Arcadie,
Phantasm of Heaven, type of Paradise.

---

[1] See Appendix.

George Long.

As the hard Miser doth, he makes a store
Of various mintage—from each learnéd tongue,
Of all the wisdom that is said or sung,
So none can count, or guess, his wealth—of lore :
And, like the Miser, doth he fret and pore,
Yet as he groweth old, as ever young—
Delving the Mine wherefrom his riches sprung,
His greed insatiate—crying more, more, more !
Unlike the Miser, he will freely yield
From all he hath, with no begrudging dole,
And still will render from the fruitful field
Wherever knowledge thrives—from pole to pole,
Till men may wonder at the hoard concealed ;—
Ah, we but gain an atom of the whole.

XXIII.

Benjamin Disraeli.

EARL OF BEACONSFIELD.

Told by a name that tells the ear his Race,
Alien, yet Englishman, of learnéd Sire,
He, dauntless, raised his standard ' Never tire,'
And noble, among Nobles took his place,—
Nature's Patrician, with patrician grace :
Great souls are unperturbed, betray not ire ;
Ah, recked they little of the latent fire
When searching curiously his statue-face,
Till the Volcano flamed, and then they knew
How passion curbed is strength to strength upon,
In flashing forces or of Tongue or Pen,
The weapons keen wherewith his foes he slew :
He scaled Parnassus, if not Helicon,
And born subaltern died a ' King of Men.'

May, 1881.

XXIV.

To Sir Robert Peel,

AFTER HIS SPEECH ON FREE-TRADE IN CORN,
22ND JAN. 1846.

Now seeth the world a high-exampled good,—
Power confessing error; onward PEEL !
Blush not thou if humanity reveal
Its *native* weakness, (which to have withstood
Were vice beginning ;) let no specious hood
Be Truth's obscurer ; sometime when we kneel
Greatest we are ; who to the right is leal
Guidance divine hath in Thought's mazy wood :
Honour to him distinguished by no deed
Which stemmed the flowing of progression's tide
To vaunt him on the eddy, who did heed
'The voice of God '[1] beyond delusive pride
And all learnt wisdom ; he shall have his meed
Though glib debaters of a day deride.

[1] Vox populi, etc.

XXV.

Wellesley.

FRIEND, I possess with joy a Gift[1] most rare,
Formed of the gems erewhile the thoughts of one
Great in all difficult things,—a mental Sun
Gilding where'er he glances, and my care
Shall be to prize it justly, and compare,
Till, like the skilled Anatomist, I've won
Conception full from fragment seen, and spun
From its sweet poesy—perspective fair !
A noble Mind ; at which I'll gaze and gaze,
By sympathy intent to emulate,
Praying all men may in the latter days
Aspire unto such high and glorious state ;
And in mine age I'll list the young men's praise
Whilst of his Gift and WELLESLEY I prate.

---

[1] '*Primitiæ et Reliquiæ*,' 1840—then first published, and sent by the Marquess Wellesley to the author. The Sonnet is addressed to the bearer of the Book.

XXVI.

John Britton,

THE ANTIQUARY, ON HIS BIRTHDAY: AGE 70.
7TH JULY, 1841.

WELL it beseems thee, BRITTON, to have gained
Fulness of years ; the Past doth honour thee
As thou the past hast honoured ; thou shalt be
A long, long age in memory retained
With those stone deeds whose glories have remained,
And hallowed now by ' hore antiquitie '
As is the storm-enduring Druid tree,
Or echoing aisle with storied windows-stained :
Ancient of days but aye a boy in heart,
Still hoping on with sympathies unspent,
Example to the Apathist thou art !
Would that thy frame might fitly represent
Thy spirit's freshness ! then should ills depart,
And the grey tyrant Time, for once, relent.

Joseph Hunter,

KEEPER OF THE PUBLIC RECORDS.

STUDENT for love, a quiet-thoughted man,
Thine is it, HUNTER, to live lustrous hours
Of gentle brooding o'er the Muses' dowers,
And, humbly erudite, the text to scan ;
Rapt with immortal memories holier than
All the tame Present issues and devours,
Thy spirit haunteth the Elysian bowers
Among the minds which, ages gone, began :
From doubt rest sacred thine hypotheses !
An honest will is all this world may own ;
In after-life, where Truth hath no degrees,
Thou'lt prove the dear conjectures thou hast known,
And see them clear, with mightier mysteries
Each to its shape immutable ygrown.

XXVIII.

Frederick William Robertson,

MINISTER OF TRINITY CHAPEL, BRIGHTON.

(Written 15th August, 1853—the day of his death.)

So might it seem—now the brave voice is still
For ever, and the noble heart at rest—
E'en as a planet leaveth in the west
No trace of the bright course it did fulfil,
Thy life, dear ROBERTSON! no deeds of skill
In marble, or in gaudy pigments drest,
Nor folios, thy labours to attest,
No monuments to mark thine earnest will :[1]
Of the Unseen—unseen, unwrought, sublime,
Thy work is woven in the Spirit of Man,
Deep meanings of the Mediatorial plan
Told by thy eloquent tongue's euphonious chime :
Hush ! the truth-tones his ringing voice began
Are echoing onward through the waves of Time.

---

[1] Nothing of any importance of Mr. Robertson's writings had then been published.

XXIX.

Sortain.

(AFTER HEARING HIM PREACH.)

IF I might envy, it should be, SORTAIN,
Thine heritage of intellectual joy,
For well I know how in this world's annoy
All other harbourage compares in vain ;
Sweet are these earthlings! but or shine or rain,
Each in fruition breedeth its alloy,
Hourling delights born to themselves destroy !
How would we have the mutable remain ?
Oh ! to *forget* them all—enough to lose
Sense of mortality, awhile to rise
Into sublimer being—as the dews
'Twixt Earth and Heaven,—gaining dim surmise
Of what, unfleshed, we may be, this endues
Man like a god—this dost *thou* realize.

T. J. Judkin.

Judkin of simple heart, who in one name
Joins pastor, poet, painter,—in one age
Blends the seven ages, or of Child, or Sage,
As mood may vary; how, anon, shall Fame
Reward thee, or thy worthy works proclaim?
Will she thy Sermons vaunt, of holy rage
And voice of Stentor? or thy metred page
Of Hymn or Sonnet? or thy pencil's aim
To reproduce the grace the poet sees?
(The phantasm of *his* mind to other's eye.)
What matters! if in each a man doth well,
Whether he sought by rivers rocks and trees,
Or by the verities he could out-tell,
Or poet's song, God's name to magnify?

Edward Lumley.

PERFECT exemplar of the London man,
True Cockney, and true Englishman withal,
A Christian too we may thee justly call,
The while devoted worshipper of Pan :
Double-lifed LUMLEY ! 'plaining of the ban
Of street-incarceration, whilst the thrall
Upon thy body cramps thee not at all
Nor narrows thy thought's compass by a span
Duty claims sacrifice, yet thy full soul
Nurtured in hopes and high imaginings
No portion loseth of its earthly joy,
Strayeth mid prairies green from pole to pole,
And, scaling Heaven with cherubic wings,
Feeds on delights unreal which do not cloy.

XXXII.

St. Preux.

Love came and spake to me, 'She is thy mate;'
I said, 'O Love, how will she know 'tis so?'
Whereat all suddenly the passionate throe
Flooded my heart, and certified my fate :
'Ah,' quoth I, 'be she heedless I will wait
Until her pulses beating fast or slow
At tone or touch in time with mine shall go,
Until together gain we Heaven's gate :'
Sweet, gentle Fawn ! caught in the silken snare
Unconscious how it wound about her charms !
She whispered 'Nay,' admonished me, ' Beware,'
Then lent her spirit unto soft alarms,
And then,—when only left for me to dare, —
Murmured 'I love,' and melted in mine arms.

XXXIII.

Abelard.

I saw, and loved,—love with no respite told ;
She answered, ' Leave me ! for thy speech is rude ,'
I, unabashed, in love's beatitude
Knelt to her, heart to heart, and cried, ' Behold
Mine is true-love, oh let me thee enfold ! '
She said, ' I pray thee rise, nor me delude,
All I can give thee is my gratitude,—
Nay, nay, I love thee not ! thou art too bold :'
Then spake I, ' I am strong, thou shalt not go !
I read thine answer in those eloquent eyes
E'en while thy ruddy lips do say me " No,"—
Thy soul elects me as thy tongue denies :'
' Ah, wherefore,' sighed she, ' dost thou urge me so ?
Can it be Love—to bid me tell thee lies ? '

Ninon.

Have I not held dominion?—ask I whence?
Truly I know not but the sweet effect
When men become my slaves; I can elect
Unto the highest heaven of soul and sense
Him whom I deem so worthy; or pretence,
When Love not lights his torch, will none reject;
This, this my sovereignty,—whilst still bedeckt
In Beauty's gifts, to yield them recompense;
My flowing hair, my never-failing eyes,—
Eyes lit to conquer when I neared fifteen,
Charms formed to madden unto fool the wise,
Must—must they wither? must I quit the scene?
Despair to think!—my spirit brave replies,
' More, by thy magic, shalt thou reign their queen

XXXV.

Delirant Reges.[1]

'—*ad hæc se*
Romanus Graiusque ac barbarus induperator
Erexit.'—JUVENAL, X. 137.

HAIL! victor Emperor; thou, erst a King,
Would'st be uplifted to transcendent state,
Dare to impersonate the part of Fate
And on thy foe humiliation bring;
And Nemesis hath heard thee pray and sing,
And given thee glory that doth ante-date
A glory ending in unending hate—
In tales of woe that shall through ages ring:
Pitiless exercise of garnered power,—
To harry helpless creatures here and there,
Robbery made righteous by the rules of war,
And death to all who did not basely cower,
Homesteads afire,—fear, famine and despair!
Such was the cost,—and thou art Emperor.

March 1871.

[1] '*Quidquid delirant reges plectuntur Achivi.'*
                    HOR. *Ep.* i. 2. 14.

XXXVI.

Photography.

1842.

By title new, for added gift, O Light!
We now shall praise thee, Limner at our will
Of all thou dost irradiate, with skill
Outrivalling the emulative flight
Of human power,—for the discriminate might
Of Nature's hand thy purpose doth fulfil:
Ye, PORTA, GALILEO, NEWTON, if that still
For earth ye care, are sharing our delight—
From pride estranged, yet glad your mundane toil
Hath glorious fruiting! and ye of to-day,
Who tracking onwards through the tangled coil
Of philosophic truth now with them may
Claim brotherhood,—nor shall your lustre soil,
NIEPCE, and DAGUERRE, and TALBOT, and CLAUDET.

XXXVII.

Ordination.

THIS day, O friend, is thy life's purpose changed,
When thou art chosen from the sons of men
In holiest cause to labour,—back agen
To call an errant nature long estranged
From primal state of virtue, and deranged,
Until, as things diverse, the Now and Then :
Be brave of heart and voice, be firm thy pen ;
Words will not fail thee whilst remain unchanged
The promises of Him who faileth not ;
Before thy mental vision will uprise
Prospects of goodness which all Sin outblot,
The tale of evil will provoke surprise,
Restored is Man, and Earth a heavenly spot :
Behold the end whereto God's agent tries.

XXXVIII.

Benigna.

O LOVELY lady of the radiant mien,
Thine aspect is a book of gentle joy,
A sweet-toned happiness without alloy,
A lake of waters clear in placid sheen;
It seemeth to me, like to Nature's Queen
Thou dost a holy influence employ,
The haughty quelling, comforting the coy—
Subduing all things to thyself serene :
Ah, surely in thine angel-face we see
Unfaded the Divine similitude—
Just as in Eve, ere of the fatal tree
She tasted,—erewhen Evil's darksome brood
Had, in the mortal struggle, sinfully,
Displaced the lineaments with fingers rude.

Tones to the Absent.[1]

MARY—mistrust not! wake the charmèd tone,
Strike! strike the chords that are too sweet for vexing :
Let thine Attendant-Spirit, else unknown,
Speak with the voice whose stillness is perplexing ;
Dread not the absence of the ears that were,
Open the heart which will not bear confining,
And there shall issue forth a holy prayer
Of heavenly music with thy thoughts combining :
More true than words or wail of human breath
Were Music to thy sorrow's full expression,
For it is abler to discourse with Death
Than any language in the world's possession ;
Court then, in love, the speech which no words needet!
The subtile tongue whose hest the Unseen heedeth !

---

[1] To a young lady who avoided music after the death of her Father

Now and Then.[1]

So, Lady, in the haven of thy will,
Meeting dear sacrifice with calm contentment,
Dost thou thine earthly destiny fulfil,
Thyself bereaving 'gainst thy heart's assentment,
Unto the Future art thou hence allied
By her in grace and good from thee proceeding,
And though the present fade, all rainbow-dyed
'Twill hold a blissful charm in its receding;
From the mind-treasures of the joyant years
Fancy will reproduce thine own sweet springing,
E'en that thou scarce shalt ken, 'twixt smiles and tears,
If then, or now, the merry bells are ringing;
But, as the Sun another clime adorning,
Merge into one the evening and the morning.

---

[1] At the marriage of the only child of a dying widow.

The Dirge of Man.

194

The Dirge of Man.

Theme of the Problem of Life.

WE live to learn, and learn to live,
We know, nor longer guess and try :
Our knowledge henceforth we outgive—
                   Until we die.

We see, and now can rightly see,
Deceived no more by erring eye ;
Sight ! thou henceforth our guide couldst be—
                   Did we not die.

We hear, and separate word from wit,
No more for truth accept a lie ;
Ear ! be henceforth our counsel fit—
                   How, if we die ?

TIME, we did hold thee in disdain—
To let the hours unheeded fly;
Now court we thee, O TIME ! in vain,—
                   Thou bidst us die.

SPRING, thy ecstatic influence,
Of life renews—we care not why—
The juvenescent soul and sense,
                   Why then to die ?

SUMMER, thy genial, sunny hours
Returning still the past outvie,
And brighter, brighter bloom thy flowers !
                   Why then to die ?

AUTUMN, thy tints, thy lessening day,
Thy saddening eve and reddening sky,
Still charm us more the more we stay,-
                    Why then to die ?

WINTER, thy cold our spirit warms,
Thy rest our rest doth typify,
And we have grown to love thy storms ;
                    Why then to die ?

We know it well the world we tread,
To wend where'er, or far or nigh,
As others will when we are dead,—
                    Like us to die.

Ye verdant plains, ye branching trees
Which oft with rapture we descry,
More, and still ever more ye please
                    Until we die.

Ye pretty flowers, ye deck the mead
And move our hearts to glorify,
More, more do we your beauty heed—
                    Until we die.

Ye elements, ye flash and roar
And, godlike, each to each reply,
More, more we wonder and adore—
                    Adoring die.

O Nature, mother Nature ! thou
Once moved men thee to deify ;
We claim our kindred with thee now—
                    E'en when we die.

Dear friends! we missed you when ye fled,
Distress and time did us ally ;
TIME! thou couldst substitute the dead—
    Were 't not we die.

And ye, our loved companions yet
Whose constancy can Time defy,
Time doth increasing love beget—
    And lets us die.

Children beloved! our hope and care
Since when ye could but laugh and cry,
Our friends to be ! but otherwhere—
    When we shall die.

Sweet confidence ! so sweet to know,
Sweet trust, we'll win thee by and by,
And trusted, sweetlier, trust bestow—
    If not to die.

Much good we knew not how to love,
Regarding not when it was by,
We covet now all else above—
    When soon to die.

Oft-seeing some affection brings,
We prize what time doth ratify,
And grow to love familiar things,—
    Then soon to die.

We've laboured much, our deeds are known,
Perchance our work doth fructify ;
Now might we reap where we have sown—
    If not to die.

For thee, O Fame! we could endure
To be interpreted awry ;
Now are we righted, and secure—
                  Erelong to die.

For wealth, the need of polished life,
We did in much ourselves deny ;
Ease now succeeds the money-strife,
                  At ease to die.

Sweet the appliances of wealth
When life is fresh and hope is spry,
Of sickly zest in ageing health—
                  And soon to die.

The talents in us, little prized
Whilst with our compeers we would vie,
If late, the world hath recognized,—
                  Nathless we die.

Honours are ours and high estate,
Our name men now much magnify ;
Is it in scorn they make us great,
                  Made great to die?

O Reputation ! canst thou not
Our joy and strength revivify ?
Or lagging long thou hadst forgot
                  Our lot to die.

Experience, trial, habitude
Tend much our lives to simplify ;
We have by use the world subdued—
                  Ourself to die.

Now apt in all our skill may test,
Or if we wits or fingers ply,
We strain our skill to manifest,—
              Brief, ere we die.

' Intricate,' ' difficult,' ' abstruse,'
Are terms which less and less apply ;
We have resolved them each by use,—
              With us to die !

Some fond idea, whereto we've wrought
Through weary years with many a sigh,
Is now to full fruition brought—
              What time we die.

Lost opportunity we grieve,
Late noting what hath passed by ;
May we not now the lost retrieve ?
              No, for we die.

Acts have we done when lacking light
Resulting much to mortify ;
Henceforward shall we know the *right.'*
              But know—to die.

In varied forms what first appears
We scan, compare, and rectify ;
Then taste the beautiful endears,—
              Most dear, to die.

Loved knowledge ! ours by sweat of brain,
It seemeth thou art ours for aye ;
Poor tree ! will then thy fruit be gain
              Though *thou* shalt die ?

Pile truth on truth from age to age,
Let knowledge mount from high to high;
Ah, then we might indeed be sage!
                              Except we die.

Alas! to each alone has worth
Experience which life must buy—
Small part whereof we leave on earth
                              When ours to die.

Wisdom may come, not lightly given,
And hard to gain, elusive, shy,
Is won by those who well have striven,—
                              In time to die.

Philosophy hath vistas fair
Wherethrough new wonders we espy;
To him their sequence is despair
                              Who sees—to die.

O Fount of language springing new,
Whence comes thine affluent supply?
Is then thy source exhausted too
                              When men do die?

Why, why O Tongue, thy wealth of words
The viewless Soul to signify?
Is thine the mission of the birds,
                              To sing, and die?

Memory, the long, instructive past
Hath made thee Reason's best ally,
And now a treasury rich and vast!
                              Shall memory die?

Ye trackless subtleties of thought
Aflight beyond our world to pry, —
Your striving shall not be for nought !
          Though men do die.

From whence ye came thereto ye flow,—
The Me divest' of mortal tie,
The very Self we best shall know—
          What time we die.

Oh highest Thought ! Oh impulse true !
Earth's highest seeking to imply ;
Our Father God—and life anew—
          What time we die.

Our Father God ! enough to think,—
Enough all thought to satisfy
And mortal with immortal link—
          What time we die.

Our Father God, Whom not to know
Doth holiest reveries belie,
Whom fain to know from Earth we go
          Content to die !

O Thou most Wise, the single Good !
Thy Work may not Thy work decry ;
For all we owe Thee gratitude,
          Most when we die.

The Tercentenary.

STRATFORD-UPON-AVON,

23rd April 1864.

The Tercentenary.

A FESTAL SONG.

I.

FULL three centuries agone
Was our gentle Shakespeare born,
And we hail his natal morn.

Shall we then forbear to sing
What the centuries do bring?
Shall we thanklessly forget
An accumulated debt?
Rather let us all confess
Our unsummed indebtedness,
Let us turn from work to play
And in joy keep holiday:

For three centuries agone
Was our gentle Shakespeare born,
And we hail his natal morn.

Cometh Spring for hope and mirth,
In the Spring exulteth Earth,
Spring renews drear Winter's dearth.
Jocund Spring gave Shakespeare birth!

With his primal, purest ray
Phœbus beamed upon the day ;
Then in glory forth he came
Putting lesser lights to shame—
Like our Shakespeare by his fame.
Avon's banks are greenest green,
Avon smiles in silver sheen ;
Stratford town this day is glad,
Streets in boughs and banners clad ;
Hour of mortal waking brings
Sights and sounds of joyful things ;
　　All people drest
　　In gayest best,
　　The church-bells ring,
　　Lads and lasses sing,
　　The birds are carolling,—
　　Earth is blest !

For three centuries agone
Was our gentle Shakespeare born,
And we hail his natal morn.

II.

Now, mustered in the Civic Hall,
The pilgrims glad obey the call
Of FLOWER, Mayor of Stratford hight,
Stalwart, portly man of might,
FLOWER—of ample beard white :

Round him and CARLISLE they gather—
Mayor and President together ;

CARLISLE, him Green Erin's king,[1]
Poet-love doth hither bring,—
CARLISLE who himself doth sing;
Round him throng the devotees,
Marking Shakespeare's effigies;
Round him lovingly they press,
They whom Sympathy doth bless;
FLOWER lifts his stentor voice,
' All be welcome! all rejoice!
Lo! our revels are begun,
Let us forth to feast and fun.'

Shade of Shakespeare.

I am here, I am here
   In æther sphere,
   As æther clear;
I am near you,
See you, hear you;
Me you not espy,
But I am all eye;
Me you not hear,
But I am all ear;
And though you not hear
Through the way of the ear,
I am whispering to you,
Passing through you;
   Everywhere
   I am there!

---

[1] The Earl of Carlisle, then Lord Lieutenant of Ireland.

Now the soul of Stratford smiles,
Shakespeare now the hour beguiles ;
Ring out merrily, merrily chime
Bells which rang in Shakespeare's time :
Ring out merrily, jubilant ring
Bells which did to Shakespeare sing ;
Ring out bells, and ringing tell—
' Here the bones of Shakespeare dwell :'
Ding dong ding, dong dong ding dong,
So to Shakespeare was your song :
Decked with medal and rosette,
   Not unwillingly displayed,
Every man doth care forget,
   Every matron, every maid
   Walks in love with Shakespeare's shade :
To the foremost favoured spot
Where our Shakespeare was begot ;
Where, when Nature him had won,
She bestowed her darling son ;—
To the little chamber, blest
More than palace golden-drest ;
To the school-room, where he caught
More of knowledge than was taught ;
To the precinct let us hie
Where he dwelt, where he did die ;
To the Church, where prayer he said,
Where he now lies buriéd :
To bright Avon's grassy banks
Conscious of his boyish pranks ;
Tread the sward his foot hath prest,
Green as it his tread confest !

This silvery stream
On him did gleam,
In its cool wave
He oft did lave,
Its mirror-face
His form did trace,—
O river! we implore
His reflex us restore!
To the meadows' chequered shade,
Where he pondered, where he played;
List to Philomela, sprung
From the choir which to him sung;
Then unto the streets agen
Where he took his note of men.

IV.

Ho! to the banquet, in a tent
Raised for this high tournament;
Grandly circled, and arrayed
With the proverbs Shakespeare said,—
Through the roof the sunbeams streaming,
    Glancing, glancing here and there,
As their presence was beseeming,
    Gleaming, dancing through the air;
Ranged at tables gaily set,
Pilgrims nigh eight hundred met,—
Ladies fair and men of thought
In one love together brought;
Snall they not, in genial mind,
Bless the blesser of their kind?
Shall they not, in Shakespeare's vein,
Loving cups to Shakespeare drain?

CARLISLE, leader of the feast,
He, the festival's high priest,
Has the duty to proclaim
Homage unto Shakespeare's name.

For three centuries agone
Was our gentle Shakespeare born,
And we hail his natal morn.

As a Poet well may prate
Of a Poet much more great,
CARLISLE spake, and full of glee
Shout the merrie companie
' *Shakespeare's honoured memorie!* '
Yet a shout! and in the clang
' Avon's bard ' the minstrels sang.

Shade of Shakespeare.

I am near you,
    Near you,
See you, hear you ;
I have been at a feast,
Nor last nor least ;
I forget not,
    I regret not ;
Drink I not, and yet I drink
In a way you do not think ;
Eat I not, and yet I eat
What is better than your meat,
Taste your viands, sip your wine,
All you do this hour is mine ;
In your cup my spirit enters,
In each soul my spirit centres ;

All you drink and all you eat
With my sympathy complete.

FLOWER told of greeting sent
From the German Continent,
From far Moscow's Domes and Spires
Through the Telegraphic wires;
HOUGHTON for the poets spake,—
For his own and brothers' sake;
CRESWICK signalized the fame
Of his great forerunner's name;
Sound the trumpet! minstrels sing
'Hail the Thespian Poet-King!'
From the dais CARLISLE sped,
And the pilgrims followéd.

Cheered by Cynthia's smile they rambled,
At the Pyrotechny scrambled,
Saw how rocket and balloon
Minished quicker than the Moon!
Rambled yielding to the whim
'Here the same Moon shined on him,—
Soothes *his* spirit too, the light
Us doth tranquilize to-night?'

V.

'Tis the Sabbath, fair the day;
Now we shall with Shakespeare pray;
To the Church the votaries speed,
Space the Gothic-fane doth need;
TRENCH, the critic-bishop, rises,
Speaks a Sermon of surprises,

For he took their hearts along
Less with sermon than with song;
More than sermon them to tell
All our Shakespeare had done well,
And to picture what we owe,
In our joy or in our woe
Shed throughout our mortal span,
To the poet-friend of man;
Near those hallowed reliques standing,
Tone and attitude commanding,
Well the Preacher then doth preach
Much to charm and much to teach.

Shade of Shakespeare.

I am the air
Of this House of Prayer;
You have well said,
I am comforted;
I bless you,
Enfold you, caress you;
Sweet to me the praise
Touching my mortal days,
For my light now so bright
Blinks not my sight
To my earth-born darkness;
I am well bestead
To be so interpreted;
I left you my best,
You hold the bequest,
In your love I have rest.

Now to Avon's banks away
Where was Shakespeare's wont to stray ;
Or in smoothly gliding boat
Floating where our Bard would float ;
Fancying, as we gently row,
We with him a-fishing go ;
Or to verdant pathways yonder
Where on Sunday he would wander,
Pacing on with quiet feet,
Lost in contemplation sweet.

' *Swan of Avon.*'

Die I never, never I,
Whilst my Shakespeare doth not die ;
Die I never, never I,
For my Shakespeare will not die ;
Sing I ever, ever sing,
Whilst my Shakespeare's voice doth ring ;
Live I ever, dying live,
Whilst my Shakespeare's name doth live ;
Sing I ever, ceasing not
Till his singing be forgot.

VI.

Every day the sun doth shine,
Every day we garlands twine,
Garlands made with flowers of spring,
Flowers by Shakespeare taught to sing ;
Every day we yoke with fun,
Frisk and gambol in the sun ;
Burthen us no sorrow shall,
For 'tis Shakespeare's festival !

Ho ! to Shottery by the path
Shakespeare's foot oft trodden hath,
When he would a-courting go,
Stepping neither weak nor slow ;
See the house where she did dwell
Whom our Shakespeare loved so well,
See the house where she was born
Full three centuries agone ;
Then o'er pleasant uplands on
To the hill of Luddington ;
See the spot where, it is said,
Shakespeare did his first love wed ;—
(Aye with Shakespeare briskly walking,
Aye with Shakespeare inly talking,)
Over Avon where he went,
Following where his footsteps bent ;
Thorough meadows green and still,
By the river-side, until
We re-enter at the Mill,
Pass the Church where Shakespeare lies,
So indulge our sympathies.

Then to Charlecote, whence, they say,
Shakespeare helped the deer away ;
Scenes that Shakespeare saw, survey.

Now the great Pavilion throng,
Listen to our Shakespeare's song ;
Songs of sad or merry note
Chaunted by a lithesome throat ;

Songs to tell the inmost mind
And the complex thought unwind ;
Songs of very soul a part,
Songs, the music of *his* heart.

Shade of Shakespeare.

I am here in the throng,
  I know my song ;
Your singing list—
    Ye Zephyrs, whist !
      Sing, sing,
The time is spring,
    Sing, sing, ever sing,
    Sing as I sung,
    Old or young ;
Sing when you can,
    Boy or man,
That was my plan ;
    Sing, ever sing,
Mother or maid,
    Be not afraid.

VII.

  Every day the sun doth shine,
Every day we garlands twine,
Garlands made with flowers of spring,
Flowers by Shakespeare taught to sing ;
Gay green earth, and heaven fair,
Leaping fish, and bird in air,
Gay the hill-side, gay the glade—
Gay in light unknowing shade ;
Never opened days more bright,
Matched with splendours of the night.

Heart in hand the votaries meet,
Unrefrained they frankly greet,
Tread the earth with lightsome feet,
On the mead, along the street,
Note the sky, the birds, the flowers,
Cheerly court the frolic Hours;
Then at eve, more blithe than sage,
Gather them before the stage,
On their Poet's visions dote,
Realize what Shakespeare wrote,
See his Juliet, Viola,
Rosalind, Olivia,
See the pictures of *his* brain,
See *him* half on Earth again.

Shade of Shakespeare.

I am here, I am here,
   In æther sphere,
   As æther clear;
I am near you,
See you, hear you;
   These were my loves,—
   I have left you my loves,
   For ever my loves;
Seek, you will find them,—
Lovingly bind them;
   Earth's gifts and graces,
      Sweet faces,
   And pleasant places,

Delights more high
    That search the sky,—
Though they pass away
        Be not vext,
Give Fancy sway!
    They are types of the next ;
I have left you my joy,
    Look above and around,
    There is more to be found,
Time doth not destroy ;
I have left you my care,
Oh ! of it beware ;
I looked high and guessed,
So do you your best ;
Old loves are yet mine
In the region divine ;
Æschylus, Euripides,
Homer strong, and Sophocles,
Plautus, Aristophanes ;
Best of the chosen few,
I dear old Plutarch knew,
    And my debt to him confest ;
Nor sought in vain
Cervantes, Rabelais, Montaigne,
Dante, Tasso, and Petrarch,
Lope de Vega, Camoens,
Spenser, and my rare Ben Jon,
    Mad Kit Marlowe, and the rest :
Strive, that when from mortals free
With the greatest you may be.

VIII.

Lo, the longest day hath end,
Every friend must part from friend,—
Though high up the Sun doth shine,
We prepare for his decline :
Devotees at Shakespeare's shrine
Knit in sympathy divine,—
'Tis the tyranny of Fate
To dissolve and separate,
But, before we part, we shall
Hold a gleesome Festival
Clad as Shakespeare's folk were clad,
And, the while a little mad,
Fancy mid the mazy dance
Shakespeare's comely countenance :
Make the Ball-room blaze sublime
With symbols of the olden time ;
Deck the walls with emblems round,
As where Shakespeare should be found ;
Don slashed doublet, ruff and hose,
Camisole with lace and bows,
And a hat our Shakespeare knows ;
Lasses, well your tresses trim,
Lace the silken bodice slim,
Look as you'd be loved by him !
Let the minstrels not forget
Jig, cotillion, minuet ;
In the time of good Queen Bess
Men were merry none the less ;
Let the hour of parting be
In Shakespearian jollitie ;
So, in after-time we'll say—
We did re-create his day !

Shade of Shakespeare.

It is well done,
I relish your fun ;
Your crew I'm among,
Your hands by me wrung ;—
To me Time is past,
The first is as last ;
But I love you, I love you,
O sisters and brothers,
I love you all well,
As I have lovéd others ;
I care for your sorrow, I join in your laughter,
I ken my kith now, and my kin who come after :
A century passes and you pass away,
But I'll be here then as I am at this day.

Esto Perpetuum.

Esto Perpetuum.

METRED PICTURES.

If happiness is perfect joy
And Heaven is true felicitie,
A happy moment Heaven could be—
          Evermore.

The little maid's first birthday-feast,
Her little head with chaplet crowned,
Her little first-loves all around :—
          For ever !

The younker with his younker friend
A ramble goeth far away,
Throughout a sweltering summer day :—
          For ever !

The schoolboy at the 'breaking-up,'
Passed the ordeal, speeches said,
Two prizes gained, the classes sped :
          For ever !

The game is cricket, and the scores
Are even—but another run-
The ball is hit and we have won :
          For ever !

I've heard of fishing, find the pool;
My heart is burning with one wish,
And now I grasp a glittering fish : --
    For ever!

The girl almost to woman grown,
Whose beauty might elect her queen,
Hath ne'er till *now* her beauty seen :-
    For ever !

The stripling, first his nature conning,
In day-dream dares the world to scan,
Thinks what it is to be a man!—
    For ever !

The demoiselle, of homage tired,
Learns, though she knows not how or when,
She has impressed the man of men :—
    For ever !

Stept out of Academus' shade
The man beholds his future clear,
And bravely forecasts a career :—
    For ever !

A day, its like not born before,
The earth in smiles, the sky in shine,
This world so beautiful—is mine :—
    For ever !

The world is mine, this world of men,
Do they not love me, every one?
Have loved me since my life begun :—
    For ever !

Dear Alma-Mater, hard thy task ;
But now—the best condones the worst—
A wrangler and a double-first :—·
For ever !

The years have flown, the fight is fought,
The care and doubt are less and less,
Yea, from this hour it is success :—
For ever !

To one I love I tell not love,—
Perchance I talk with her awhile
And win a smile beyond a smile :—
For ever !

My love is with me, and I prove
There is no doubting in her love ;
How more than this the gods above ?—
For ever !

Mid meadows green and Summer's sheen
I track the winding of the brook,
And now and then a trout I hook :—
For ever !

A-wearied in the summer heat
I stand upon the River's brim ;
A 'header' and a mighty swim :—
For ever !

Who cometh nigh? what lovely face,
What form of grace, what eyes divine !
She passeth, but one look is *mine* :—
For ever !

Ecstatic vision, thou art gone ;
Gone ! as the meteor glideth by
Its splendour leaving in the eye :—
       For ever !

My nag is fleet, the sward is soft,
I turn my back on men and towns
And madly scamper o'er the downs :—
       For ever !

The wind is south, well soaked the soil.
The sky is grey—hark, hark ! the horn :
For sure, good hap, a hunter's morn :—
       For ever !

The hound gives tongue, Fox breaks away,
Away ! o'er mead, or hedge, or stream ;
I claim the 'brush,' in pride supreme :
       For ever !

I've wooed in vain, and woo again,
This notelet comes to ban or bless ;
I break the seal, the word is 'yes :'—
       For ever !

We meet and kiss, and talk, and walk
In winding path and coppice green,
By all but each by each unseen :—
       For ever !

The time is May, the Earth is new,
And warm and bright and blossoming,
The soft air stirs, the birdies sing :—
       For ever !

How like to life the tale is told!
So true, a fiction it is not
To me who have all else forgot :—
> For ever !

Or, with our Laureate we rejoice,
Till with his Fancy so at one
We e'en forget 'tis Tennyson :—
> For ever !

A friend, front *coupé*, train 'express,'
A Novel, or the World's Gazette,
A gossip and a cigarette :—
> For ever !

White, graceful hands now strike the chords,
A lithesome throat doth deftly sing,
Whilst I, the loved, am listening :—
> For ever !

'Tis calm and warm the summer night,
And clear the moon, when on the lawn
We linger, linger till the dawn :—
> For ever !

Or on a sultry day of June
Beneath the canopy remain
For music of the thunder-rain :—
> For ever !

Some work is done, some part achieved,
No more to-day but talk and joke,
Serenely rest, serenely smoke :—
> For ever !

O hand unfaithful! in my mind
The very touch is clearly wrought;
There, there it is! I *see* my thought:—
                    For ever!

In intellectual being blent,
With chosen friend I calm converse,
Or here and there a line rehearse:—
                    For ever!

The middle row, a central stall,
The zest of youth, the rest of age,
As Hamlet, Fechter on the stage:—
                    For ever!

The lake is smooth, the mountains shine,
My skiff I steer amid the isles
Whilst to my glance my sweetheart smiles:—
                    For ever!

A truce to toil, a truce to care;
Shipped are we not for sunny France?
Be ours to laugh and sing and dance:—
                    For ever!

The music inchoate in my soul
Hath by the lute been made a voice!
Supremely doth my soul rejoice:—
                    For ever!

To think mankind henceforth shall hear
From out the sweet supernal store
A cadence never heard before:—
                    For ever!

Now Costa leads, the viol sings,
And each ingenious source of sound
In perfect synthesis is found :—
>> For ever !

Her eyes are lustrous, large and full,
Their icy beauty men admire ;
For *me* they now are flashing fire :—
>> For ever !

The Mother first her child caresses,
Whereat the thought her life-blood stirs
Henceforth on earth two lives are hers : -
>> For ever !

Now done it is—a noble deed ;
Prolonged the toil, mid doubt and blame,
But men shall much repeat my name :—
>> For ever !

The sweet forgetfulness of ease,
Assured all things are good and true—
And nothing in this world to do :—
>> For ever !

The game is Whist, the players are four,
Old friends well-loved, of kith and kin :
All savage in desire to win :—
>> For ever !

Where chamois haunts and glacier gleams,
Stupendous Alp amid I pause,
More high than Alp to think the Cause :-
>> For ever !

A truth I ween words cannot prove :
Come arc and angle, point and line ;
O perfect Reason ! it is thine :—
> For ever !

Through me, by geometric art
A thing invisible is shown,
A vital consequence beknown :—
> For ever !

Humane philosopher, distressed
At ills unthinking men endure,
Propounded hast thou cause and cure :—
> For ever !

Thou, with severe, inductive search
The Earth's Arcana hast unsealed,
The hidden mystery revealed :—
> For ever !

Indulge the beatific thought
How through the ages yet to be
The world shall own a debt to thee :—
> For ever !

Consummate mechanician, thou
Hast well the combination sought,
Taught iron to perform thy thought :—
> For ever !

Thou know'st that by thy shrewd device
Some hurtful toil in filth and pain
Will ne'er be done by *hands* again :—
> For ever !

The analyst a solvent needeth,
Nor from his craving knoweth rest ;
'"Tis mine, 'tis mine ! the single test :'—
                    For ever !

Rapt poet ! vext by subtle view,
With urgent throes thy thought hath birth,—
A new creation on the earth :—
                    For ever !

Astronomer, despair not yet,
The star *is* there, compute again ;
He searches, searching not in vain :—
                    For ever !

The long-continued effort closes ;
My Book is nearing to the end,
The final word one day is penned :—
                    For ever !

At ease reclined, in waking dream,
For overwork by rest atoning,
No neighbour but the wind amoaning :—
                    For ever !

The air is fresh, the day is young,
This day I act my long desire ;
Who tells of toil, who talks of tire ?—
                    For ever !

Of feeble breath, in fading hope,
The weary weeks have crawled along ;
' Hail ! blest Hygeia,—I am strong :'—
                    For ever !

Fatigue and peril press too long,
The fruits of toil with us will die ;
Ho! to the rescue! hear, they cry :
        For ever !

O'erpast the danger and the dread
Once more I breathe unbated breath ;
' Hurrah ! no more I dance with Death : ' —
        For ever !

I loved onetime, the love did die ;
Since then I've striven the sordid strife :
Anew I love, am loved—new life :
        For ever !

On foreign land, perchance in Spain,
I ride and rove amid the wild.
In freedom freshen as a child :—
        For ever !

This pain doth stultify my mind,
Will in its rage the Mind destroy ;
'Tis dead the pain ! new-born is joy : —
        For ever !

Oh, anguish ! and oh, deeper grief ;
Why life and health mid cloud and care ?
Outshines the sun, my sky is fair :
        For ever !

Cathedral dome beneath, I list,
The Anthem riseth to the skies,
The mortal ' *in excelsis* ' dies :—
        For ever !

Far, far from land, the ship rides well :
I view the restless, shoreless sea
At one with its infinitie :—
                    For ever !

How still the night ! the stars are bright,
They see me with their myriad eyes;
My Soul unto their gaze replies :—
                    For ever !

The world forgot, perception clear
From mazes free of doubt and strife,
I live a new, unbounded life :—
                    For ever !

The past into the future passes,
And all experience I see
Determine in an endless Me :—
                    For ever !

Dissolved in prayer, in longing lost,
I know no speech of thought or word,
Entranced I know my prayer is heard :—
                    For ever !

A joy there is above all joy,
A thought beyond all thinking dear,
The thought to be where God is near
                    Evermore !

A Canticle.

240

A Canticle.

Unto God the all-pervading, Whence we came, in Whom
    we live,—
    Men for aye your voices raise
    Unto God, in songs of praise!
Unto God Whose gifts are boundless, let us give all man
    can give.

Of unconscious earth made conscious, conscious earth of
    God aware;—
    Men for aye your voices raise
    Unto God, in songs of praise!
Knowing God, shall man unknow Him for a moment out
    of prayer?

Sole indued with admiration, sole conceptive of applause,—
    Men for aye your voices raise
    Unto God, in songs of praise!
Sole on Earth enraptured gazing, more enraptured of the
    Cause.

Witness diverse shell refulgent, glistening crystal, ore, and
    gem,—
    Men for aye your voices raise
    Unto God, in songs of praise!
Witness egg of bird or insect, or the germen in the stem.

Witness living things quiescent, varied flower, and herb,
    and tree,—
    Men for aye your voices raise
    Unto God, in songs of praise!
Witness zoophytes perceptive though they neither hear
    nor see.

Witness ye ephemera lasting the duration of a breath,—
    Men for aye your voices raise
    Unto God, in songs of praise!
Witness parasite and fungus springing beautiful from
    death.

Witness animated creatures, of the water, land, or air,—
    Men for aye your voices raise
    Unto God, in songs of praise!
Witness complex works whose working silently their God
    declare.

Witness myriad modes of instinct new in beings number-
    less,—
    Men for aye your voices raise
    Unto God, in songs of praise!
Witness each existence ordered a superior life to bless.

Witness well, ye orbs of glory! balanced by a mighty
    spell,—
    Men for aye your voices raise
    Unto God, in songs of praise!
Witness meteors and comets, forces which their course
    compel.

Witness agencies of Nature—they which winds and seas
  control,—
 Men for aye your voices raise
 Unto God, in songs of praise !
Witness mysteries electric, and the needle to the pole.

Witness verities of Science lighting to the vast unfound,—
 Men for aye your voices raise
 Unto God, in songs of praise !
Witness philosophic visions unexpressed by verbal sound.

Witness godlike power of Reason scanning the sublunar
  scene,—
 Men for aye your voices raise
 Unto God, in songs of praise !
Witness higher reason rising to the search of things unseen.

Witness habitudes unreasoned tending always to the
  best,—
 Men for aye your voices raise
 Unto God, in songs of praise !
Witness human heart confessing more than reason has
  confest.

Witness Fancy daring farther than the farthest planets
  roll,—
 Men for aye your voices raise
 Unto God, in songs of praise !
Witness inspiration prompted by the whispers of the
  soul.

Witness awful voice of Conscience—voice at war with
    mortal sin,—
  Men for aye your voices raise
  Unto God, in songs of praise!
Witness God in man residing—making man with Angels
    kin.

Witness Mind of Man revolving of the future and the
    past,—
  Men for aye your voices raise
  Unto God, in songs of praise!
Witness Man the God-perceiving, seeking to the first and
    last.

Witness Providence prevailing omnipresent though un-
    sought,—
  Men for aye your voices raise
  Unto God, in songs of praise!
Witness God's unmeasured goodness — mercy passing
    human thought!

Meditation.

()

Eikonoklastes.

A REQUIEM.

ONE by one our gods are broken,
  One by one they fade and fall,
And as auguries betoken
  Time will overthrow them all.

Fallacies of inculcation,
.   Or of ignorance the brood,
Or of fatuous imitation,
  Or the spawn of reason crude :

        One by one our gods are broken, etc.

In the dream of life's fresh morning
  Did the years unheeded fly,
Till, surprised, I met the warning
  Once my turn must come —to die :

        One by one our gods are broken, etc.

Fancies born of misconceiving,
  As abortions turn to nought ;
Tenets held in firm believing
  Perish at the test of thought :

        One by one our gods are broken, etc.

Or the rainbow's transient glories,
  Or the Guardian Angel's care,
Or the flittings of the fairies, —
  Vanish as the mist in air :

> *One by one our gods are broken, etc.*

Zeus enthroned in orient splendour,
  Moon and stars were made for *me*,
Till I knew they must surrender
  To *their* laws, or cease to be :

> *One by one our gods are broken, etc.*

Loved pursuits, in love increasing,
  Always with a keener zest,
Fondly held to be unceasing, —
  Death-struck, lose their interest :

> *One by one our gods are broken, etc.*

At the birth of admiration
  Things or theses were adored, —
On acuter observation
  Into limbo are restored :

> *One by one our gods are broken, etc.*

Thus, to art I paid devotion, —
  Objects perfect to *my* sight
At the critic's cultured motion
  Changed, as withered by a blight :

> *One by one our gods are broken, etc.*

I had made a god of friendship-—
    Friendship to life-long endure,
Till experience cooled the worship,
    Found ingratitude the cure :

        One by one our gods are broken, etc.

On a day love's flame was lighted,
    Furthermore her love was proved,
And I thought—her love is plighted,—
    Loving ever as I loved !

        One by one our gods are broken, etc.

Rhapsodies of perfect virtue,
    Perfect truth and honour fair,—
Till the deity was shivered
    Into fragments of despair :

        One by one our gods are broken, etc.

I had made a god of error—
    Taught by some who claimed to *know*,
Judged the god an empty terror,
    It demolished at a blow :

        One by one our gods are broken, etc.

As a god is firm opinion,
    Fixed, immutable as law,
Some day ceases its dominion—
    Banished, as not worth a straw !

        One by one our gods are broken, etc.

In my prime the Star ambition
   Glowed with emulation's flame,
Guiding to, perchance, perdition,
   Or to vantage—in a name !

        One by one our gods are broken, etc.

Surmise of regard omniscient—
   Providence o'er chance to rule,
Fathomed by percipience prescient
   Is as gewgaw to the fool :

        One by one our gods are broken, etc.

Faith in dogmas of the elders
   Burns with zeal's illusive light,
Wanes and flickers in the embers —
   Dies, as day is merged in night :

        One by one our gods are broken, etc.

Only in the realms of Nature,
   Or of Genius, Nature's child,
Shall I keep the gods unbroken
   Till with Nature reconciled.

Alpha—Omega.

THE urchin, elated at feeling his feet in the dame-school,
Ingrate looks back, with the firstling of scorn, to the
    Nursery—
' Its trumpery toys ! its infantine triflings !'—
The germ of the sad thought,—our Earth-life is
    nothingness :

Next the manikin schoolboy struts in defiant pretension,
Ignores, with half-shame, the fore-enjoyed games of the
    dame-school—
' Those childish pranks ! those paltry simplicities !'—
Begetting the sad thought,—our Earth-life is nothingness :

Then the brave adolescent, unconscious as yet of
    ambition
Disdains the athletic amusements — a year gone his
    life-joy ;—
' Mere sports ! unproductive of glory or lucre,'—
Begetting the sad thought,—our Earth-life is nothingness :

He is man now—and, in his strength, goes forth to his
    purpose,
Essays, and achieves, and with rapture possesses the
    guerdon,—
Contemning the prize so yearned for and fought for,—
Begetting the sad thought,—our Earth-life is nothingness :

He has loved—a true love, a frenzy which knew no
     confining;
This the sum of all hope,—to have won the true-love of
     his mistress,—
Won also the insight of loving more wisely !—
Begetting the sad thought,—our Earth-life is nothingness :

Oh, for learning ! he ponders full-puffed with the pride of
     the pedant,
To-day's blush but faintly atoning for yesterday's
     rashness,—
' Time lost ! in acquiring some fruitlings of error,'—
Begetting the sad thought,—our Earth-life is nothingness :

And now hath he learnt, and his knowledge has mounted
     to wisdom ;
O Wisdom miscalled, if thou too must soon be
     exceeded,—
The Mind's superessence attainted as folly !
Begetting the sad thought,—our Earth-life is nothingness :

Again, and again, and again for the goal looming furthest,
Again, and again, to acknowledge the foregone is
     worthless,
Again to the stretch, for the loftier and nobler,—
Begetting the sad thought, —our Earth-life is nothingness :

Then a STAR rose to him,—and he saw with a far-sighted
     vision ;
He said,—' In the Hereafter is transcendency final,
This world as a dream awaked from and over,—
I shall see thence, exalted,— how Earth - life is—
     Nothingness.'

Vapores.

GLIMMER of the light of Heaven,
Inklings of the life of angels,
Voices reaching me though heard not,—
            Forgotten !

Grateful sentiments engendered,
Priceless favours unrequited,
Native impulses to virtue,—
            Forgotten !

Thoughts of fire—they flashed and faded,
Clear, infallible deductions,—
[Fitful visitings of genius,]
            Forgotten !

High resolve and passionate purpose,
Schemes which unto Fame were tending,—
Haply marred by false ambition?
            Forgotten !

Loves which grew without incitement,
Loves of flame the whitest glowing,
Loves of sympathy sincerest,—
            Forgotten !

Loves of places, things, and persons,
Loves made loves in love unconscious,
Real loves, though unresponsive,—
            Forgotten !

Friendships genial, spontaneous,
Softer friendships more than friendships,
Friendships true though uncontinued,--
              Forgotten !

Ah ! the years of seeing, hearing,
Thinking, reading,—storing knowledge
Gladly found and fondly treasured,—
              Forgotten !

Incidents of signal import,
Strange events of poignant pathos,
Synchronisms to strike with wonder,—
              Forgotten !

Gifts of God ! outreaching reason,
Gifts exceeding mundane value,
Gifts we knew not how to ask for,—
              Forgotten !

Gifts no less by self-denial,
Gifts of guidance forth from danger—-
Gracious gifts, of blest prevention,—-
              Forgotten !

Dire unreason and delusion,
Errors having worked for evil,—
Keen chagrins—abortive offspring ;
              Forgotten !

Much is gone, but more remaineth,—
Their residuum who shall reckon?
Are the numberless conceptions
Lost in Mind's mysterious storehouse—
              Erasèd ?

Fuerunt.

O FRESHNESS and newness of all in this earth-world,
O simple contentment, acceptance undoubting,
O future unending, and sweet without bitter,—
No more !

The world was for *me* in its beauty and grandeur,
The beings I loved were for *me*—a charmed circle,
All places and things had endurance eternal,—
No more !

O dreams of perfection, in waking or sleeping,
O pure admiration unknowing abridgment,   .
Perfection of hope in a hope seeming perfect,—
No more !

O faith dwelling in me, a faith yet unshaken,
A faith in all promise, a faith in pretension,
A faith in the rightness of all things existent,
No more !

Sweet Truth ! with no stain on her heaven-born whiteness,
Sweet Trust ! resting calm as the sleep of the babies,
Devotion unstinted, and boundless as æther,—
No more !

O warmth of the heart which has never known chilling,
O impulse forth-springing, the cost never counting,
Emotion outwelling—a river of gladness,—
No more !

O joy of the thoughts I believed to be primal,
O joy of invention by no man preceded,
O joy of observing what none had erst noted,—
No more !

Wild wonder—delight to me daily and nightly,
Holy awe—unobservant of cause or conclusion,
A dread, with no fearing, in glimpses supernal,--
No more !

O zeal, as the flame unto heaven ascending,
Desire for all goodness—expedience unknowing,
O sentiment glowing untold and unmeted,—
No more !

The zest of the spirit, the zest of the senses,
Each sight or vibration a new-born enchantment,
Enjoyment upsprung from the fountains of Nature,—
No more !

O charm of the vision, and charm of the hearing,
O pride of the soul quick in mental perception,
O marvel of life in a life full of marvels,—
No more !

O dreams beyond Earth in the region of Fancy,
O fancy ecstatic to soar as the angels,
O life more than life, in a state beatific,—
No more !

Ye error, delusion, or bootless expectancy,
Thou base discontent, eldest born of unreason,
Thou fatuous conceit of a self proved so feeble :—
No more !

Imago Mortis.

In my youth I went a-roving,
Roving on beyond the oceans,
Men and things I saw, rejoicing,
Many marvels,—unforgotten !
                        Dead to *me*.

What a man was he ! I dwelt with
In a city of Achaia :
Great in virtue as in knowledge,
Well I love him—for he liveth ;—
                        Dead to *me*.

Oh ! the learnèd disputations,
Oh ! the subtleties expounded,
Fondly think I he is speaking
Ever with enlarging wisdom ;—
                        Dead to *me*.

Wondrous scene ! amid the Andes,
Mountain over mountain towering,
With the terror of volcanoes—
Fire, and frost, and sky commingled ;—
                        Dead to *me*.

Fertile plains, and shining rivers
Flowing on in sacred silence,
Flowers and birds of gorgeous colours,
Regions of primeval nature :—
                        Dead to *me*.

Pleasant cities! where I rested
Till their novelty grew home-like,—
Mosque, and Temple, and Cathedral,—
They have been and are for ages;
    Dead to *me*.

And the people of those cities
For a while my social circle,
Or philosophers, or poets,
Graceful ladies all-accomplished;—
    Dead to *me*.

Ah! the one of my election,
Moving with a queenly grandeur,
Smiling with a smile that blesseth:
And she still is smiling, blessing;—
    Dead to *me*.

So, it seemeth, will the earth-gods
On and on, in turn, be dying,
Whilst I live in thoughts unceasing,
And increasing, till they all are
    Dead to *me*.

Arcus Cœlestis.

Though thou art on the ground
With things of baseness found,
Be not to baseness bound,—
           Look up.

The lowly may be high,
And loftiest be nigh,
Canst thou not see the sky?—
           Look up.

Hast thou some work to do
And canst, with false or true,
Or low, or high, endue,—
           Look up.

Hast thou thy place to take,
And wouldst some merit make
For self and others' sake,—
           Look up.

If, as a latent fire
Prevails some strong desire,
And well thou dost aspire,—
           Look up.

If much with grief perplext
Mid complications vext
Thou doubtest of the next,—
           Look up.

If, having open choice
Thou hearest honour's voice,
And after, wouldst rejoice,—
> Look up.

In disappointment crost
Thou hast essayed and lost,
And tremblest at the cost?—
> Look up.

Exists the world in joy
Undimmed by Care's alloy?
Lest thou the charm destroy,—
> Look up.

All dark the world appears,
Depressed art thou with fears,
And fails thy heart to tears?—
> Look up.

They say fair Truth's a flam,
Honour a mere whim-wham,
And Honesty a sham?—
> Look up.

Art thou both mean and grand,
Thy life seems darkly planned
And hard to understand?—
> Look up.

Thanatos.

What is this which cometh o'er me,
Makes me so suspend my breath
And begin to think of death?—
       'Tis the shadow of the tomb.

Why so caring and comparing?
Why doth thought through memory ranging
Moralize—the world is changing?—
       'Tis the shadow of the tomb.

Chosen friends! I think—where are ye?
Whither doth such thinking tend?
Thou thyself shalt have an end;—
       'Tis the shadow of the tomb.

So do all things have an ending,—
Folly! thus thy heart annoying
With things made for thy enjoying;—
       'Tis the shadow of the tomb.

Knowledge I have loved thee dearly;
How this heresy of thought,—
Knowledge tendeth unto nought?—
       'Tis the shadow of the tomb.

No! it tendeth unto wisdom;
Yet, when faculties are failing
Wisdom will be unavailing!—
       'Tis the shadow of the tomb.

R

Or, if Wisdom cometh truly,
She shall teach thee for thy earning
All the littleness of learning!—
  'Tis the shadow of the tomb.

Ay, but Fame shall be my guerdon;
Fame, I think, not far extendeth,
And like other things it endeth!—
  'Tis the shadow of the tomb.

From me time is fleeting, fleeting,
[Once my slave, become my master,]
Like a torrent, faster, faster!—
  'Tis the shadow of the tomb.

Is it well when I, so earnest,
Sicken at the worldly strife,
Feel the nothingness of life?—
  'Tis the shadow of the tomb.

Sweet contentment, wert thou darkness?
Have I hallowed wrong for right?
Why perturbeth me the light?—
  'Tis the shadow of the tomb.

More to Heaven I bend my vision, -
More and more in God confiding,
More and more in God residing,
  Past the shadow of the tomb.

Golden Moments.

Of itself the soul is conscious,
Knoweth it exists sublime
Out of space and out of time :

Love begot is unconfinéd
By the Earth or Arc above,—
All the world shut out by love :

Each on each, abstracted, leaning,
Eye to eye, and cheek to cheek—
Musing more than tongue can speak :

Friend, my friend, O friend eternal !
Sympathy hath whole control-
When we see each other's soul :

Gaily we converse together,
Strive wherever words can reach,
Share oblivion in speech :

With a waking dream I dally,
Thinking out and writing thought,
Coining treasure out of nought :

Thought abstruse by others written
Weans me from the mortal strife,
Charms me in a charméd life :

Words of praise alone are sounding,
Words of praise the trump of Fame;
Have I made myself a name?

Heart-still in a holy silence,
Lost in awe exceeding fear,
Doubting not of God anear.

Ignis Fatuus.

WAIT, oh wait! for life is new,
Time will bring thy heart's desire,
Thy young hopes shall tell thee true,—
            If thou aspire.

Wait, oh wait! though sped the boy,
Let not care precede the day,
Thy long future hath of joy
            For all you pray.

Wait, oh wait! though manhood's prime
Hath not satisfied thy will,
Be not out of heart with time,
            It cometh still.

Wait, oh wait! if love to thee
Hath till now been bitterness,
She is coming, fair and free,
            Thy life to bless.

Wait, oh wait! the world as yet
Heedeth not thy voice or pen?
Wiser growing, thou wilt get
            The praise of men.

Wait, oh wait! though knavish fools
Take the prizes rightly thine,
Providence o'er Fortune rules—
            Then why repine?

Wait, oh wait ! if thou hast past
The climacteric of thy years,
Highest honour comes at last,—
   Suppress thy tears.

Wait, oh wait ! if strength decays
And thy future seemeth brief,
Note thou those who wear the bays
   Have greater grief.

Wait, oh wait ! if hope no more
Trick thee with delusions fond,
Are thy merits not a store
   In life beyond ?

The Skylark Caged.

WHAT wouldst thou tell, winged voice so singing—
    Imprisoned there?
Prisoned! a lot to man, whenever, bringing
    Untold despair:

Is it then joy forth from thy narrow cage
    Escapes in song,
Or but the passion of poetic rage
    To vent thy wrong?

Or hear we some vibrations from the spheres
    Expressed by thee?
Less sadly telling than with sighs and tears
    Thine agonie;

Or dost thou cry unto some far-off mate
    Hid in the skies,
The empyrean searching for her fate
    Until she dies?

Caged—doth the burthened Soul, like thee rejoicing
    On music's wing—
Mount, the loud beatings of the heart outvoicing
    As thou dost sing:

Caged—doth the laden Soul, like thee upsoaring,
      Seek heaven for balm,
Till, from its thrall released and its deploring,
      It rests in calm :

O Soul of man ! regard the pent-bird's rapture—
      In sorrow gay,
If dark-stoled Melancholic would thee capture,
      Sing her away !

Leniter Ridens.

When we sit with folk about us
Wisting not of those without us,
Recking not of such as flout us,-
    Then we smile.

When away from our belongings,
And alone, in nights or mornings
We survey our rightings—wrongings, —
    Then we smile.

When of those who should believe us
Some we love by coldness grieve us,
Some we love not misconceive us,—
    Then we smile.

When some vaunt them holier, better, —
Virtue proving to the letter,
By their thoughts our thought to fetter,—
    Then we smile.

When some pique them richer, grander,
And to wealth would have us pander,
Or denounce the truth as slander,—
    Then we smile.

When one claiming to be wiser
Of his knowledge is a miser,
Yet would be our proud adviser, —
    Then we smile.

When with chosen friends conversing,
Our plerophories rehearsing—
Studious gatherings dispersing,--
  Then we smile.

When, ingratitudes forgetting,
We have cease of useless fretting,
Thinking but—our Sun is setting,—
  Then we smile.

When at last to Nature bending,
On the law divine depending,
We reflect upon the ending,—-
  Then we smile.

The Sun=Dial.

('*Horas non numero nisi serenas.*')

ONLY the sunny hours !
    The home of gloom
  Is in Oblivion's tomb :

Only the sunny hours !
    Hold—for they haste ;
  Let care as shadows waste :

Only the sunny hours !
    The clouds between—
  As if they had not been :

Only the sunny hours !
    Truth can but shine,
  Error to shade incline :

Only the sunny hours !
    Honour is clear,
  And baseness shrouds in fear :

Only the sunny hours !
    Count gain—not loss,
  The ore, and not the dross :

Only the sunny hours !
    If love hath flown,
  Rejoice how once it shone :

THE SUN-DIAL.

Only the sunny hours!
    Thy friend decays?
  Think of the joyous days:

Only the sunny hours!
    Some hopes have failed?
  Cherish what hath prevailed:

Only the sunny hours!
    Dark—is distress,
  And light is happiness:

Only the sunny hours!
    Our Life is Light,
  Our Death is as the Night:

Only the sunny hours!
    So—when 'tis done,
  Mark, with the Dial's powers
  As do the fruits or flowers,
    The record of the Sun.

Emotion.

Carmen Amoris.

My Love's a miracle ; to *me* alone
  Her beauty liveth,
Whilst from her eyne alone to mine
  Love light out-giveth :

Men else her mortal countenance may scan,
  And find it fair,
But oh ! they see not as I see—
  The *lustre* there :

She comes—when as by th' enchanter's spell,
  Earth disappears,
And I am living out of Time
  Amid the spheres :

She looks—and I beholding am abashed
  Her soul to see ;
For when she looks—her form and face
  My vision flee :

She speaks—and I suppose some other ears
  Hear woman's voice,
The while for *me* soft tones of heaven
  My heart rejoice :

She moves—and from her course obstructions fade,
    For lo, it seemeth
In passing she doth glide or float
    As one who dreameth,—

But that her motion harmonies attend,
    Supernal, sweet,
And cadences, in pauses true,
    Fall with her feet :

She smiles—and instant flashes forth the Sun—
    All round so bright,
Distraught I fain would turn away,
    As dazed with light :

She laughs—when with ethereal echoings
    The sky resoundeth,
And in the glee, from height to height
    My spirit boundeth :

She sings—all other earthly sounds are hushed,—
    The Angels list,
And I am with them flying, flying,
    On wings of mist :

My Love is gone—how blank and dark it is,
    And hope how vain !
Except, on any day my Love
    Shall come again.

Sybil.

HER face uplifted, and she looked—
    The mirrors *spake*,
    Not—not to *me;*
But, to see her eyne so grand and bright,
Enough—enough for my delight,
I blessed her for another's sake,
    As the slave blesseth the free :

Her face uplifted, and she smiled—
    Her soul a smile !
    Not—not for *me;*
Yet, to see her face so heavenly bright,
Enough—enough for my delight,
I blessed her who could so beguile,
    As the slave blesseth the free :

Her face uplifted, and she blushed—
    The heart a blush !
    Not—not for *me;*
Yet, to see such sight of pink and white,
Enough—enough for my delight,
I blessed the face one else could flush,
    As the slave blesseth the free.

Primevères.

Ah, I bethink me, dear, longing still on and on,
Numberless wonderments are there to see ;
And I'm rejoicing me now in foreshadowing
Bliss in beholding them
                    Lucy, with thee.

Spring will be coming soon, trees will be budding forth,
Flowers will be blossoming over the lea,
Birds will be carolling,—and I'll be happy then
Looking and listening
                    Lucy, with thee.

Are there not rivers, lake-mirrors mid mountains high,
Countries and cities beyond the broad sea?
Are they not waiting, and glowing, and flowing on,
Until I visit them
                    Lucy, with thee ?

Endless the marvels of nature and skilfulness
Spread o'er the world we shall rove when we're free ;
Blest are they all to me, smiling or terrible,
Thinking to witness them
                    Lucy, with thee

Jewels, and pictures, and sculptures, and palaces,
Rare things and fair things of highest degree
Beaming in brilliancy, grace and magnificence,
Only to gladden me
     Lucy, with thee.

Nought it concerneth me Wiseacre's mutterings,
' Ever these have been and ever will be ;'
Worthless they'd seem to me, as dust and ashes all,
Were not my wanderings
     Lucy, with thee.

Perdita.

WHEN her eye no more discourseth
  Language more than tongue can say,—
Then be sure the spell is broken,
  Then true love will fall away :

When her touch no more respondeth
  To thy touch, from heart to heart,
Counsel thee true love declineth,—
  Dæmons whisper, 'Ye must part :'

When no more her smile entranceth,
  Raiseth up the soul of joy,
Question not true love hath flitted,—
  Helen hath gone out of Troy :

When her lips have ceased to sweeten,
  Sweeten more the more they press,
Let not hope belie thy senses,—
  True love every hour is less :

When no more her patter-patter
  Moved thee as it went and came,—
True love's warmth was of the ashes,
  Not enlivened by the flame :

When no more the silken rustle
  Of her robe doth charm thine ear,
Then in vain thine invocations,
  Cupid will refuse to hear:

When no more her voice hath music
  Sweetest strains of earth above,—
Waste not life in sighing, weeping,
  Go thou seek another love.

Coqueta.

My day is over !
  My pride all past !
No more a rover,—
  Have married the last !

· Ever adore you,
  Ever mine own ! '
Bah ! now I bore you,—
  When rivals are flown !

Worse than a zany—
  Listening to such ;
Were there not many
  Who loved me as much ?

The men admire me,—
  For *them* the fun ;
Wherefore desire me,
  Belonging to *one ?*

Onetime their fury,
  Duel, or toast !
Sit as my jury,
  Pass me as a ghost !

' Bright your eyes ! Minna,
    Bosom how fair !
Slender waist, Minna,
    So silken your hair !'

No one to praise me,—
    Beauty all lost !
Surely to craze me
    Is what it will cost !

What does it matter ?
    Live so ? alas !
Only to flatter
    Myself—in the glass !

Heart-ache to cover
    Laugh I in pain,—
Not—*not one* lover ?
    COQUETA again !

Aenigma.

True of heart as false of tongue,
Old in art, in years so young,
Deftly hiding whence she sprung :

Pretty lips with smile so sweet,
Pretty lips with fibs so fleet,
Pretty lips with kiss to greet ;

Placid smile, no sign of guile,
Syren smile of subtle wile,
Winning with a winning smile ;

Eyes of fire without desire,
Eyes the same for love or ire,
Eyes compelling to admire ;

Somewhen wild, or somewhen mild,
Somewhen praised, anon reviled,
Simple as a prattling child ;

Free of care as passing air,
Flinching not to do and dare,
Boldly facing blank despair ;

Deaf to heed, but fair in deed,
Generous to grant the meed,
Never failing at the need ;

Rash of speech, discreet to teach,
Patient listener when you preach,
None the worse or better each !

Words do flow you should not know,
Fables out of nothing grow,—
Playthings of her puppet-show !

Somewhen wise to your surprise,
Volatile as butterflies,
Sparse of truth, diffuse of lies ;

So Ænigma passeth life,
Smiling on, evading strife,
Making many wish her wife.

Brunetta.

BEAUTIFUL eyes so bright,
  Are ye shaded never
Till ye close in night,—
Their effulgence full
  Beaming ever, ever?

Beautiful eyes so bright,
  Do ye never gloom
Ere ye close in night,—
Pitiful for hearts
  Lingering in doom?

Beautiful eyes so bright,
  Do ye never weep
Ere ye close in night,—
Martyrs by their shafts
  Writhing though they sleep?

Beautiful eyes so bright,
  Will ye ever fade
Ere the final night,—
When their tenement
  In its shroud is laid?

Love-Stricken.

THEY tell me the King will be there,
   His Queen with her dainty-clad dames ;
They tell me much honour I'll share
   In their venturous, chivalric games,—
             Ah, what is it all to my love ?

They say there'll be worthies of state,
   Ambassadors, Princes, and Peers,
And scholars of merit most great
   Whose fame hath advanced with their years,-
             Ah, what is it all to my love ?

They say there'll be music and song,
   Fair objects the eye to delight ;
Sweet sounds to the ear do belong,
   Gay colours have charm to the sight,—
             Ah, what is it all to my love ?

They say there'll be feasting and glee,
   And frolic, and dancing, and wine ;
Oh, these are as nothing to me
   Who have found a companion divine !
             Ah, what is it all to my love ?

Finitus!

I.

I LOVED My Love,
And my love was as the Sun at his ascension,
    Resplendent, clear and strong ;

I loved My Love,
And my love was as the Sun at his declension,
    Calming—as coming sleep :

I loved My Love,
And methought my love is, as the flambeau flickers,
    Uncertain of its life,—
    Flaring, fading,
    Brightening, decreasing,
    Somewhiles nearly dying !

II.

    The torch is out !
  What can relume it ?
    The torch is out,—
  My heart is cold and void :

    The torch is out !
  Say'st thou relume it ?
    Not so—not so,—
  It will not kindle there :

    The torch is out ;
  Who would relume it
    Must fuse a heart,—
  Create a Soul !

The Song of Othello.

SHE is my soul's delight,
    Mainspring of feat and glee,
Sun, Moon, and Stars are bright,
    Less bright—less bright to me !

She is my soul's delight,—
    Ah, could she faithless be
The dark of darkest night
    Were darkness less to me !

She was my soul's delight,
    I know her false to be,—
Oh, dark of darkest night
    Less dark—less dark to me !

Duales.

LOVE me, my love, why or whether,
  Love me,—love me as I love thee ;
So the time when we are together
  A foretaste of Heaven shall be :

What matter the world or the weather,
  If lost in the thought—we are met?
We know only we are together,
  And everything else forget :

What matter, or flower or feather,
  Are not four eyes better than two?
Whatever we see not together—
  Is empty to me !—or to you?

Love me, my love, why or whether,
  Love me,—love me as I love thee ;
So the time when we are together
  A foretaste of Heaven shall be.

Love and Time.

Said'st thou the time was brief?
   Who stole the hours away?
   Stern justice bids me say
Thou wert the thief!

Shall I reproach thee for
   The theft a source of joy?
   Then, lest thou Time destroy,
Flee from thy presence, or

Shall I, contented, bless
   Thee, Charmer! and the charm
   Which me did, painless, harm
In blest forgetfulness?

Prithee increase thy crime,—
   So, if from day to day
   Thou steal the hours away,
There'll be a death to Time!

Leonora.

TURNING, her face shone on me—to my sight,
In grace surpassing speech : the vision dwells—
My memory haunting as a ghostly guest ;
Or chance, or change, or trouble, space, or time,
To *me* dim not the apparition fair :
Glow, melting eyes, to *me* ye cannot freeze,
Smile dimpled cheeks, to *me* for ever smile,
Pout coral lips, to *me* for ever pout,
Beam sunny brow, on *me* thou canst not cloud,
Shine seraph-countenance, for ever shine,—
To *me* the same whilst constant is my mind,
Seen, though in darkness, or though eyes be blind !

The Love Test.

Oh ! frank, fond kiss—oh ! honeyed kiss
    Of lips to lips, and clinging,
Oh ! heart rejoice the while her voice
    Mine ear within is ringing :

If e'er the kiss do quit my lips
    I'll think she feels offended,
When those dear tones mine ear not owns
    Alas ! her love is ended.

Felicia.

LADY, the nightingale did sing full-hearted
    As on my homeward way
    I lingered yesterday,
Oppressed with sorrow since from thee I parted;
    Ah! tuneful, happy sprite,
    To trill thy roundelay
    Of all true-love can say
    Throughout the charméd night!
Why is our lot, alas! so different,—
Art thou more blest, or I less innocent?

    Dearest, if the soul do wander,
    As the Orientals tell,
    Into various tenements
    Still on earth to dwell,
    Then I pray, whate'er my fate,
    Thou a nightingale shalt be,
    Hymning, aye, at Heaven's gate
    From a spring-time tree;
    Never but in music speaking,
    Smiled on by the listening stars,
    Soothing man in his distress,
    Joy attained yet keenly seeking,—
    Only varying the bars
    Of a sweet-toned happiness!

Impromptu.

Ah! Lady, pity the poor fluttering mite
   Which maddened by the radiance of thine eye
Ventured to taste of the intense delight—
   Blindly to feed ambition—and to die!

The memory cherish of the tiny bird
   So proudly scornful of the taper's flame—
In orbèd brightness instant death preferred
   To the spun pleasure of a joy more tame:

Thus have I sought, when those twin meteors blazed,
   A moment's rapture in their fervent fire,
Yea, at the flashing beacons have I gazed,
   Unconscious e'en to look was to expire!

------- >•<------ —

Violetta.

Violet on her bosom white,
   Did its loveliness decoy thee?
Soon thou sheddest thy delight,
   Quickly will its warmth destroy thee!

So the lure knew I too late,
   In the magic of her eye,—
Violet, happier thy fate
   On her bosom lone to die!

The Blush.

In blushing, thou charmest me most, my dear,
For it's then I am sure thou art all mine own ;
When blushing, I know thou'st forgotten to fear !
And I know thou are loveliest then, my love :

I think when thou blushest thy heart overflows,
Then thou lov'st me with all thy large heart, my love ;
The tint is as rosy as rosiest rose,
Only warmer—much warmer ! is't not, my love ?

———>•◄———

Pity or Envy.

Love me ! or pity not,
Mine image quite outblot,—
Lest I the wretch should be
Pitied for *losing* thee !

[Can love from pity grow ?
Cold reason tells me—no ;
Does greater spring from less ?
Hope faintly whispers—yes !]

Give thou thy *love* to me,—
Pity to hell be hurled !
Then am I, *gaining* thee,
The envy of the world.

The Inconstant.

So you think she deserves not my love,
  She is fickle, and may be untrue?
Well, why should I fret or complain
  If she seems not to me as to you?
  For I love her, I love her, you see,
  And I fancy she much loveth me:

I have looked into eyes beaming grander,
  Or enfolded a bosom more fair,
Taken honey from ruddier lips,
  Or toyed with more soft silken hair;
  Yet I love her, I love her, you see,
  And I fancy she much loveth me:

I've rejoiced with a spirit more frank—
  A more bland and beneficent grace,
I have won me a tenderer smile
  Than the bright sunny beam of her face;
  Yet I love her, I love her, you see,
  And I fancy she much loveth me:

Ha! you tell me she's like to bestow
  The same favour I thought only mine?
Well, it's pity, and serveth to show—
  Being mortal, she is not divine;
  For I love her, I love her, you see,
  Though 'twere certain she *not* loveth me.

A Lament.

HE is gone : our hopes and fears
 Are ended now—by death,
 Whilst from his parting breath
  Outspring our tears :

Gone,—ah ! wherefore was he born
 Merely to mock our love,
 To smile, to soar above—
  To make us mourn ?

Yet not mourn without relief,
 For, loving, we shall own
 Him never to have known
  Were deeper grief ;

Never Davy to have seen,
 His simple, gentle face,
 His unlearnt baby grace,—
  Regard serene ;

Not the quick though steady eye,
 The mounting forehead fair
 Clustered with Saxon hair
  In 'brutus' high ;

Davy's eye, observant, blue,
 His brow of noble traits
 Thoughtful in infant days,
  Of promise true ;

Never list' his laughing joy
  Proving by every sense
  A clear intelligence—
    All, all the *boy :*

It were greater loss and woe
  Not to have seen him—dead,
  In loveliness unsaid
    On th' earth below ;

For to him a beauty came
  New when earth-life had past,
  And hovered to the last—
    A lambent flame ;

Beauty yet unshed, innate,—
  As bud involveth bloom,
  Subliming to assume
    A saintlier state.

The Last Good=Bye.

MOTHER! no more we'll see thy face,
   No more will hear thy voice,
Lost—lost the sympathetic tones
   Which made our hearts rejoice :

Yet will the Seasons come and go,
   The Sun, the Moon will shine,
But all our consciousness will lack
   The portion sweetly thine :

So now begin we life anew,—
   Past, present, future changed ;
Full many an old, accustomed thought
   Will be from us estranged :

Dear Mother ! absent though thou art,
   To *me* thou livest still,
For carnal Death is impotent
   The Life in Love to kill.

𝕷𝖆𝖈𝖍𝖗𝖞𝖒𝖆̈.

*An ELEGY written at the instance of the early
death, by fever, of my schoolfellow
ROBERT SKINNER.*

YESTERDAY—thrice yesterday, we twain
    Together played, learned, thought;
Thus soon outspun the skein,—
    To Earth, to *me* thou'rt nought;
Friends wander comfortless, bereft,
    Thee nowhen do they find,
Save in their hearts—where thou hast left
    The impress of thy mind.

Ah wherefore? wherefore changed to stone,
    Pale, cold, the features senseless
Where late thy smile hath shone,
    From every foe defenceless—
In the silent tomb,—alone?
The Soul thy comrade bade to be,
    In thy disarmèd state
Unpitiful deserteth thee,—
    Consenting to thy fate!
False Pilot! so to quit the helm,
Pass—pass away to Pluto's realm:
But yesterday the final hour,
    I striving not—to save,
      To soothe a pang or stay a sigh,
      And oh, perchance when death was nigh
E'en as the perfume fled the flower,—
    I laughed above thy grave!

We were in life alike, together found
  Complacence or regret ;
Thou hearest now no sound.
  On Earth I linger yet—
Of joy the toy, the sport of sorrow,
  O'er things attained to fret,
To prove them froth to-morrow ;
With aim and hope one time the same,
  How shattered ! in thine ending,—
I toiling on for praise or blame,
  Thou lone to Hades wending ;
Ah, if awhile those moments dread
  A thought did rise
    Of my forsaking,
Within me sympathy is dead,
For surely else my heart had bled,—
  Or listing not her cries,
    My dormant Soul is deaf to her awaking !

Goddess with the golden hair,
Thou beneficent as fair,
Sweet as Zephyr music-fraught,
Subtile as the thread of thought,
Thou with Seraph-wings divine
Visiting the soul thy shrine,
Hail ! holy Sympathy, be near,
Nor desert this lower sphere,
Leave not *me !* permit me hear thee,
More I'll court thee, more revere thee ;
Whisperest thou of things above,
Or, of Earth, inspirest love,
Or whether with obscure portent
Thou warnest of some dire event,

Me attend, aye whisper on,
Touching soul in unison,
And if, in thy high vocation,
Thou wilt yield such intimation
As may spare my friend a throe,
Thine accents soft mine ear will know,
Though it woundeth, bless the smart,
As 'twere done by Cupid's dart;
Be *my* heart *thy* favoured spot,
Shun me not, oh, shun me not!

Dear ROBERT, thou art gone,—the veil
Withdrawn; the mystic tale
      Supernal,
For *thee* no more hath wonder
  Where immortality is brought to light;
    For *me*, 'tis left to mourn—
When we are reft asunder,
  When thou, in woe, art taken from my sight,
    No farewell said,—o'erpast the bourn
      Eternal.
Ah! I have promised me for long to hold thee
  With an enstrengthening chain,—
    By trial closer, firmer to be wrought,—
In still more perfect friendship to enfold thee,—
  Have I then yearned in vain?
    For 'tis a weird, a solemn thought,—
  Shall we be friends again?

Various.

300

Last Words to my Lorgnette.

COMPANION of serenest hours,
  Good genius of mine eyes,
To aid me with thy magic powers—
  Rich in thy memories!
O constant friend through fleeted years,
  Since part we must ere long,
List, whilst I mingle smiles and tears
  In valedictory song:

Involved within thy crystal arc
  Are countless lovely things,—
So musing now thy frame to mark,
  Rich recollection brings;
Yet, to recall what thou dost hold
  Were more than I may hope,
Nor would I wish thee all unfold
  From thy kaleidoscope:

Ah! dost thou memorize our first day—
  When we began delight?
A multitudinous array
  Of dames in colours bright:
Then wert thou new, I then was young,
  And it were rash to tell
Some sights discreetly left unsung,
  Of joy us then befell:

Those eyes, those lineaments, those smiles,
    Those glances slily soft,
Till, to assure ourselves the whiles,
    We spied again—too oft !
Thou know'st we saw a damsel's cheek
    So reddened with a blush,
Thy two clear orbs, so cold and meek,
    Partook the crimson flush ;

We peered again and saw, beside
    The fair face looking down,
A dark brow blanched with jealous pride,
    Dark with portentous frown ;
Thy firm frame shivered at the shock,
    And when I thee withdrew
I saw thy hard pellucid rock
    Bedimmed with frigid dew :

Dost thou remember one grand dame,
    Castilian, high-born,
Of whom we wist not e'en the name,—
    So beauteous in her scorn ?
Her now I see beyond thy view,
    Though thou didst it foretell,
For by thy help rejoiced I knew
    The smile of Ysabel :

Recallest thou, anent the stage,
    The dancing fairy-fair,
How we her notice did engage,—
    Trod she on earth, or air?
She flew, bird-like, again—again!
    As if our glance to greet,
Whilst wondered we what *could* sustain
    Her pretty twinkling feet:

A noble lady once we found,
    Endowed with eyes of fire,
We met them as they roved around,
    And asked, ' Is't love or ire?'
And then we pried again, to heed
    A sign pretence above!
Then, in our beating hearts agreed—
    ' It is the blush of love;'

We felt it—burning through thy lens!
    Who would her mien define
Will need a power beyond the pen's,
    A cleverer tongue than mine;
I laid thee down in sudden fear
    And trembling—for thy sake,
Lest, by such heat, thy mirrors clear
    Should into atoms break:

Canst thou forget the Actor great—
    Whose features we did scan
Whilst wrestling with a hopeless fate,—
    In semblance more than man ?
I felt thee shudder in my hand,
    And pitied thee thy pain,
Yet thought, with thee—' It is so grand,
    We'll suffer it again : '

Rememb'rest thou—a face malign,
    At distance dimly guessed ?
I sought thy help, and, with thine eyne,
    Good hap—perceived the rest ;
We marked his movements, saw his hate,
    And said—' 'Tis very clear,
Right well, dear friend, 'tis not too late,—
    We stay no longer here : '

Some secrets are there us between
    Which fain with us must die,
And some of such a kind I ween
    To seal our sympathy ;
I thank thee for unreckoned smiles
    Which came through thee to me,—
Let us, when life no more beguiles,
    Together buried be.

L'Abandon.

BURTHEN base of mortal cares—
It of the godlike nothing spares,
Takes the soul from out us wholly;
Joy and jollity rise unawares,
Then away with melancholie,
Vive la folie!

Weary, bored with life's humdrum,
Waiting for joy so slow to come,
Wit and fancy fly us wholly;
Tipple and smoke and sing fee-fo-fum,—
Ho! away with melancholie,
Vive la folie!

Work is good, and work is dry,—
Live a little before you die,
For a while forget it wholly;
Fiddle and dance and laugh till you cry,—
Ho! away with melancholie,
Vive la folie!

Grind and grind, and gather wealth,
And have everything—but health,
Zest for joyance losing wholly;
Off for a rollick, (sweeter by stealth,)—
Ho! away with melancholie,
Vive la folie!

Pore and fret, let knowledge grow,
The more we learn the less we know,
Till content deserts us wholly;
Summon the Ladies, and shout ho, ho,—
Ho! away with melancholie,
Vive la folie!

U

Belle=blonde.

A PORTRAIT TAKEN FROM IRIS' MIRROR.

FEATURES, English, purest type,
    (Let the Painter's tint compose
    Of the Lily and the Rose,)
Ruby lips, or 'cherry ripe,'
Lips that wreathe and speak in smiling--
Heart of saddest man beguiling—
Oft a string of pearls displaying;
Nimble tongue in wit unstaying,
Or, by silence sense betraying;
Archéd eyebrows rivalling jet,
Shading azure eyes—which met
As Nepenthe make forget,—
Eyes that should Eternal be,—
Ceaseless in vivacity!
Hair of Saxon, touched with brown,
Ample forehead well to crown,—
Front so fair and frank that there
Truth and goodness emblemed are;
Movement or of frame or face
Charmedly instinct with grace;
Form of Phidian Venus, shaped
As she were the Goddess draped;
Did Olympus give her birth?
Can she be a child of Earth?

Dulce Sodalitium.

OFF to the woods with my Myra,
 Through thicket or glade,
 In sunshine or shade,
Wandering away with Myra :

Ranging the woods with my Myra,
 Wait under the trees
 To list the wild bees,
Thridding the maze with Myra :

Under the trees with my Myra,
 The Zephyrs play round
 To the vari-tuned note
 Of the feathered sprites' throat,
 And the rivulet's sound,—
Resting and harking with Myra :

Roving on, on with my Myra,
 Now sit on the grass,
 Watch butterfly pass—
Happy as I with Myra :

Far, and more far with my Myra,
 The world is all ours,
 We gather gay flowers
 Just for botany's sake,
 Or garlands to make—
Garlands to make for Myra :

Over the hills with my Myra,
   Aye talk as we walk,
   And laugh as we chaff,
   Looking up to the skies—
     To hear the lark sing,
   Or in each other's eyes—
     Mute music to bring ;
Over the hills with Myra :

Far, and more far with my Myra,
   For ever to roam,
   To never go home,
Ever at home with Myra :

Down to the Lake with my Myra,
   Eftsoons in the boat
   Together afloat,
   Mid lilies to steer
   In ripples so clear—
Bright as the eyes of Myra :

Home at the eve with my Myra,
   Enchanted in glory
   Of Song, or of Story,
Only—not lonely, with Myra.

The Eddystone.

BLITHE Winstanley came unto Plymouth one eve
  His Fisher-friend hailing, 'What ho!
I am bound for my Lighthouse to challenge the storm ;'
  But his Fisher-friend answered, 'No, no!

'There is bane in the welkin, and fury and fume,
  Such as only a seaman can guess;
Those who venture to-night will not many return ;'
  Blithe Winstanley said, 'None the less!—

'I couch in my Lighthouse to laugh at the storm,
  Shall I not to mine offspring be true?
I built it for centuries, not for a night,
  Must it perish, let *me* perish too!'

Then he came to his Tower, and his brave watchers
    cheered—
  Saying, 'Though now 'tis so sunny and warm,
They tell me there's terror wrapped up in the night,
So here have I hastened to save you from fright,
  To be near you—to laugh at the storm!'

And fondly he looked on the pride of his life—
  With its minarets gilded and gay,
'On this shall men gaze, or from ship or from shore,
Or by night or daylight mid the Ocean's mad roar,
  A long age after I pass away!'

Darkest dark came the sky, wildest wild rose the storm,
  Bringing ruin to ship, house, and tree ;
Men saw the gaunt reef bare at day's dawning hour,
The dread reef alone—for the Man and the Tower
  Were at one with the Infinite Sea!

Sevilla.

IN after-days I oft shall praise
The towers and flowers of fair Sevilla,
Her sun and shade and busy ways
Graced by the Doñas in mantilla;
Her grand Cathedral's solemn gloom,
Her zephyrs sweet with orange-bloom,
Her *patios* cool with pure azúl,
And all her Moorish maravilla;
But chief in memory will rule—
(As far above as bright Orion!)
　　　　A sprite or bird
　　　　Which there I heard—
　　　　An English tongue
　　　　Which spake or sung
　　　　In simple sooth
　　　　Or careless truth,—
The clear, frank laugh of Dame Carlyon!

SEVILLA, 1st *May*, 1860.

Vale!

LADY, believe—
Though but few hours ago
Each other's face we did not know,
　　Tearful I grieve
When hopelessly we part,
Thine image shrining ever in my heart;
　　Oh, happy fate!
To be enchanted with a deathless mate.

Weber's 'Last Waltz.'[1]

AIR.

BE still, be still my soul, is this delusion,
Or is my spirit free from earthly bondage?
Those strains seraphic cannot be illusion—
Ah, no! they are . . for sure . . from heaven   from
      heaven :

INTERLUDE.

Mortal—mortal! thou art not translated,
Yet art thou habiting this lower sphere ;
O soul! to hear those accents hast thou waited?
Why, having listened, dost thou linger here?

AIR.

Hark, hark—oh list! again, again 'tis sounding—
Now—now I hear their echoing melody—
Now—now 'tis ringing through the host surrounding,
In tones . . divine . . decreasing . . softly slow :

AIR.

Rest, rest, my heart—for thee this world is over,
Rest, spirit! thy celestial home is nigh,—
I hear—I hear! and they are Angels' voices,—
I hear—I hear!—and . . now . . I die—I die.

---

[1] Verse 1 is to be played *tempo giusto*, except last line, which is
rallentando ; the Interlude, *mezzo piano ;* verse 3, *con fuoco, allegro,*
diminuendo ; verse 4, *adagio è calando.*

A Hymn for all People.

ALMIGHTY Father, hear !
Our voice to Thee we raise
In gratitude and fear,
And tunefully to praise
Thy holy Name, confessing
Our faults with humble mind,
Beseeching for Thy blessing
Great God so long forbearing
With us the while transgressing,
So oft for Thee uncaring,
And to Thy goodness blind ;
We have done ill unknowing,
Have thanklessly received,—
But Thy mercy much exceedeth,
As our feeble nature needeth,—
Oh ! cease not Thou bestowing,
Lest we be all-bereaved !

Impromptu.

SOME acts there are of human kind
    Surpast our earthly sphere,
Some thoughts in other worlds to find
    The home they have not here.

Yea, such will be the kindred traits
    O'erspread the heavenly face,
Whereby the loves of mortal days
    Affinity shall trace.

To Sarah at School,

ANTICIPATING THE HOLIDAYS.

PRETTY, merry-laughing Sister,
  This I wot will find thee gay,
Brimming-full of hope and joyance,
  Looking for a happier day :

From the mirth thy heart o'erflowing
  Couldst thou wisely make a store,—
I may wish not, yet there will be
  Times when thou shalt want it more :

What a fund of bliss for after !
  Fairy Sister, fancy-free,—
Precious fund of merry laughter
  Rich enough for thee and me :

Through the years, however lengthened,
  Thou shouldst from thy hoard dispense
Balm divine for every sorrow,
  Joy evolved of innocence :

Life may cheat thee, merry Sister,
  So laugh out thy little span,
Making it your rule of living
  To be merry when you can.

Impromptu.

The mirror broken? never mind!
Let not its fragments breed dejection;
Nor will I scold whilst yet I hold
The object of its lost reflection.

———

The Sermon.

Madam—when, sitting in the Church,
I see thee near the parson shining,
Howe'er recondite his research
I, gazing, list without repining;
And whilst in fairness I agree
With those who deem the sermon prosy,
Mine eyes (as shut they could not see,)
Forget entirely to be dozy.

———

Impromptu.

Shut, shut bright eyes! turn, turn away fond face!
Tend not wherefrom next moment ye must sever;
Yet oh! let sorrow soon to joy give place,—
For what at sight I love—is mine for ever.

Rosa to the Rose.

SWEET Rose! from thy kindred severed,
From thy parent stem—alone!
In spring-drops pure I place thee—
Ah, did I hear thee groan?

May not Rosa share thy feeling?
Thee echoing with a sigh
Her sympathy revealing,—
Like thee to bloom and die!

An Answer.

Ay, lady dear! whate'er—I'll go to see thee;
For in thy presence time is very sweet,
And in thy presence joy is very great,
Yea, in thy presence I escape my fate;
Then cometh soon the moment I must flee thee,
The term most bitter brought by time too fleet,
In anguish keenest when we separate!

Prelude

TO A COMMON-PLACE BOOK.

NOUGHT to me e'er pleasure brought
Like participating thought;
If silent, deep the joy we feel
To find our own another's weal;
The crude conception unexprest
Yet to ourselves, by others drest,—
Truly and touchingly foreshown
Thoughts we had deemed were all our own;
This mutual insight of the mind,
Or glimpse whereto a third is blind,
New interchange of feeling, this
Sincere, if momentary bliss,—
Should it,—as bliss had been the cost,
Henceforth be to memory lost?
Should aught which were a joy to stay,
All unremembered pass away?

1835.

With 'Ibood's Annual.'

(1840.)[1]

LADY, the books herewith thy favour claim ;
Thou shalt find Wisdom drest in Folly's garb,
Good-sense instilled with all the force of smiles,
Truth its own language speaking to the heart ;
Thou shalt know Virtue when she doth not frown,
And pathos undisturbed by groans and tears,—
To learn, by pleasant proof, how laughing out
Doth better recreate than doleful dreaming :
The keen though bloodless weapon Satire named
(Sometimes misused in aid of personal spite,
But then most weak,) doth in these pages strike
With cunning aim and guileless artifice,—
Wounding for cure, chastising faults which else
(Congenial being and in colour like
To an imperfect nature,) had remained
Uncared-for or unseen : albeit—on *thee*
The shafts of satire hurtlessly must fall.

---

[1] This date was prior to the general recognition of Hood's high
place in the rank of *genius*.

The Fifth of November.

THERE was once a time, my brothers,
Ere to man's estate we came,
When the fifth day of November
To us brought a merry game;
Oh! the banging squibs and crackers,
Blazing rockets, whirling wheels,—
Still memory smells gun-powder,
And the trepidation feels:

Then Guy Fawkes, the wretched hero,
Was reduced to ashes quite,
As the red remorseless tar-tub
Ycrowned our fierce delight,
Yet, like the famous Phœnix,
From the flames to re-appear,
And make this day, next winter,
Unlike other in the year:

Now, the fifth day of November
To us brings—perchance a fog;
'Tis a Monday or a Tuesday,
Or—a day to burn a log;
We wonder much those simpletons
Their 'guy' should hawk about,
The boys with squibs and crackers,
Make such an infernal rout.

Sage and Disciple.

MASTER, for thy learning
Much my soul is yearning ;
Why don't Man live longer,
Longer live, and stronger,
Wisdom always earning?
This is my surprise :

Son, thy thought hath reason,
With thy youth in season ;
Yet, to wish life longer,
Longer life and stronger,—
To thy Maker treason !
Man would grow too wise.

———

Impromptu.

As a cloud athwart the Moon,
So is Life, in passing soon ;
Such is life to mortals given,
Hindering sight, not hope of Heaven.

Pyrrha.

Thy golden tresses, Pyrrha,
  Illume my silvery pate,
As oft the sunshine blesses
  A wretch disconsolate :

Thy golden dowers, Cleon,
  To me much more are worth,
As oft the summer showers
  Refresh the thirsty Earth :

Nay, nay ! *thy* gold, my Pyrrha,
  Is finer gold than mine,
For these resplendent tresses
  Around my *heart* entwine :

My heart thou bindest, Cleon,
  About with cords of gold,
Else, lover though the kindest,
  Might Pyrrha think thee old :

Ah ! lovely, saucy Pyrrha,
  Thy gold is more than gold,
For near these glowing tresses
  I never shall be old !

IN GERMANY.

1844.

Bastei.

SPOT from primæval chaos unsubdued,
Or haply left by the Creative Word
An instance of the Earth's disorder crude;
We gaze and tremble ! man's calm spirit stirred
To deep emotion by this shapeless herd
Of things material; and thus we own,
In all our pride of destiny deferred,
A kindred nature with the senseless stone,
And bow, small block to great, as we to fear are prone.

Brandt.

METHINKS the countless orbs in Space revolving
At the beginning were concrete in *One*,
The mighty throe, its vast compact dissolving,
Casting enruined, when the wrack was done,
A city which Man's work should equal none;
Bases stupendous, taller than our spires,
Pillars sky-searching though but yet begun,
Portals at whose assize the mind retires,
Grandeur beyond our means, not passing our desires.

X

The Dresden Gallery.

TREASURE of atoms of great souls translated,
Sparks of the inextinguishable fire
Erst in the upward struggle scintillated,
Relics bequeathed to comfort and inspire
The future earth-worm destined to be higher,
Beautiful sublimations of high thought
Prisoned for centuries in dense attire,
Glimpses in heavenward flight by Genius caught—
To thousands aye unknown if not to vision brought.

———

Cologne Cathedral seen from the Rhine.

LIKE a dismembered stone-god thou appearest !
Knowing the course of ages will restore—
Thy giant limb and front sublime thou rearest,
As he, bold Titan, proudly did afore ;
Even to-day is thy abasement o'er,
When man redeems a long-neglected right—
Resolving to endure its shame no more ;
Lo ! where the weed had growth, the owl delight,
Again the chisel clinks with hundred-handed might.

A Full Moon at Ehrenbreitstein.

I SAW at Ehrenbreitstein the still Queen
Crowning, refulgent, the embattled height,
On all things smiling with as pure a sheen
As it had been her first created night ;
Such sweet communion held she by her light—
A hapless mortal gazing from afar
Forgot his earth-born nature, and, despite
Whate'er of ills his aspirations mar,
Became for little while as her attendant star.

The Novice.

THERE, in the ancient Convent art thou hidden
A jewel in a casket, yet mine eye
Straining, lacks not thine image ; spirit-bidden,
Her loved form as an angel standeth by ;
Ah, if indeed unwilling, would she hie
Unto the mountain-top, of aspect mild,
And, with a mocking presence, hear me sigh ?
This were to prove true love but Fancy's child,
Or sympathy, alas ! no more than notion wild.

The Ariadne.

A GREAT deed, Dannecker, thus well to earn
Thy perpetuity objective, so—
If the unending lot whereto we yearn
Not unto to us were granted, *thou* wouldst know
Prolonged existence whilst men come and go,
Thy soul in stone,—a name for ever new;
Nor would man's Maker thus on man bestow
The skill creative, and unpleasèd view
Of our decaying form this lasting image true.

The Ariadne.

IT's very well; her arm reposeth sweetly,
Wholly uncared-for by the eager mind;
The graceful form is fashioned so completely—
It were too difficult a fault to find;
If to profess a choice I were inclined,
First would I praise the limb depending low,
As proof in art than nature more refined;
Persuade me it is nerveless ere I go!
Or, if she liveth not, what *will* supports it so?

Stigmata Loweri.

CARPTOR INHABILIS.

READ AFTER DINNER—25TH JANUARY 1860.

Mark Antony Lower's a prince at '*palaver*,'
But, plainly to speak, a most rascally carver ;
Twice his aid at the table no host will employ,
Having seen the arch-spoiler hew, hack, and destroy ;
As Hecuba's dire the despair of the wife
Who ever has trusted his hand with a knife ;
At instant all reason and sense fly away,
He seizes your prog as a tiger his prey,
Your Beef he saws thick, your Down-Mutton thin,
Or if it be Fish serves out nothing but fin ;
If Chicken—he causes beholders to groan,
Tearing flesh into ribbons, and sinew from bone ;
Seeing near him a Ham, you ask him for *that*,
When straightway he gives you a dollop of fat ;
In the matter of Pie put not in him your trust,
Lest wishing for fruit you get nothing but crust ;
He's been known, many times, to be very profuse
With the savoury stuffing, forgetting the Goose,
And, wisely avoiding your steel blade to tarnish,
Help the lady who's next him to nothing but garnish ;
He can cut with a pen, and concoct you a dish
Out of fine modern ink with an ancient rel*ish*,
But in carving, and sarving, of Lower beware,
Else, though you be parson, he'll cause you to swear,
Thus whilst in the higher you recognise Lower,
In this art which is lower you love him no more !

QUÆSTIO LITERARUM.

MARK ANTONY LOWER enjoys his 'vacation,'
But says there's no time in it for—recreation,
And then for long months he pursues his 'vocation,'
Like a wretched mill-horse—without any cessation;
Hence a problem provoking no small botheration,
Namely—which is vocation and which is vacation?
For the difference herein between vo and va
Should value the same as between work and play,
Or even as much as between do and say;
(Not to mention the contrast, in aim foul or fair,
Nor if 'tis your purpose to spoil or to spare :)
But whether in vo or whether in va,
Or whether in work or whether in play,
Or whether in do or whether in say,
The metamorphosis is with O and A;
So with LOWER—a slave who ne'er kicks off his fetters—
Call it work, call it play, it's a question of '*letters.*'

The Curate.

FOUNDED ON FACT.

In a village not far from 'the city of smoke,'
Where more bitter the scandal the better the joke,
A place much infested with (very) old maids,
Who declining are pining for spiritual aids,
Where tradesmen learn brotherly love at 'the Shades,'—
There dwells a young Curate, ah, so interesting!
He wins by a look, by his mode of requesting,
And so sweetly retiring, 'tis said by his friends
His beginnings so modest, he can have no ends:
When he took to the parish, most sad to relate!
Original sin was its terrible state,
No light in the darkness, no star in the sky,
Of the whole population—not one but must die!
Then—then came the Curate, and surely no change
Since order from chaos, so marvellous strange
Has been known or conceived; in one little week,
No lady need summon a blush to her cheek,—
The thieves all decamped, tongue-tied were the liars,
The sellers, converted, told truth to the buyers,—
The maids grew seraphic, angelic the men,
The old 'roaring lion' durst not from his den,—
Decorum and piety, virtue and peace,
Half ruined the lawyers, made null the police:
Now the godless and graceless flock gladly to church,
Now the sick and bed-ridden are left in the lurch,

Pew-openers are harassed and big beadles strut,
Free seats are *not* free if the church is not shut ;
Now balls are deserted, and plays unremembered,
And all the May joys prematurely Decembered ;
It was reckoned all men who had fathers before them
Penance did for *their* sins, and but lived to deplore them :
The Curate proved truths with a force mathematic,
He proved without meaning the old word fanatic,
He proved to his listeners, by counting their heads,
Exactly the number at home in their beds,
He proved—and fair Truth ne'er seemed sweeter or
    grander—
How man is not rightly a goose, but a gander,
(Which fact he asserted could clearly be shown
In a very particular friend of his own :)
The Curate did more,—a blunder irrational
Had mis-named the school of the village 'the National ; '
The boys had their duties ; the principal thing
Was aloft in the old church to make the walls ring,
And like cherubs encourage the people to sing ;
Now these cherubs sang badly, all out of tune sadly,
And the Curate at first bore the dissonance madly,
Until he determined, mind-peace to restore,
They could not sing worse, if they sang as much more !
It followed herefrom the dull people improved
By the Curate's exertions felt piously moved
To some cheerful diversion,—for saints do not thrive
Without something worldly to keep them alive ;
To give them full justice it here should be said
They wisely consulted and patiently read
To find a pursuit which their hearts need not grieve,
Nor even a speck on their spotlessness leave ;
They searched through the Fathers, they little there found,—
But just when despair their perplexity crowned

St. Thomas Aquinas the friend-in-need stood,
In writing of Music as 'holy and good;'
They shouted the dictum, they felt quite delighted,
They thought all their labour was doubly requited,
But ah ! one suspicion their joyfulness crost,
If the Curate objected their pleasure was lost !
The Synod agreed on the Pastor to wait,
And, or banning or blessing, discover their fate ;
The Curate received them with looks calm and gracious,
And nice as his favourite food farinaceous ;
The purpose propounded, the visit explained,
They await the decree with suspense nothing feigned ;
Alas ! why so dark his erst radiant brow ?
Why quiver those eyelids ? why rises he now ?
He lifted his book, the table he slammed,
' Why, gentlemen, surely you would not be damned ? '
The worthies first wondered, then meekly begun
To mention their reasons ; but when they had done,
   ''Twas lost on the Curate,
   Who still was obdurate,
And venting his fury he spluttered out 'Zounds !
Whilst you talk to me this way my zeal has no bounds,
If your taste were thus heightened in every degree
Who the deuce will be caring to listen to *me?*'

1843.

King Sham.

A SKETCH FROM LIFE.

'Il n'y a point de sots si incommodes que ceux qui ont de l'esprit.'
—ROCHEFOUCAULT.

ONCE on a time—there dwelt upon the Earth
One unendowed by genius or by birth,
With knowledge unencumbered, as with worth;
He swaggered forth, and said, 'I'll have my day—
Hey, for King Sham! let men say what they may;
What others know, I can as well *profess*,—
And take the credit for it, none the less;
I apprehend how diffidence doth lag,
How Talent, toiling, is cut out by Brag,
And he who claims the merit—takes the swag;
To modest pleadings gates and ears are shut,—
The port potential is to swell and strut;
Let honest zeal, unsordid, sweat the brain,
For me, prepared to grasp, the *fruits* remain;
Of Truth, with Pilate's question I agree,—
Truth is a branch of high Philosophy!
Learning and virtue and all gifts divine
May work their purpose—so the spoil is mine!
Bethink what game will best your wiles repay,
And then, with tongue in cheek, say—*That's* the way;
A noble project! Go ahead, my boys!
Who gets the guerdon? I, who make the noise;

The brainless boobies, aimless, fail to see
Their zealous striving is, at last, for *me ;*
Wheedle, incite, and when the battle's won
Forward I stand, and vaunt what *I* have done ;
Then, with a flourish, sheathe my bloodless sword,
And, in due sequence, claim my just reward ;
If other foremost in the fight would be,
Bamboozle him ! he leaves the field to *me ;*
Oppose, denounce, and put him on the shelf—
Next, to the front—and do the job myself ;
Flattery goes far, and homage bringeth grist—
Few men (or women) can such siege resist ;
Yet, though your words be soft, and sweet as honey,
They are as empty wind, unbacked by money ;
Therefore my cry shall be 'gainst joke or jibe,
(Indifferent for what) " Subscribe, Subscribe ! "
When for the race of life you get astride,
The filly Charity's the one to ride !
What wots the world or if you die or live
Unless you seize on something still to *give ?*
He has the thanks by whom the dole is dealt,
Enough if leaps the largess from *his* belt ;
Cajole and twit, caress and promise high,—
Suppose you *fail,* to give the world the lie
Suggest a " Testimonial " by-and-bye,—
Sign me this paper—testify your debt
To *me* who never did *your* good forget ;
Some scruples ? tush ! a fig for your pretences !
At them at once ! and bring them to their senses ,
What ? recreants, cowards, meanlings, to refuse
A fair return to whom you owe your shoes !
Downcast, ashamed, they all before me creep,
And do my bidding like a flock of sheep ;

Then they the bantling bring—to me who got it—
And I exclaim—God bless me ! who'd have thought it?
Ho ! to oppose me who shall be so bold?
Who can bestow, can he not too *withhold?*
Your *friends*—are those who fawn, or those who sneer,
For some are held by hope, and some by fear ;
If one, enraged, against me dares to preach,
I say he's "personal," and stop his "speech ;"
Or if sometimes they flat refuse to hear you,
Tell it instead to the Reporters near you,—
They'll find to their surprise, defeat, and sorrow,
It's in the Papers all the same to-morrow ;
This is not all, good-living maketh bill,
For this the best thing is to share a Will,—
Fools work, and what they earn must go to some one,
And then—what *does it* matter to the dumb one?
A noble maxim—all mankind are brothers,
Nor less a truth—some born to work for others ;
Such useful, slavish industry you shirk,
Then manifest the glory of *their* work ;
Janty alike, be it to saints or sinners,
Feed them with eleemosynary dinners ;
Some one to couple beg-and-boast presumes,—
Don't you look quite as well in *borrowed* plumes?
The art of life ! to be *not* what you seem,
Cozen the world by impudence supreme,—
Gross, and yet unsubstantial as a dream !
When the good parasites would bow the knee,—
" Nay ! it is *you* men honour, honouring *me ;*"
But if they rashly breathe contempt or blame,—
Reply " On *you* alone descends the shame ;"
I pray no prophet from the sky be sent
To reckon all the good—I did *prevent,*

Or, of my deeds, interpret to the letter
What, but for me, had certes been much better!'

'Have you not seen a damsel fair as day,
Whilst all-deserving, pine herself away?
Have you not seen a woman bold as brass,
With nought to flatter her—except her glass,—
Proud in success, with her third husband pass?
So to succeed in honours or in pelf,
Wait not for courting, but "propose" *yourself.*'

'Though much is gained, yet further must be done,—
Some for to-day, and more for future won;
Forsooth, the future is beyond my ken,—
The dreadful difference of now and then!
In this how true *Bis dat qui citò dat!*—
I know my men too well to count on *that!*
It's good to batten on the things that be,—
A grander aim—to gull posterity!
Make thine own Statue! or thy ghost will rue it,
Lest when thou'rt gone there be no fools to do it.'

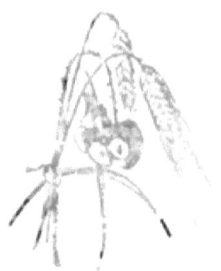

Stylites at Brighton.

AN INSCRIPTION.

1878.

WE saw, when all was over, and too late,
When our magician had succumbed to fate,
When now no more the sophist tactics charm,
Specious pretences, or the ' itching palm,'
When to the stimulant succeeds the qualm,—
Our god of gold was but a thing of clay,
(Eke with a demon guiding men astray);
As some usurping king deludes his troops
Till, at his fall, they know they've been his dupes,—
' Diabolus !   To his Manes let us pray !
Let not the world suspect that *we* were less
Than him who led us,—falsely we confess—
Yet told us so much truth—when he was mellow,—
Hence will we, though we look a little yellow,
An effigy raise of this confounded fellow !
Then shall they think the man who reigned and ruled
O'er us, hoodwinked, and every way befooled,
Deserved of us the homage we have paid him
Blinded by flattery, (as the purpose swayed him :)
Besides, alas ! the world knows he has done us,
Posterity will laugh ! in shrouds to stun us ;
So, as revenge, the Devil knows, to sinner
Is sweeter morsel than of any dinner,

We'll set him up (albeit 'tis unkind)
To expiate humbug "in the parching wind,"
Then as we pass we'll nod, and grin, and mutter—
Stand there! thou type of wile, and guile, and " butter ; "
Placed by thy puppets on that gairish spot
Still to proclaim thou wert what thou wert not !
Doomed to perpetuate, though tongue be mute,
The *fiction* of thy virtue and its fruit !'

. *Here follow the names of the purblind.*

Ye Battel Daye.[1]

Ho! a joust of joyance rare,
The Sussex chivalry was there,
Maidens, matrons, knight and squire,
All the flower of the shire;
(In the tilting of this day
Was there nought of warlike play,
Only (g)lances aimed to fly
Peacefully from eye to eye,
And the combat's rage was spent
In a learned argument :)
From afar, with aim æsthetic,
Philosophers peripatetic,—
Britton,[2] ancient antiquary,
History's depositary;
('Tis conjectured he is able
To describe the Tower of Babel,
Even knows the secrets hid
Under the great Pyramid,
And was with his [*Briton*] clan
At Stonehenge, and made the plan !)
Mantell,[3] wise in fossil stones—
Very conjurer with bones;

---

[1] The General Annual Meeting of the Sussex Archæological Society at Battle, 23d July, 1852.

[2] John Britton, F.S.A., author of *The Cathedral Antiquities of Great Britain*, etc. etc.

[3] Dr. Gideon Mantell, F.R.S., F.S.A., author of *The Geology of the South Coast of England*, etc.

Hunter,[1] munimental student,
Sage in dates, in phrases prudent;
And in force numerical,
Scholars lay and clerical,—
All to Battel Abbey came
In the Ladye Webster's name.

To the ancient hall with glee
Flocked the goodlie companie;
On the dais, as of old,
Sate the wisest and most bold;
Chiefest, like a warrior brave,
Was the Thane of Waldegrave;
Then the Minstrels at command
Sang the deeds of fatherland;
Lower[2] first, the bard of Lewes,
Told the conquering Norman's prowess,—
Sad as dying swan he caroled
Of the final woe of Harold,
Of the ground whereon he stood
Drenched with Sax and Norman blood,
Till all saw ere he had done
England lost and England won:
Hunter next, with modest grace,
Occupied the minstrel's place,
And the burthen of his song
Wrought eftsoons a passion strong,
For he quashed, with accents bland,
A tradition of the land,—
Swore the famous 'Roll of Battle'
None it was but housewife's prattle,

---

[1] Joseph Hunter, F.S.A., Keeper of the Public Records.
[2] Mark Antony Lower, F.S.A., author of *Patronymica Britannica*, etc.

And in softest tones denied
Fame to those who fought and died ;
Shrieked the ladies, horror-stricken,
Antiquaries' hearts did sicken,
Men of high ancestral pride
Wished him stoned or crucified,
And the spirits hovering near
Groaned in anguish—sad to hear ;
Fled the companie in haste,
Hunter honeyed words did waste,
B****w[1] of Beechland raised his voice
In a chaunt of wond'rous noise,
Essaying to soothe their fears
With a song of 'nuts and pears ; '
But in vain—for some do know
When to stay and when to go ;
Pitying their loss that day,
B****w of Beechland strode away.

    Now the mid-day meal was spread,
Where the monks of yore were fed,
In the vast Refectory ;—
'Twas a pleasant sight to see
Such a joyous companie
Ranged at tables, o'er and o'er,
Twice two centuries and more
Of gay dame and cavalier ;
So they wassail—till their ear
One in phrase polite doth crave,—
'Tis the Thane of Waldegrave ;
Then they pledge the Queen around,
With their shout the crypts resound ;   .

---

[1] W. H. Blaauw, F.S.A., author of *The Barons' War*, etc.

To the Prince a cup they quaff,
Him, Victoria's 'better half;'
To the Ladye Webster's name
Next they drink with loud acclaim ;
Then a mighty shout they gave
For the Thane of Waldegrave ;
Spake the Thane, and well said he,
Spake the Thane right gallantly ;
Britton spake, and worthie Lower,
Hunter meek, and many more ;
B * * * w of Beechland then begun,
But the dames effrayed did run ;
As a dream by noise is sped
The assembly vanishèd.

Shone the sun, the zephyrs played
Lightly in the chequered shade ;
Type of human life, the day
Marked unnoted its decay :
Phœbus loath the joy to mar,
Pitiful, restrained his car ;—
On the lawn, among the flowers,
In the cool of archèd bowers,
Paced the fairy feet so light
Of the dames with visage bright,
Smiling, laughing, full of glee,
Laughing out right merrilie,
Passed the happy companie,
Backward, forward, here and there ;
Music floating in the air
Blended with the voices' hum—
The climacteric had come :—
'Tis the superpenal doom,
All things ripen to their tomb ;

Lo, they ripen, ripen on
Unto their perfection,
Unto dissolution :
Like a phantasy of mist,
Which but now the mountain kissed,
Fringèd round with beauteous dyes
    From the golden orb, at even,
(Minor whisperings of the skies
    By reflection fresh from heaven,)
So is gone the happy host,
    Whilst hill and abbey both remain,
So its elements, not lost,
    Elsewhere shall be condensed again.

𝔄 𝔣𝔞𝔪𝔦𝔩𝔦𝔞𝔯 𝔏𝔢𝔱𝔱𝔢𝔯

ADDRESSED TO JOHN GURR CHAPLIN.

1837.

THINK not, dear Sir, because so long
You've lost my presence in the throng,
It is of dread to meet your looks
From a design upon your books,
Or that, forgetting them and you,
I'm unpolite and thankless too,—
Rather, believe me, they have been
A flowered medium between
In severance, by the Fates decreed,—
They've some time been retained indeed
(Eke all the while me lonesome cheering)
As hostages for your appearing;
Yet doth it seem there now should be
A sentence of apology;
For who has ever lent a book
And failed to cast an anxious look,
With passing thought of doubt and pain--
' Ah, when wilt thou be mine again?'
Severe, prolonged in fear, I ween,
Must your anxiety have been;
But I have an excuse to state
Which one in twenty cannot prate,
One true as truth before the fall,—
Of having duly read them all!

This last, if a forgiving creature,
You'll own is a redeeming feature ;
One book, or ten, I'll ne'er reject
Of his for whom I have respect ;
I should not think it more unkind
To spurn a portion of his mind,
Than to reject, indifferent,
A book which he, in faith, hath lent ;
I will not trouble you to heed
The scanty time I have to read,
Perhaps it's why I more enjoy it,—
Satiety doth not alloy it ;
Be this my comfort,—yet, alas !
Such solace may itself surpass ;
For oh,—to escape the point I try,—
Illiteracy the penalty!
This clear conviction too accrues,
I'll ne'er retrieve what now I lose ;
Past will be youth, and in its train
The sympathies then sought in vain,
The energies which early flow,
Desire and aptitude to know ;
For thought alone there is not time,—
Such idleness would seem a crime
As spending hours to form opinions,—
So act we money-seeking minions !
I do not wonder how so much
The world at large should make a crutch
Of priests and bigots, and then die
In empty, false credulity !
Nor longer puzzle me how men
Yclept of sense,—and deep of ken,
Should take their notions second hand,—
Interest sole spur to understand,

Their moral code a rope of sand :
Ask thou, my friend, the first you meet
In office, *salon*, club or street,
One honest and without pretence,
Possessing *more* than common sense,
The upshot of his latest thought
On all philosophy has taught—
But of one thing ; what speed ? alack !
You'd better take your question back ;
He'll either choose the mode subversive
And get immediately discursive,
Showing his ignorance in an hour
While one small word had had the power :—
He'll straightway give the fire a poke—
Your question shirking as a joke,
Or else he'll worship truth in kind,
And say he's not made up his mind ;
Pursue it further, he'll confess
Unread—it has been thought of less,
While using one hand eloquent,
Concealing where his mind is bent,
His other hand supplies the link
Where (in his breeks) the shillings chink,
And he in sooth will only tell
What thousands must admit as well,
That when he ponders 'tis about
Who now are in, who now are out,
Which way he can a hundred earn,
And which side best will serve his turn,
Or if he think with ' high emprize '
Which way he can *through riches* rise ;
This *know* we,—though the fact offends,
His mind by intuition tends
To some dank hemisphere which best

Will suit the *sordid interest ;*
Let but a man—with grave resolve
Repose, an axiom to evolve,—
Determined ere he rises thence
To moralize on 'future tense,'
Eradicate a solemn doubt
By thinking till he hunt it out,
Or cogitate with pious care
On some benevolent affair,
Do I say well?—it's 'ten to one '
In minutes few his fancies run
Vagarious, or if they keep
True to their point, he falls asleep,
And wakes of a deduction short,—
Such things are not by dozing caught ;
Thus fleets a life,—from day to day
Still is deferred by most to pay
A solemn debt to reason due,—
'Tis true, 'tis pity, and *'tis* true.
India, when Europe was unsung,
When blest philosophy was young,
When men had nought their thoughts to guide
Save things which we like them deride,
Cold scepticism came to be
A dire and sad necessity ;
Then, if men thought, and searched their text,
'Twas but to make them more perplexed ;
E'en the magnanimous—high-souled,
Whose deeds were great, whose purpose bold,
Shrunk ! when they sought the great First Cause,
The mysteries of Nature's laws, —
For though the intellect were bright,
The book it studied was as night
Lit by some dim and fickle rays,

Lacking cognition's Sun-like blaze ;
Then did the mass live on their life
Doubt and belief through youth at strife,
Till deaf their ears and blind their eyes
As superstition's votaries ;—
But for *our* world where knowledge meets
The mind, and lights—as gas our streets,
What say we, if in God alone
For data,—Hope's foundation stone,—
And Science, in itself a light
To render our horizon bright,
We have enough to chase away
Delusions of a darker day ;
Yet more, oh more,—throughout the land
Knowledge is teeming, every hand
Doth hold a book, and many a voice
Proclaims new theories for our choice ;
The ancient adage doth indeed
Come true, and he that runs may read ;
But lo ! no change in minds, which still
Their in-born tendencies fulfil ;
Men now, as ever, hear one side
The other hear,—then *not* decide ;
Now thoughts are units—not a sum,
Minds imitate a pendulum,
They rise to sink,—then soar to drop,
And never settle till—they stop :
Yet why complain ?—whate'er endures
The shock of time, a *right* secures ;
Alas !—'tis but a right to show
How man improves not here below ;
A moral teaching for all time,
To man debasing, yet sublime ;
Let youngsters study wisdom's page

Ere on the world's enerving stage
They enter, not with notions crude
Dismiss them, let no lies obtrude
Their minds to harass, then a few,
Fixed, vital truths with them endue ;
Let them be taught—this the true end
Of knowledge, how all thought should tend
Unto an object, which perceived
Must be in probity believed ;
Firm and undoubting in their youth,
With Reason on her throne of Truth,
They will decide how far to go,
To stay when conscience whispers—no ;
Or, if belief should e'er fall out
Be renegade,—not rest in doubt !
If in the grove one tree decay,
Let it be rooted quite away—
So that another planted be
In the new-made vacuity ;
Thus and thus armèd send them forth,
I think they'd prove of sterling worth,
And leaven, mind in action free,
The impure beast 'Society :'
To shallow wits no sorer terror
Than earnest faith—in truth or error.
(Grace if I tire you, but, 'sdeath,
I can't leave off till out of breath.)

I thank you for the books, and next
Will make them, each in turn, my text ;
First, Eugène Sue,—he is your friend,—
Which doth from harshness me forefend ;
His writings are but of the mass
To their dishonour made a class

By Frenchmen of the present age,
Else must we curse them page by page ;
They're better meant if not so smart,
And more do vice and virtue part
Than other tales with vile intent
Wherewith *belle France* is redolent ;
Sue doth partake, with nearly all
His *camarades* who have learned to scrawl,
A lack of purpose, writing on
Where'er an uncurbed craze may run—
Unto they care not what, and tending
To ends the moral sense offending ;
Thus 'tis with these,—they nothing teach
In morals, manners, or in speech :
They have no unity, nor show
At least, the path we're *not* to go :
I apprehend and love romance,—
A blissful spell, a waking trance ;
On novels I impose few strictures,
They are for us as mental pictures ;
Poems I love for Fancy's sake,
Some good from most books man may take,
But Monsieur Sue all these hath sipped,
And made a sort of nondescript
With blasphemy and license larded,—
Yet good intent is not discarded ;
Au contraire, there is little doubt
The scribbler meaneth well throughout,
And that his private character
May be '*chez lui*' without a slur ;
Thus has it been with them the most
Of writers bred in France, a host
Of heedless and licentious authors,—
At best their books are merely frothers,

The effervescence and the scum
Of their fermenting minds ; —the stum
Viscid not spirituous being
They'd fain prevent the world from seeing !
You may remember how Louvet
A patriot proved in peril's day,
And boldly rose in Freedom's cause
When dastards broke his country's laws,
Then fled the scaffold to evade,
His name proscribed, a beggar made :
Behold a problem, which to solve
Must often in the mind revolve ;
Might we, at guess, a verdict find,
'Twould be, I think, ' not sound o' mind ; '—
Your Sue I place apart from these,
Though him such preference may not please ;
For I protest that more of good
May be educed from logs of wood ;
They serve not even time to kill,
At nought they aim, and nought fulfil ;
What are they? this I ask of *you ?*
But, being alone, must answer too ;
Those dandy covers do environ
Five paraphrases of our Byron,—
And by my troth below the par
As imitations always are ;
They're copies from our own bard's Hell
Of fiends angelic—pirates fell,
Five types of Lara and the Corsair,
Though one be silk, the other horsehair ;
Yet what doth most our wonder strike
Is—they are every one alike,
Except that John hath tones more harsh,
And Dick a little more moustache ;

They've more than Byron's mal-prepense,
Without his high-toned excellence ;
They've with the properties of evil
No poetry to paint the devil,
No sweet Medoras to their aid,
But harpies of a pirate's trade,—
Of such these precious tales are made :
'Tis plain what scenes must hence arise,
What situation for surprise,
What play for impious imprecation,
For blood and fire and deep damnation,
What opportunity to show
How far in vice a man may go ;
Nor is neglected any chance
Which could profanity enhance ;
Ruffians are free to curse their fill
And rave in rage as rascals will,
To scoff at holiest things, and seem
To be jocose when they blaspheme :
One episode of different mould
Alone is seen—impure and old,—
Its interest centering in a tale
Which, at the least, 'twere best to veil—
Not making prurient thoughts be *said*,
As sacrilege emblazonèd ;
Moreo'er I doubt if much which we
May deem original to be—
Because such guilt we rarely see,
Is novelty to else, forsooth,
Than unsophisticated youth,
Or say for those who, haply, hie
Where such putridity may lie ;
Therefore we hesitate to grant
Some praise which else were relevant,

Or point to pages bright and clever,—
For wit whate'er is pleasing ever;
Fail not to note his grand oration
In the parental dedication;
Two-and-a-half to *père et mère,*
And half a tale to *mon grandpère;*
This looks a joke,—for he'd be hissed
Who here so played the egotist
As in this book doth Monsieur Sue;
Mark you the spacious margins too,
The thin fly-leaves to every chapter—
With awe to take the judgment captor;
I nauseate humbug,—and do think
Of *it* these books do loudly stink;
Worth all the rest,—though least pretending,
Regard the story at the ending:
Oh, how refreshing 'tis to turn
From Sue, to find somewhat to learn—
In Richard Sharp,[1] and wisdom's page;
Oft may such truths our minds engage:
This is indeed a book !—a gem
To place in England's diadem,
A book throughout with learning fraught,
A rich epitome of thought !
Wherein each sentence is an axiom,
Where every pause contains a maxim;
Each page doth more respect inspire,
The more we read we more admire,
Exclaiming as the text we scan,
'Ah, this is like an English man !'
Time does not let me,—or I well
For hours could on its beauties dwell,

---

[1] *Letters and Essays,* (anonymous). London, Moxon, 1834.

I'd make its words of wisdom mine,
An Essay write on every line ;
I spare you likewise,—and, alas !
Unto a different theme do pass ;
Poor Julia ! who can tell the cause—
Whene'er we hear the word we pause,
Uncertain as we speak her name,
To love or pity, praise, or blame ;
Can you not answer? nor can I,
But I suspect 'tis sympathy.
And now, dear Sir, your pardon pray
For all sins perpetrate this day
On you, your eyes, and finer senses,
For bore in all its moods and tenses :
One Joseph Ellis thee assures
He is, as erewhile, *truly yours.*

A Chase of Echo.

z.

A Chase of Echo.

AN IDYL.

[The legend of Ovid reversed—Echo pursued instead of pursuing:
Echo lives—is the object of love—love as an abstraction, real only
whilst unreal, lost when found: Laon is the love which dies at the
moment of disenchantment.]

LAON.

VISION of sleep,—and Dream of waking hours!
Why is it, Echo, why I find thee not?
Thou livest, doubtless, for the heart is true,
And in my heart thou livest:

                      Echo dear!
Soon shall I find thee, for I think, nay, know
Thou art anear me,—answer to my call!
Be Nature blessèd for these yearnings sure,
Be Nature blessèd for unfailing hope.

   *   *   *   *   *   *

Where from me hidest thou?—where art thou, Echo?
Thou knowest I have sought thee o'er the plain,
In meads and groves, and in the haunts of men;
Sweet, answer me! that I may be where *thou* art;
Echo!—not here:

                   Echo!—alas, not here:

   *   *   *   *   *   *

On, on I wander, wander, wander on,—
Aweary wandering, alone, alone!

Ah! *with thee,* I would tread the Earth like air,
Thy presence giving each a two-fold life,
Thy soul with mine us winging o'er the hills!

    *   *   *   *   *   *

Here, by this lucent lake's smooth, smiling face,
The woods and rocks around in holy stillness,
Here thou awaitest me; I'll find thee here :
                   Echo !
                   Echo.

She is here !

                   Come to me !
                   Come to me.
There,—there ! 'tis sure,—across the lake I'll swim ;
                   Dearest, I come !
                   Dearest, I come.

    *   *   *   *   *   *

Alas ! not found—again—again not found ;
Come to me, Echo ! so together we
May see, and hear, and live the self-same life ;
Come to me, sweetheart ! to my longing come !
No joy without thee can be quite a joy,
What *thine* eyes see not, brings no joy to mine,—
To look on cheerless what *thou* seest not ;
Thus, thus to know thee near me,—it is pain,
Pain to be near, nor see thee, nor embrace ;
List Echo ! hear me !
                   Pitiless ! she is gone !
As I approach and think to clasp, she flies ;
Oh, I am breathless, and must faint, or sleep. (*Sleeps.*)

        (*Murmurs in sleep.*)

Dear love, but this is well ; come—come to me
Now, now I see thee, now I hold thee near ;

We shall not separate—shall never cease!
Such love for ever lives:

(*Wakes.*)

           No more! no more:
Yet shall I chase her, if she will not stay,
Where she hath cheated me,—away, away!

   *   *   *   *   *   *

Out of the maze at last! I pant with speed;
But where—where is my Echo? Echo, hear!
How on these spreading down-lands so evanish?
The velvet sward too soft for resonance,
Too smooth the print to take of her light feet,—
How shall I guide me?

           Swelling on and on
The earth is undulate like waving waters,
Now high, now low—an ocean though of land;
Yet, in yon trough I think she may be found,—
There could she gain some harbour; I'll descend;
The place is silent;—now, if she but speak,
Though lightly, I'll pursue her o'er the wold:
             Echo!
             Echo.
Whence was the voice? I heard it very clear:
             Echo!
             Echo.
Lo, she hath flitted, but I'll call again;
        Echo, where art thou?
           Where art thou?
             Echo!
             Echo.
          Hearest thou me?
          Hearest thou me?
Yea, love, I hear thee! and do straight come near

The spot wherefrom thou speakest; I am here :
Echo, my Echo! prithee speak again ;
Oh, flee not from me,—flee not from me, love !
    Echo !
She waits not, cruel ! I must follow her !
I faint—I faint ! once more,—once more will call :
    Echo !
    Echo.
    Answer me !
    Answer me.
    Thou lovest me ?
    Thou lovest me ?
Thou knowest I do love thee, Echo sweet !
Forsake me not ! for I am broken-hearted ;
My strength declineth as the day doth wane ;
I sleep, or die :
    Be with me, Echo, now ! (*Sleeps.*)

    Echo *speaks.*

Yea, I'll be with thee, Laon,—in thy sleep—
Fain would I pity thee, fain prove to be
The love thou seekest, and so lose delight,
Thy pain my bliss,—the bliss to be besought !
For aye evading and for ever loved !
So *shalt* thou see me, more to give thee life,
Fire to thy heart, and frenzy to thy soul.

    LAON (*in sleep.*)

Echo, loved Echo, now I see thy face,
Yea, hear thee breathe, yea, know thou art mine own ;
Thou'lt never leave me ! fly from me no more :

    Echo *speaks.*

Fond, foolish boy, then were thy chase at end !
I must away, lest thou thy pastime lose !

Laon.

Oh, horror! sleeping live, and waking die!
Echo, dear Echo:
                She hath fled me, fled:
Must I then sleep to make her live to me?

   *   *   *   *   *   *

The dells o'erpassèd, on this arid plain
The merest sprite can hide not; let me rest;
Oh, void in heart! oh, heart an aching void!
Oh, languid limbs sustaining heavy heart!
This mossy bank—how soft!   (*Reclines.*)

Fairest, why fadest thou always away from me,
   Here and there answering, never appearing,
Somewhiles approaching, or whispering low to me,
   What shall I think, is it loving or fearing?

Is it of will, or of fate thou art lost to me,
   Near me to hear me wherever I'm straying!
Is it in gladness or grief thou escapest me,
   Mocking my call, and thy presence betraying?

Yet, while thou answerest, dear one, I'll follow thee,
   Wooing the voice and its origin blessing,
Lovingly hearing, thee calling unceasingly,
   Till eyes shall behold, till arms shall be pressing.

   *   *   ?   *   *   *

And next oh whither, whither do I wend—
Abroad this dreary field withouten bound?
The dim horizon is, I think, the Sea;
Its mark I'll reach, and then no farther go

   *   *   *   *   *   *

It is the Sea,—and on the shore are crags :
There doth my Echo hide ;

> I come, sweet Echo.

*   *   *   *   *   *

Here, in this sea-cave, will my phantom be !
"Tis deep and wide, the voice of Ocean list !
If she be here, I'll win her,—winning, hold :

> Echo !
> *Echo.*
> I follow !
> *Follow.*

O happy me !   I'll enter ;

> Echo, love !

Echo, kind Echo ! kill me not with scorn !
Echo, kind Echo ! kill me not with woe !—
Sure then she spake, but now again is dumb ;
Why in these dark recesses should I bide?
Here, from the beach I'll call her, o'er the Sea :

Echo ! hark—Echo ! list—my Echo ! list,—
Nought but my sad voice moaning o'er the main ;
What worth to me is life when hope is dead ?
My heart is failing fast, mine eyelids droop ;
Come—come, blest sleep, my feet approach the flood ;
The waves will mount, upon them I shall float
Another world unto,—and to my Echo: (*Sleeps.*)

Echo *speaks.*

Doomed Laon, thou wilt die : nathless I love thee !
So will they hear me ! and indulge in vain
A love which doth not to their world pertain ;
See me once more, dear Laon ! dost thou not ?

LAON (*in sleep*).

Echo, I see thee, and methinks thy beauty
Sublimeth more and more; turn not away
Those dove-like, dreamy eyes, look on me yet,—
The rhapsody of thy seraphic traits
Shall live with me in mine eternal rest;
Now I regard thee—ne'er to lose thee more!

(*Wakes.*)

Despair!—despair!
                    I think the world is false,
My Love a Voice—mine idol but a Shade;
All hope is dead,—is higher life a dream?
The life of dreams is love and joy to me;
My heart is void and life is nothingness;
Then rather let me sleep the long, long sleep
Where vain hope is not, or where love abides—
Where, dreaming only, I my Echo see:

The heaving billows lift me from the Earth; —
Echo, sweet Echo! Daughter of the Air,
For aye, in dream, with thee!

L'Envoi.

Go, go my book, go tuning tell
Conceits which haply me befell
Or in my youth or later age,
   And set my soul a-singing ;
Away, to bear upon the page
Some traces of my pilgrimage
   To them whose life is springing :

Wend well, my book, wend wide and find
The true-born brotherhood of mind,
Con-natural souls who me not know—
   Albeit they have been yearning ;
Their kindled love may serve to show
The boons we but on self bestow
   Are little worth the earning :

So speed, my book, so gainful speed
Perchance in coming men to breed
New motions of the heart and brain
   To send their wits a-flying ;
Thus shall I not have writ in vain,
But charmedly live on again
   And never quite be dying.

Appendix.

THE following complimentary Sonnets, etc., now first published, are added in the desire to preserve, so far, a few valued Reminiscences of Friendship. Be this their apology.

The Friend of Friends.[1]

INSCRIBED TO JOSEPH ELLIS, AUTHOR OF 'CAESAR IN EGYPT.'

Who is the Friends-of-Friends?—not one who smiles
While you are prosperous,—purse-full, in fair fame,
Flattering, ' Come, be my household's altar-flame,'
When knowing you can bask on sunny isles ;
Not one who saith, ' Thy brain's a mighty mould,'
With base-coined hints about alloys in gold ;
Not he who frankly tells you all your faults,
But drops all merit into vampire-vaults ;—
No ; the true friend stands close 'midst circling storms,
When you are poor,—lost,—wrestling thro' a cloud,
With whom your ship rides high in friezing calms,
Its banner ghostly pale, to him still proud,—
Whose heart's Blest-Arab-spice dead hope embalms,
The same, tho' you sate throned,—or waiting for your
     shroud.

December 26, 1879.

---

[1] By R. H. Horne, author of *Orion*, *Cosmo de Medici*, etc. See p. 165.

To Joseph Ellis.[1]

FRIENDS meet in paths unsought,—and when dire Care
With pitiless gripe hath fixed its gnawing tooth
Among our heart-strings, and, for love in sooth,
And those bright visions of diaphanous air—
Quick Fancy's brood of all that's pure and fair,
Instead of home-lit peace, the dream of youth,
Linked with a help-mate who, or pain or ruth,
Occasion claiming, smiles nor tears would spare,—
We prove, alas! how one of womankind
But gained a trust implicit—to betray,—
Then twice-told welcome is the hap to find
A kindred being on life's darkling way,
Whose deeds and converse, rich in heart and mind,
Shed through the gloom, like thine, a sunny ray!

T. J. J

---

[1] By the Rev. T. J. Judkin, M.A., Caius Coll. Cam., author of
By-gone Moods; The Spirit of the Psalter; Original Hymns, etc. etc.
See p. 182.

To the Author of 'Caesar in Egypt.'[1]

ELLIS ! no slipshod muse is thine ; robust,
 Incisive, musical, thy lines beguile
 The hours away, and yet inform the while :
The mighty ones of ancient days thou dost
Recall ; Great Caesar, shrewd, urbane, august,
 Lives on thy page anew ; and her whose smile
 Made him her thrall, the ' Serpent of old Nile,'
Thou limnest in true tints, proportions just !
Next, o'er Costanza's heart-enchaining tale
 I weep, rejoice : anon, upon mine ear—
 Solemn and sad as sound of funeral bell—
Vibrates the sore-tried world discoverer's wail.
 Sing on, dear Bard ! 'tis thine to wake the tear,
 Or tune to mirth the Minstrel's magic spell !

H. C.

April 5, 1877.

---

[1] By Henry Campkin, F.S.A.

Horace, Odes I., IX.[1]

WHITE with deep snow, behold, Soracte soars,
And scarce the struggling forests bear the load,
    And bound by winter's frost
    The rivers stay their course:
Dissolve the cold, pile on the hearth the logs,
Bring without stint—the wine of four years' growth
    Bring down in Sabine jar
    O Thaliarchus dear:
Trust to the gods the rest; when they have laid
The winds contending on the yeasty deep,
    No more the cypress waves,
    Nor antient ash is shaken:
Seek not to know what lot the morrow brings,
And count as gain each day that chance shall give,
    Nor thou my boy despise
    Sweet love or joyful dance:
While youth is green, and peevish, gray-hair'd eld
Is not yet come, at nightfall's trysting hour
    In field and open place
    Let gentle whispers breathe:
Now let the pleasant laugh from inmost nook
Betray the lurking girl; seize then the pledge
    Snatched from the maiden's arm
    Or finger unresisting.

April 7, 1868.

---

[1] Rendered by George Long, M.A., Trin. Coll. Cam., author of *The Decline of the Roman Republic: Translations of the Thoughts of the Emperor M. Aurelius: The Discourses of Epictetus: An Old Man's Thoughts*, etc. etc. See p. 174.

𝔖𝔬𝔡𝔞.[1]

' Fies nobilium Tu quoque fontium.'—*Horat.* Od. xiii. l. 3.
' Fontium Qui celat origines.'—*Horat.* Od. xiv. l. 4.

O Fons Salutis !   Vita !   Fides mea !
Tumultuosi qui mala pectoris
    Compescis, et morbi furores
       Attenuas, saliente lymphâ ;

Musis sodali sub Camerario [2]
Præstes novellam Castaliam mihi ;
    Salvumque dilectis amicis
       Restitues, animosque reddes :

Sparsim remotas condis origines
Arcana rerum subter, et abditus
    Nascentis ad terræ recessus,
       Primigenique elementa mundi :

Unde ausa in auras Te trahere, et leves
Miscere doctâ particulas manu
    Cohors Medentûm, ut rivus orbi
       Mirificâ fluat auctus arte.

Agnosce Patris munera !   Quem Deum
Agnoscit, omni parte operis Sui,
    Ad Solis occasus et ortus,
       Terra, Mare, æthereumque Cœlum.

August 22, 1842.

---

[1] Written by the Marquess Wellesley when at the age of eighty ;
as also the Translation : these are not included in his *Primitiæ et
Reliquiæ.* See p. 177.

[2] His physician was Dr. Chambers.

Translation.

Fountain of health! and hope! and faith! and life!
That quell'st my tortured bosom's restless strife,
And to relieve my agonizing dreams
Pour'st forth thy crystal, cool, bright, salient streams!
Under the hand of classic Chambers placed
A new Castalia freshens to my taste,
Inspires new life and spirit, and again
Leads me revived to the gay haunts of men:
In Nature's secrets hid thy birth-place lies,
Far scattered, deep, remote from human eyes,
Amid the germs that first gave Nature birth
And the primæval elements of earth,—
Whence dared to draw Thee to earth's airs, and blend
Thy lightsome texture in one glorious end—
Machaon's Race, and spread thy wholesome streams
Where'er the Sun extends his living beams:
Acknowledge God's good gifts—whose bounteous hand
His works acknowledge all through main and land,
Where'er the sun sinks low, or rises high,
The Earth, the Sea, and the æthereal sky.

[Another Translation.
2 A

*Another Translation made at same period
by Joseph Ellis.*

O SALUTARY fountain !   Life ! my confidence,
Thou allayest the disorders of my troubled breast,
Alleviating the ragings of disease
                    In limpid sprightliness ;

Handmaid of the Muses ! gladdening my chamber,
Thou affordest to me a new Castalian spring,
Re-invigorating my spirit, and restoring me soothed
                    To my dear, chosen friends :

Scattered remote within the secret places of the Earth,
And hid in the recesses of first-formed matter,
Amidst the elements of the embryonic world
                    Is hid thine origin,

From whence the band of healing men have boldly brought
        thee forth,
Mingling with discriminate hand thy aeriform particles,
And causing thee to flow with admirable influence—
                    A stream miraculous !

Confess the gifts of our beneficent Father !
Whom the Earth, the Sea, and Heaven above acknowledge
In every part of His work from the rising to the setting
        of the Sun
                    As very God supreme.

Charles Hatchett,¹ Joseph Jekyll,² and James Smith.³

(*This anecdote was written by Mr. Hatchett for J. E. 8th October 1836.*)

On the 29th of January 1836 Mr. Hatchett, of Belle Vue House, Chelsea, sent an Engraved Head of himself to his old friend Mr. Jekyll, and on the next day Mr. Jekyll returned the following Note :—

'*30th January* 1836.

Thanks for a kind memorial of our long friendship, though it looks somewhat radical on the 30th of January to thank the Hatchett for the Head of Charles.

JOSEPH JEKYLL.'

Some days after this, Mr. Jekyll again wrote to Mr. Hatchett,—' I told my merry friend James Smith how I had thanked you for the Engraving : he sate down directly and versified it.

'An Answer, Charles Hatchett, thou claimest,
    So take it both pithy and short,
For surely so able a Chemist
    Can never reject a Retort :
Your Portrait no Painter can match it,
    So I scorn all their envy or snarls,
And like Cromwell I owe to a Hatchett
    What I gain by the Head of a Charles.

JOSEPH JEKYLL.

NEW STREET, SPRING GARDENS,
    February 13, 1836.'

¹ The eminent Chemist :   ² The Wit :
³ Brother of Horace Smith.— [Authors of '*Rejected Addresses.*']

AD PERFAMILIAREM MEUM.[1]

LAST time I wrote to you in rhyme
My lowly muse you charged with crime ;
For cant, I will say nought about it,
My conscience tells me I'm without it,
And want of sense is quite in season,
For who expects both rhyme and reason ?
But I will take another theme,
Which less absurd I hope you'll deem ;
I'll strut in Epicurus' gown,
And praise the pastimes of the Town :
For joy alone let's live, my friend,
Be it of life the aim and end ;
Why pass our time in strife and care,
In melancholy and despair ?
Our days are but a little span,
We must enjoy them when we can,
While fortune, youth, and fate allow—
Ere to fell Death we're forced to bow ;
        We'll leave ambition to the Great,
        With all the cares which on it wait,
        In governing this stormy State,—
An Island torn by turmoil more ;
Than are the seas which round it roar :
        In Eastern pomp we'll sit elate ;
Bring us then perfumes, flowers, and wine,
The Lily with the Rose entwine ;

---

[1] This classic Epistle was addressed to J. E. by his schoolfellow-
friend, George Houldsworth Theakston.

Whilst black-eyed girls, with chaplets crowned.
In mazy circles beat the ground ;
Our Company should be but small—
Men of complacent manners all,
Gay, yet endowed with cultured mind,
By arts and poetry refined :
Let Authors preach—poor starving wights—
Of Intellectual Delights :
Or mental or corporeal sense
To gratify is no offence ;
Either of these if you despise
You know not in what luxury lies,
And, of true Epicures the laugh,
Of all your wealth—you use but half !

But, when of wit and wine o'er-full
Our friends begin to be but dull,—
Some time before the break of day
All unobserved I'd steal away
Unto the bower, or snug boudoir,
Where new delights are yet in store ;
There the bliss of Love I'd prove,—
How poor the joy uncrowned with love !

Let me describe this charming place,
The fane of beauty and of grace ;
The bower to which I next repair,
    Unlike the room I late did quit,
Is free from noise, or pomp, or glare,—
    Which all for love are found unfit :
The ceiling's arched and painted blue,
    To imitate Italia's sky,
Such as in Summer's eve we view,
    When not a cloud doth meet the eye ;

Around it naked Cupids play,
And modest nymphs, and Graces gay ;
The wainscot is with tapestry hung,
  Showing whate'er, in colours bright and strong,
Of Love or Arms the bards have sung,
  Whether in ancient or in modern song ;
The coloured lamps reflect a mellowed light,
To favour vision, not bedim the sight,
And so designed as shall inspire
Soft thoughts of amorous desire ;
With silence, of true love the sign,—
  Which loquacity most hates,
Though solitary it would pine,
And ever, with ground-seeking eye,
And unpresumptuous modesty,
  The puny god's decrees awaits,
  Yet scarcely dares to make reply :
This Temple's Deity is fair
As famed Circassia's beauties are,—
See, in her cheeks the young blood glows !
The pouting lips, the well-formed nose—
Are so described by every bard
To tell them newly were too hard ;
Her eyes are of the varying hue
Which seems to change at every view,
Now they in liquid softness swim,
  And now they seem with lightning fired,
Just as may suit the moment's whim,
  Or by the passing thought inspired ;
And on her neck and snowy breast
The fair-haired curls in clusters rest ;
She on a couch of roseate tint reclines
  Fixing her anxious eye on the arch above,
Her slender fingers in her locks entwines

While with impatience she expects her love.
So the fair Goddess sits on high,
Not to be viewed by vulgar eye.
So Love's alluring altar stands,
Not to be touched by impious hands,
And thence she graciously invites
The favoured swain to share her rites.

Brief time in sluggard sleep we'll waste,
    The vital hours run quickly on,
Each to our journey's end we haste,
    The winged moments fly with speed,
    And endless dark and night succeed,
  We shall have time to sleep anon !

                Vale !

                  G. H. T.

August 26, 1833.

Richmond Hill.[1]

THE treatment of the subject in this Sonnet was suggested by the following anecdote :—

Captain Vancouver on return from his 'Voyage of Discovery to the North Pacific Ocean and round the World in the years 1790–95,' went direct to Richmond Hill,—arriving there at night ; the season was Summer ; in the morning he saw for the first time the beautiful prospect and, enchanted, exclaimed 'Here will I live, here will I die !' He lies buried near, in the church of Petersham.

---

[1] See p. 173.

www.ingramcontent.com/pod-product-compliance
Lightning Source LLC
Chambersburg PA
CBHW021711110726
47902CB00005B/1145